Time and The Place

A NOVEL

Will Goede

Edited by Marilyn Brulhart

Rock's Mills Press
Rock's Mills, Ontario • Oakville, Ontario
2023

Published by
Rock's Mills Press
www.rocksmillspress.com

Contents

PART ONE

The Place

1

I heard the back porch screen door yarr and snap and looked up and saw my uncle coming into the kitchen and taking off his cap. "Ned," said my old man, and my mother, "Why, you look like a man needs a cup of coffee," but Ned said, "No, I already et." I kept out of it. It wouldn't've mattered anyways. My old man always acted like I wasn't there, and you want to know something, I wasn't. *There* I mean. I wasn't there, sitting at the kitchen table with him. Oh yeah, well sure, I mean I was there of course, but if you went looking for me you'd have had trouble finding me because I wasn't *there* there.

I was invisible there.

It didn't just happen, you know. I had to work at it. I would start working at it the moment I parachuted down the stairs and dropped across the living room and into the kitchen, saying, "G'mornin' Mama," pulling the ripcord and landing in the chair across from where the old man sat gobbling away at his scrambled eggs and back bacon. I was pretty well invisible by then. That way you see he didn't have to say anything to me. He didn't have anything to say anyways, and of course I had nothing to say to him either. It didn't matter if for some reason I did have something to say because he would have gone on acting like I hadn't said it, or maybe even worse, he would have said something and then I would have found myself in hot water.

You see my point. I wasn't there, so how could my old man say anything to me?

My mother launched a kitchen chair across the floor at Ned, who leaned back against the doorframe and studied the chair with those blackberry eyes of his as if he didn't know what it was. "Oh for goodness sake, Ned," she said, "set down, you won't get electercuted!" He snuffed out a smile and lowered himself onto the chair as if he wasn't at all convinced, and then he began to flick his eyes about the room searching for something he wanted to talk about if only he could find it.

My old man looked at Ned and said, "So what brings you to town?"

"Vera, she run out of oyster chips." Ned cast a glance at my mother to see if that explained everything. It didn't, and so he said, "Goes into chicken mash." My mother wrinkled up her nose as if she could smell the oysters on him. "Hardens the eggshells," he explained and looked to my father for help. My old man knew all about oyster chips and eggshells, but he was done with farming, had been ever since he got out of high school, and he wasn't going to be reminded why you added oyster chips to chicken mash. "Cost me seventy-five cents a bag, too," Ned growled. "Everything going up now because of the war."

Ned's forehead was smooth and white and clean as snow because he lived most of his life outdoors and never took off his cap, but the rest of his face – the high cheekbones, pointy chin, scrawny neck, the Adam's apple – it was the colour of horsehide all the way down to his shirt collar, and there it turned white again. He tried out a sad nervous smile on my mother because of the high cost of chicken mash, lifted a hand and smoothed back his thick coal-black hair, and then stuck a finger into an ear and dug out a fingernail of wax. He looked exhausted trying to explain the mysteries of oyster chips and threw himself once more into a study of the wrinkled yellow and green linoleum floor at his feet.

Something was up.

My old man said, "Gonna be a scorcher, up in the nineties, maybe a hunnert."

"Yeah maybe."

"Peas poddin' out yet?" asked my mother, who knew Ned never talked about the weather but had a certain endurance for conversations about agriculture.

"Good big pods!" Ned giggled like a proud father. "Inch or two for sure. Lots of blossoms still though."

"I hate shakin' a barn in this kind of heat." My old man turned to look out the window. "Cloudin' up though, maybe it'll rain."

"Corn's lookin' good too," said my mother, refusing to knuckle under to my old man. "Knee high by the fourth of July, you think?"

"Yeah, you bet. Down in that bottom forty cobs is maybe six, seven inches." What was up anyways? Ned continued looking around the room for something he couldn't find. "Needs cultivatin' right now. Needs *somebody* to go out and cultivate it."

"Probably hunnert and ten working up on a roof in weather like this."

My mother said, "What about your pa? Couldn't he just take his team out cultivatin'?"

Ned shook his head as he flicked his eyes like small brooms into the far corners of the room.

"Worst place to be in the summer's up on a barn roof when it's hunnert and ten."

Ned finally pulled his eyes back into his head, ran his tongue across his lips and sucked in a pool of air. "You know, you just can't tell Pa nothin' no more," he said sourly. "You can't even stop him from goin' out . . . and then when he's out, you can't get him in again!" He spat the words out as if they were too hot to hold in his mouth. "He won't listen to me nor Ma nor Vera nor nobody. Gets up from the breakfast table and goes straight out and harnesses up MackandJack and takes them over to the shed and hooks them up to that rusty old gangplow Uncle Hermann give him when he first moved onto The Place. You remember that one? And then he heads out to that sandy marsh – you know the one I mean, that low ground down alongside No Nothin' Creek where it runs out from under the railroad bridge

– and what does he do? He ploughs it, and it don't bother him none that he ploughed it just yesterday and the day before that. Back and forth, back and forth he goes, jabberin' away to hisself. German of course. Ever since that stroke everything's German. Don't matter if you're a fencepost nor a cow nor you nor me. You can say somethin' in English if you want to but he won't answer you back. Why, just yesterday I asked him, I says, 'Pa, why don't you speak English no more?' and he looks up at me and he says, *'Hab' nur noch ein paar Kröten in der Tasche.'*"

Definitely, something was up. I'd never heard Ned string more than a half-dozen words together unless of course he was already launched into one of his hunting yarns. My old man looked over at Ned and said, "Bet you never worked up on a barn roof when it was hunnert and ten in the shade."

"Oh goodness gracious, Colvin!" my mother said, "Ned's talkin' about your pa, we don't need to hear more about shakin' a barn."

Ned didn't seem to hear what she said. "I got to go all the way out there and tell him to come back to the house," he said, "otherwise he'd plow away in the dark."

"It's true, he's sort of peculiar nowadays," Mother said. "Vera told me Nettie flew off the handle last week when he was schpricken de Dootch, and she had to go and pry her off'n him."

"Yep, got to keep an eye on Nettie when he comes up to the house." I knew Aunt Nettie didn't have all her buttons, but I didn't like everyone treating her like she was a child, which in fact she was. "As I said I had to pry her off'n him yesterday."

My old man spoke up, said, "I told you we should put her away before somebody gets hurt!"

"Oh, you don't have to worry none about Nettie, but what am I goin' to do about Pa? I can't count on him to help out harvestin' peas nor cultivatin' corn this summer . . . and then there's all that hayin' to do in July."

"Oh no!" I said to myself, *"that's what's up!"*

"Too bad about Buck," said my mother. "I'm sure he'd come home if he could and help out." Uncle Buck had gone off to war a year ago and was at that very moment down in Texas learning how to fly a secret new airplane. "Maybe if'n you wrote and told the Army he was needed to home they'd let him out for a month or so."

"What about Amos Victory?" my old man offered. "He helped you out last fall when you was fillin' silo."

"Amos? Why, I'd have to spend every morning combin' the taverns lookin' for him, and if'n I ever found him, then I'd have to dry him out and try and keep him sober the rest of the day. You can't pay Amos nothing either. The minute you pay him, he's out drinkin' it up."

"Well, don't look at me!" said my old man when he saw my uncle looking at him. "I can't do nothin' about it, I got to go out and shake Bert Himmelfahrt's roof in a hunnert and ten degrees heat."

Ned suddenly squared his head at that moment and narrowed his eyes and trained them on me. But how could he see me when I wasn't there?

"Well, it looks to me like Junior's put on another inch or two since Christmas," he chuckled. "What you feedin' him, Bonnie?"

"Oyster chips," she said.

I had to do something fast now that I figured out Ned had been looking for me ever since he walked through the door. I dropped my hands below the table and twisted my Little Orphan Annie ring four times to the left and four to the right, and then for good measure recited the secret pledge of The Phantom just as Ned shifted his voice into a major key and said, "Well, that seems to work because he's sure growed up just like mustard seed in a hayfield."

"You got *that* right!" said my old man, snickering. And he looked at me like I was a weed he was going to pull up by the roots, and I gave up on Little Orphan Annie and switched over to my table manners checklist. My old man had that look in his eyes. I knew the look. Something was going wrong around him, and he was an expert at finding out what it was.

Why, he could find something wrong with God if he knew just where to look!

My mother could see it coming and yanked the chair with me still in it back away from the table. Seemed like I could watch one of me separating away from the other me still sitting there. "Okay, boy," she said, pulling me to my feet, "upstairs you go, and brush those teeth of yours real good and get ready for school."

I started walking backward toward the door.

Then Ned said it: "Maybe I *could* use Junior out to The Place this summer." His eyes shadowed me as I backed away. "All he'd have to do is learn how to drive that new tractor I bought last week. It's a Ford-Ferguson, a new kind of tractor, smaller than a John Deere but just as tough. Guzzy Sieg said he could probably get me one maybe even next week, just in time for cultivatin' corn."

"Junior drive a tractor?" squawked my old man as he jumped to his feet and slung himself at the coat rack, screwing his carpenter's cap down over his ears. "Why, he can't even push a lawnmower across the yard without runnin' into a tree and he sure can't keep the woodboxes full, and he's broke every damn plate in the kitchen . . . why, he walks into walls, he falls out of bed, he chews his fingernails right down to the blood. "

"All right, Colvin, all right!" said my mother.

"You let him onto that new tractor of yours, the first thing he'll do, he'll run over a cow!"

My old man grabbed hold of his lunch pail and fired his eyes at me one last time and then barrelled out the door and across the porch and down the front steps. Then I heard a dog barking. I looked out the kitchen window and saw my old man stomping across the yard toward his car and then stopping and chucking a stone at Old Lady Herrick's howling beagle.

2

I stared at myself in the mirror and thought . . . but this is summertime, wrist-flicking time, double-undertime, taws, big eyes, aggies, keepsies, plunkingtime, why you were champion last summer, now someone's going to take that away from you, school's out, nobody can tell you what to do until Septembertime, now's the time you can roll hoops up and down the street all day, you can chew tar jelly when they come around to fix potholes, you can lick shards of ice left behind when the iceman chips a block for your mother's icebox, you can race bikes over railroad ties, you can go skinnydipping in the woods along Bridge Creek, you can trade off your stack of Supermans and Dick Tracys, the ones with the covers still on to show them you paid a dime for it, you can play all day in the dusty haymows of the old barns around the neighborhood and smoke ragweed and get good and sick and puke, you can go to the Gene Autry movies Saturday night, you can wait for the Barnum and Bailey circus train and the Rottner Brothers' trucks and pester them until they hire you to help pitch the big top, and then you get free passes . . .

"Where are you, boy!" my mother called from the bottom of the stairs. "You're going to be good and late now!" I parachuted down the stairs and grabbed my Hopalong Cassidy lunch pail on my flight through the kitchen. "And don't you dare short-cut through Mrs. Horton's garden!" she shouted as I raced out the door. "You remember what happened last time!"

I came back and said, "I don't have to go out and work at The Place this summer, do I, Mom?"

"You have to git to school, now git!"

I tore down the steps and took a short-cut through Mrs. Horton's garden and across Old Lady Herrick's back yard and past the feed mill and across The Iron Bridge until I came to The Pussyfoot, the path that snaked down through the weeds and alongside the creek till it reached the other side of town, where the old brick school squatted in a field just like a jail.

But just as I crossed the bridge heading for The Pussyfoot, I heard a truck pull up behind me. It was Uncle Ned, of course. He'd been waiting somewhere until he saw me on my way to school and shoved the door open and yelled, "Better get in if you want to get to school on time!" I climbed up beside him. He drove down long tunnels of giant oak and elm without saying a word until we drew up in front of the school, and then he reached across the seat and laid a hand on my shoulder. "If you wanted to," he said, "you could pack yourself a suitcase and come on out and spend the whole summer with me and Vera and Gramma. Why, you could even sleep in Buck's room."

"You didn't mention Nettie."

"And Nettie too."

There was no time to think. "I'll have to ask my mother when I get home from school."

He giggled when he said, "That ain't it, and you know it. You think you'll miss your Pa too much."

I could see myself swimming around in the pools of blue water that were Ned's eyes. "Him?" I said, the thought of which took my breath away, and I giggled too. "Well, who'd he have to pick on all summer?"

"And you wouldn't have to worry about walkin' lawnmowers into trees. Nettie, she does all the mowin' at The Place. And I could work it out so there ain't one woodbox to fill the whole summer."

I thought about it again and laughed, said, "Yeah, but what about running over cows?"

"Don't you worry about them cows. Cows's smarter than you and me. And also your Pa, come to think of it."

* * *

The doors to all the classrooms were all shut.

The narrow floorboards of the empty hallway snapped at my heels as I ran toward my classroom. I twisted my Orphan Annie ring and recited all the creeds I could think of and then felt that black cloak of invisibility settle over my shoulders so tight that when I looked in the mirror above the water fountain there was nothing to look at. Then I cracked the door to the classroom and tiptoed across the back of the room. It was working! Miss Hiller was busy looking at the blackboard and yakking away, and all the kids were sitting there trying to figure out what she was saying. I thought I'd got away with it when my lunch pail touched Norma Wolfgang's desk and rang out like a fire bell, and at that very moment the cloak was torn from my shoulders and I fell into my seat with a bang.

Miss Hiller came and stood over me like a shadow. She put her hands on her hips, which meant I had to come up with a reason for being late, and of course I had one ready for her.

"It's all my Uncle Ned's fault," I said, too loudly. "He came to our house just as I was getting ready for school and said Uncle Buck can't help out this summer because he's away in the army . . . and my Opa, he takes a team of horses out to an old sandpit and talks German all day, and Amos Victory, he can't help either because Uncle Ned has to go digging him out of the taverns, and Gramma, she's too old now and Vera and Nettie . . . well, they're just women, you see . . ." I had gone too fast too far, but now I was stuck, I had to keep going. "Well, you can't expect them to go out and do the field work." Miss Hiller scrunched up her eyes the way she does when you misspell words like 'receive' or 'cemetery', and then everyone started to laugh. "What I mean is I'm the only one left, I have to go out and drive it."

"Drive what?"

"That new tractor Ned bought."

Dorothy Livermore laughed out loud, and Miss Hiller swiveled about and paddled Dorothy with her eyes. "Why, you're only nine years old, Junior," she said it as if it were a curse. "You can't drive a tractor, it's way too dangerous for a boy your age."

"That's what my old man – oh, sorry, Miss Hiller - my father, that's what he says."

"Well, you listen to your father. Fathers know best."

"Yes, Miss Hiller."

I wanted to tell her she was wrong. I wanted to tell her I never listened to my old man. I wanted to tell her too that my old man had never listened to his old man either, and his old man to his old man, and so on and so forth.

I wanted to say that that was the way things were done in our family.

That night my father came home from shingling his barn in a hunnert degrees, and by the time he got to the supper table, I was totally invisible again. I knew that because he talked to my mother about me as if I wasn't there. "So Ned thinks he's old enough to drive a tractor?" said my mother, standing at the stove stirring buttered carrots in a pan. My old man says "Why shucks, he's way too small, he won't be able to reach the clutch and brake pedals, and what about the steering wheel? It's twice't his size. He'd have to climb up on top of it to run it and jimmy those baby toes of his down into it and push off with all his might just to turn a corner." He cackled as he pictured it in his mind. "And as I said, he'll kill every cow he comes to. And then what about them hills? Sure as I'm sittin' here, he'll tip that tractor right over on top of him first hill he comes to. Those new tractors they build nowadays, they tip over real easy. I read about this kid over at Brandon, he was pulling a load of hay with a brand-new Farm-All and what did he do? He flipped it right over right on top of himself, squished him flatter'n a pancake! Nobody could get him out from underneath. They had to hire a rig somewheres to come out and pry the tractor off the top of him."

"Think of it this way, Colvin!" cried my mother. "If the boy goes out and stays at The Place all summer, then he won't be in your way until school starts up again in the fall!"

This was something he hadn't thought out because thinking came hard for him, but now that she had said it, he thought maybe he *could* appreciate having me out of the way.

My mother carried two hot plates and slammed them down on the table and turned and went into the living room and tossed herself down onto the sofa. He sat and stared at where I sat saying nothing. He loaded up his plate and began to eat, staring over at what should've been me. I knew without my mother at the table, I would have trouble keeping down the small steelball potatoes, the pellets of green peas, the concrete slabs of chicken. I thought again about what Ned had said that morning and watched my old man filling his mouth and right then and there, I made up my mind to spend the summer at The Place. I was ready for him now! I hit the ground in full flight and pulled in my parachute, and right in front of him loaded up my plate. Eight potatoes, four spoons of peas, three slabs of chicken. I was going to sit right across from him and eat it all. And I was going to swallow it and keep it down. When school let out in a week or so, I was going straight out to The Place and drive that new tractor straight at the first cow I could find and drive right on past her and head for the steepest hill in the south fields and go up and down and all around it without tipping over.

I wasn't going to listen to him!

As I said, he hadn't listened to his old man and his old man hadn't listened to his old man.

It was my turn now.

So summer came at last and Ronnie Lighthouse showed up at the house just after breakfast. He was rolling a brand-new wheel this summer. He had yanked it off his sister's stroller, and I could see he had made himself a new handle and fresh crossbar. I recognized the handle. It was the broom he'd lifted a week ago from his father's bakery store. It was neatly notched for the crosspiece pusher, and he'd screwed it down just right. It was a slick machine, and I could see he was going to rule the streets this summer.

"I can't go hooping today, Ronnie," I said. "And I can't go tomorrow neither and not the day after that. Fact is I can't go out at all this summer because I'm going out to The Place and I'm going to drive the new tractor my uncle Ned bought for me."

My mother came out of the house and looked back and forth at the pair of us. She could see the new difference. She set down the suitcase at my feet and handed me the key. "You can probably roll your hoop out to the cemetery with Junior if you want, Ronnie," she said, stifling her laughter as she picked up the small belted suitcase and handed it to me. "But maybe you should ask your mother first if it's okay."

"She ain't to home," he spat. "Anyways, she don't care where I go since I can go anywhere I want in the summertime."

"Now, Junior," ignoring Ronnie and said in a Mother's voice, "remember to ask Vera if you can help around the house, and make sure you don't just leave your clothes on the floor like you usually do, and listen now . . . I packed you a toothbrush. Remember what Dr. Ziehr told you if you want to stay away from him next fall."

I said, "What about that new Superman comic, did you pack it? I just bought it. And my little radio?"

"Yes comic, no radio. You know they don't have electricity out at The Place."

She reached down and kissed me on the forehead.

"I guess I'm off," I said, shoving the suitcase out in front of me. "Coming, Ronnie?"

"Yeah sure. I'll go as far as Schefchick's is all."

Mother stood watching us until we turned the corner down toward the bridge. I could see she had her handkerchief out waving. Ronnie wheeled around me in circles and did some spin-outs to show me how he was going to rule the roads this summer. He kept ragging me about the old swimming hole and the promise of some new dirty pictures old man Stark had given him, and all the other miracles that were going to happen while I slaved away all summer on the farm. I could tell he was worried. My life was going somewhere, it wasn't just another summer of hooping, hanging out at the creek skinny-dipping, going to Saturday night cowboy movies and reading comics and looking at dirty pictures and smoking weeds down behind von Schoen's barn.

I ignored him and concentrated on my suitcase, and then after a while, I realized he wasn't following me anymore. I turned around and looked for him. There he was, standing in front of Shefchick's gas station. He was holding the hoop in one hand and the stick in the other. I waved back to him, but he just stood there watching me as I stepped right over the edge of the world, and on purpose.

3

You couldn't tell just where the town ended, it just broke up a little at a time until it became the country. And it didn't really matter which was which. *Country* was where you farmed a quarter-section of oats and timothy and corn and had thirty, maybe forty cows, and *town* was where they put you when your hands were too stiff to milk a cow and when your sons had finally learned to fix the hayrake on their own and when they sold the horses to the fox farm and then wanted you out so they could move their kids into your bedroom.

In between town and country and below the cemetery was a narrow sandy creek with a collar of pine woods and reedy swamp they called 'No Nothin' Creek' because it didn't amount to much, some calling it 'Piss Creek' because the sandy bottom made the water look like pee juice.

You could smell country in town, and town – the feed mills and stores and garages and the canning factory – in the country. Nobody ever groused about it one way or another. It was just something to talk about. "Well, Lonny Erdman was out early this morning spreading pig manure in that sandy pasture down by the creek," Art Lampham says to Ray Korth, come to the post-office to pick up the mail for his Red-and-White Food Market, and Ray says, "You can't grow nothing on that piece, I don't know why he keeps trying to." And Lonny Erdman cleaned out the pig pen and said, "They must be canning wax beans now. You can smell the brine and those stinky boots they wear cleaning out the cookers."

* * *

We called our family farm 'The Place.' It rose above No Nothin' Creek right there where town and country reached a fine balance. The house was in the middle of a long blue lawn and a grove of glossy oak and maple trees. It was a small house. On the first floor there was a tiny mudroom, a kitchen, dining room, living room, and one bedroom. There were two bedrooms on the second floor. That was pretty well it. If you looked north from Uncle Buck's bedroom, you saw white houses and streetlights, the canning factory and the silver water tower, but if you looked south from Aunt Vera's bedroom, you saw nothing but hayfields and cow pastures, creeks, hills and woods. The gothic barn lay to the southeast of the house, down and across the sandy driveway and in between two concrete silos and an iron windmill on the slope that sounded like an airplane crashing when it got too windy. In between the house and the barn was the cement-block milkhouse, and just east of it the machine shed with the old sleigh in it, the pig pens, and granary.

Out at the roadside stood Aunt Nettie. Nettie was built like a football player: short, square, a neck like a tree trunk. She was tilted forward and dancing about as if tugging at a leash that kept her staked to the yard. I loved her a whole lot. They said she wasn't all there, but what *was* there was enough for me. She was my girlfriend and my pal. Standing there she was mouthing words, but I couldn't make them out until I was halfway up the hill.

"The tractor's come, the tractor's come!" I heard her say, eyes blinking, "Hurry up, Junior, hurry up! They're all down at the barn, Ned and Guzzy Sieg, him and whole bunch of fellas, they come in a great big white truck, you should see it. They had the tractor inside it and drove it right into the yard, and it's sitting down there just waitin' for you. Ned's down there too!"

She reached out and scooped me up when I got to her and bounced me up and down and bound me up into her fat old sweaty armpit and hustled me across the lawn and beneath the old oak trees bundled now with green acorns, and around the corner of the house, and there it was.

It sat in the yard between the machine shed and the horse barn. Everyone was gathered around it and staring at It. Grey, it was. Grey grey. The door to the horse stalls stood open, and Mack, the older Belgian, kicked at his straw bedding as he fixed his eyes upon the thing that had come to get him. A few black and white heifers had gathered in the yard and stood gazing through the slats of the pasture gate, chewing their cuds and wondering what the ruckus was all about, and a gaggle of red pullets strolled nearby clucking and scratching at the ground, thinking it was an occasion promising earthworms. Three old geezers sat on the tailgate of the big truck, legs dangling over the edge, their caps hung over their knees, sitting and whispering solemnly and pointing at the tractor as if, instead of having brought the thing to the farm themselves, they had heard rumours about it and come running to see what it looked like. Gramma was there too and had abandoned her chores and stood leaning on her pitchfork and smiling as if all her prayers had been answered.

Uncle Ned was kneeling before the tractor, a wrench held up to the front axle attaching a metal bar that looked like an upside-down T. Aunt Vera was there and had climbed up onto the back of the tractor and was tying a yellow pillow to the seat. And while everyone stood admiring the new tractor, we heard the kitchen screen door slam and turned and saw Aunt Esther, all gussied up and ready to go to work in town, hurrying toward us and carrying a sheaf of papers. Guzzy Sieg stood above Ned waiting for her. He was a big man with a red face and nose, but giggled like a kid when he pulled off his cap and bowed while she handed him the papers.

"Now, the Ford tractor was five hundred sixty-five dollars," she said in a chippy official voice, ignoring me, "and the Ferguson attachments – the cultivator and the harrow and the plow – they came to two hundred twenty."

"That's very good of you, Miss Esther." Guzzy's face went redder still, and he tried to cram his voice into a small place. "Now, I know this sounds like maybe a lot of money and all –"

"I've made the cheque out for seven hundred eight-five dollars."

"Miss Esther, that's a whole lot of money, you don't have to pay me all to once't."

"Guzzy, you know Mama," she said, and the two of them looked over at my grandmother, who still stared at the tractor with something like tears in her eyes, swaying from time to time as if listening to something it was saying to her. "She always pays up front, it's the way she does business."

"Well, then, that's mighty fine of you folks."

"Ned's milking fifty cows now, you know. He's got money in the bank."

"Well, all right, Miss Esther, if that's the way you want it!"

Aunt Esther then came over to me and swung her hip and laughed, "So you're finally here, Junior. This is just for you, I hear." She crammed my old man's voice into hers. "I just hope you don't run over some cows and tip over on a hill."

Guzzy folded the cheque and stuffed it into his bib pocket and turned to watch Ned lifting a large red can shoulder-high filling the gas tank. Vera climbed off the tractor and came and stood beside Nettie as if waiting for the curtain to go up on some kind of show. "Think you can do it?" she whined. "Your pa don't think you can."

"What does he know?" I laughed.

"Of course you can drive it!" laughed Vera. "Ned says you can drive it, you can drive it. Ned ought to know. When you come and take over The Place, you'll have to know about things like this."

The tractor didn't look much like the ones on the other farms: the big green monster John Deeres, the big tall red Farm-Alls, the dark orange Allis-Chalmers . . . old clanky iron monsters with ugly faces. This one was sleek and grey and hugged the ground like a kind bully with smooth muscles and a sassy torso and an I-can-do-it! grin on its face.

"This's a new kind of tractor," explained Guzzy Sieg, barely able to contain himself, walking all around it as if announcing the birth of a god. "It's called 'the Harry and Henry Special'. That's because of Henry Ford, he built it to carry Harry Ferguson's three-point hitch and power system. Ferguson's a Limey, you know. Henry Ford went over there to see him before the bombs started fallin', and then the two of them got together on this little baby with only a handshake. It's got a power take-off. That's brand new. You see how it works. You can move that hitch there just behind the seat up and down, depending how high you want the blades of the plow or the rake or the cultivator to run. Power runs straight back to the implements, and another thing is, you can slide the front wheels in or out, dependin' on whether you're cultivating or plowin', and those rear wheels, they can be turned inside out for different jobs, mud or no mud. It's a godsend for farmers runnin' early in the spring or late in the fall."

We watched then as Ned climbed onto the tractor and started it up. You could barely hear the motor. "You can see the Ford's way quieter than all those big ol' John Deeres. And to help out with the war effort, it uses half the gasoline, but it's still just as powerful."

"But why's it grey, Mr. Sieg?" said Esther. "Have we run out of colours?"

"Right you are, Miss . . . colours gone off to war. Grey's about all that's left."

The driver's seat was like a yellow lily on a pond. The large black steering wheel, almost horizontal, leaned out over the long grey hood and seemed to ask the driver to give it a good hug if he intended to drive off somewheres.

After Ned started it up, we backed off and gathered together in the shadow of the machine shed to see what would happen next. He shifted into low gear and backed up and then drove it around in a small circle, stone-faced, worried, and when he straightened out, shifting into second, and took off toward the chicken coop, we decided to run after him. The three men in the truck jumped off the tailgate and joined us. It was like a cicus. Guzzy Seig waited in the middle of the yard and clapped his hands like the ringmaster. As Ned looped around past the dog pens, now in high gear, his bloodhounds leaped into the wire fence howling like mad, and then Ned turned toward the outhouse and headed toward the woodshed and the milkhouse, and we ran faster, laughing and pulling each other along. Gramma was way behind us and breathing hard until she stopped and held her side, we came around the milkhouse, we watched Ned pull up and park beside the horse barn. He jumped to the ground, calming the Belgians dancing about in their stalls, and we surrounded Ned, and the three men from the tractor company pounded him on his back, congratulating him.

"It sure is a fine machine!" they roared. "We couldn't catch up!"

"Yup," said Ned. "It's sure-footed all right."

"Now, if it needs any fine-tune, Ned," said Guzzy Sieg, coming over and putting his arm around Ned's shoulders, "you just bring her on down to the shop, or if it don't start or it runs ragged, why I'll come out and fix it right here. You know there's a one year warranty on it."

Ned looked over at me and said, "All right, Junior, it's your turn."

"No, no, no!" cried Nettie, changing her mind. "He's way too small. Why, he ain't but nine years old!"

"Oh, Nettie, who asked you anyways?" said Vera, pulling me away from Nettie. "I don't suppose you got those potatoes peeled for dinner tonight!"

"Nettie's right, you know," said Guzzy. "Nine's a tad small for the job."

Ned ignored Guzzy and came over and wreathed his arm about my shoulders and steered me toward the tractor. "You remember how I taught you to drive the pickup?" he said. "Well, a tractor's about the same thing as drivin' a pickup, don't you think?"

Ned climbed onto the tractor seat, and I sat on his lap. He took off his cap and crowned me with it. The cap came down over my eyes. I placed my hands on top of his as he held tight to the steering wheel, my feet over his resting on the clutch and brake. With him there, I felt safe and secure and warm, lean and powerful! Ned's voice stroked my ears, his instructions easy to follow. He pressed down the clutch on the left and we were off. We made a circuit through the yard, this time a little slower, the hounds shouting, chickens flying into the trees, the horses thundering, and everyone walking along this time, weighing Ned's instructions, and when we eventually circled and came back to the horse barn, I jumped off his lap and was grabbed, hugged and petted by Nettie, and then Guzzy Sieg pronounced everything in good order and took his three men and drove back to town in his big van.

I looked toward town and imagined Ronnie running his hoops up and down the sidewalks and bragging.

The next morning it was good and hot. Ned and I drove the new tractor out into the barnyard. The cows were lying all about, resting up from milking and chewing their cuds and thinking about maybe heading out for some lime greens in the pasture. When they saw the tractor coming, however, one by one they got to their feet and slunk off into the fence corners. They bunched up there as we headed for them. They scattered and proved impossible to hit. Then we lit out for the fields to find a good hill. It was cool riding into the wind. The Place was mostly flatland, but there was one minor hill back near the Wadley Place, just this side of the railroad tracks. When we got out there, Ned climbed onto one of the high fenders. "Okay," he said, "she's all yours." I sat all by myself in the seat then and drove the tractor up and down and all around the hill three or four times and didn't come even close to tipping over.

4

That first summer I slept with Vera.

Not with Esther, though her bed was just a foot away from Vera's bed, and certainly not with Nettie, who had inherited Uncle Buck's bedroom. Nettie had for years slept in Esther's bed, but Esther took it back when she came home after her husband Pug sat on his mother's tombstone and stuck a gun into his mouth and pulled the trigger. It would've made perfect sense to put Esther into Buck's bedroom because Esther wasn't going to hang around The Place too long, but even if she did and then Buck came home from the war, he probably wouldn't want his old bed back.

As I said, soon as Pug was in the ground, here comes Esther, and so Nettie got shoved into Buck's room. That's the way it went with Nettie. She could be stored anywhere, like an extra chair or a broken lamp or an old set of dented silverware. Because as I said before she wasn't all there. That's what Vera told me, she said, "Nettie's not all there, you know." I used to sit and stare at Nettie and wonder what part was missing.

Of course I knew *something* was.

One thing, Nettie used to sit and sway back and forth and blink her gray rubber eyes and model the air in front of her with her stubby fingers. The fingers were what upset Vera most. She'd reach over and slap at Nettie's hands and say, "You stop that, Nettie, you stop it right now!" Nettie would wait a while and when Vera wasn't looking, she'd start the elaborate finger ballet all over again, and next time Vera would smother the dancing fingers with her hands and say, "We can put you away, you know!" That's all it took. Nettie would stomp out of the house and straight into the woodshed, where she'd stand and foam at the mouth in front of a hundred cords of yellow elm and box elder. We'd sit in the house and listen to her going off by herself and stare at each other and feel somehow cursed that we were a family that had one of *those kinds* of people in it. Talk always started up again and and Uncle Emil, if he was there, would lecture us all over again about the invasion of Poland and how we should change our name from 'Draeger' to 'Dreyer' or even better 'Smith.' Some said yah let's do it, and others, especially Aunt Esther said but how would we get the mail? and Uncle Emil would say, "We will have to call you 'Esther Smith.'"

I'd wait until I had a chance to slip out to the woodshed and walk up behind Nettie and put my arms around her and tell her Vera would have to put me away too if it came to that.

I finally figured out that Aunt Esther had the part that was missing from Nettie. She had high Prussian cheekbones and stout jaws for clamping down on ideas and grinding out large and difficult words. Her hair was shiny sleek and bobbed in town style, and she wore brown cloche hats and three strands of pearls and bright silk dresses that came to just above her knees. And she seemed always to be in motion.

Not long after Esther moved back to The Place, she got a job in the bank in town, went into it a teller and came out the loan manager and vice-president. She drove a butter-yellow 1938 Ford Roadster and filled up the rumble seat with giggling women whose husbands had gone off to war. We used to see them laughing and crooning some jazzy tune as they headed for Clearwater, where we heard they went bowling with men and afterward sat around drinking beer and dancing in smoky bars. And sometimes she took her girlfriends out to her cabin on the far side of the lake, where they paddled along the lakeshore wearing two-piece lavender swimsuits, or kept their neighbours up as they drank and danced the night away to the Victrola on the screened porch. Esther occasionally drove around town a little too fast for Fatty Cameron, our town cop, who always sat on a stool at the water fountain on Main Street and scowled at the Illinois cars speeding through town on their way toward the fat muskies waiting for them at the bottoms of lakes in the far north. He'd yell at them and blow his whistle, but none of them ever stopped. One day he blew Esther to a stop and made her leave her keys under water in the fountain for the rest of the day because of the way she drove her car.

Before she moved back home, Esther and Pug Pabst lived in a town about ten miles away from our town. It was even smaller and had nothing much to show for it, except for Carole Landis being born there. Esther used to invite my sister Bits and me down to her house for the weekend. It was a whirling dervish of window ledges and end tables strewn with gewgaws and gadgets that moved and went clickety-clack and flashed out colours, and she had a big wood radio with a green eye that watched you when you turned it on. She made chocolate cakes and told us wild stories about the people living in big old houses built by rich men in the 1870s when it was a railroad town. I don't remember much about Pug Pabst. I know he drank four cups of coffee at breakfast and wore a monocle and ate his one piece of toast without butter on it and smoked three straight cigarettes and then walked over to his dry goods store every morning at five minutes to eight and came back every night at five past six and poured himself a drink and dropped into a chair and smoked three more cigarettes as he vanished behind a newspaper. One Monday morning, as I said, instead of going to the store, Pug took his .22 rifle down to the cemetery and and ended it all.

Right after his funeral, of course, Esther came and got her old bed back.

So that first summer I slept with Vera. Until the end of July. It was a Sunday, if I remember, and we were getting ready for church and Vera came to me and said, "This afternoon you're going to empty out your drawers in that highboy and take your stuff to Ned's room."

I looked at her, but she refused to look back.

"How come?"

"You're sleeping with Ned starting tonight."

"How come?"

"Because."

"Because why?"

"Just because!"

"Why don't I just leave everything in the highboy and move over to Esther's bed?"

"No."

"How about Gramma's then?"

"You know that bed ain't safe!"

That was true. Something was wrong with every darn bed in the house.

Even Vera's. It had sprangy springs and sagged in the middle and sometimes I woke up in the middle of the night and found myself rolled flat up against Vera. She'd roll me back up my side and stick a pillow between us to keep me there. And then too it was always hot in that bed. Vera loved flannel sheets even in summertime. Still, I loved the heavy old star and moon quilt fraying about the edges, and I used to lie on my back in the morning after she went out to the barn and lift my knees and the quilt into the air and then let my imagination run up and down the cotton sky and watch the stars and the moon vanish and slowly reappear. My stars, my moon, my sky. I remember running my hands around the white curlicues of the metal headboard, feeling safe in a little world of flowers and leaves.

On the far wall stood Esther's bed, a mahogany temple, its carved head and footboards and four tall pillars calling to one another. It had once been Gramma's bed, and it still wore her heavy tufted cotton mattress, very hard and full of stains Vera said were Nettie's, when she slept there, and Nettie said were Gramma's. Esther hated that bed. Every morning at breakfast she sat up and rubbed her back and complained about it, until at last Gramma, whose bedroom was downstairs just off the parlour, said she'd be happy exchanging and getting her old bed back, but Esther always said, "No thanks, I don't want to wake up in the middle of the night and find myself laying on a cold floor."

Gramma's bed had been fetched all the way from back East in a covered wagon. It took up the whole room and had tall fancy bedposts. You had to climb up onto a chair to crawl into it. Gramma told me it fell out of the covered wagon and had to be nailed back together, and you just couldn't trust it any longer because sometimes in the middle of the night for no reason it would suddenly disintegrate, starting with one corner, then another . . . sagging, splintering, clattering inward until it was just a pile of rubble. Everyone would wake up when Gramma would shout, *"Ned! Ned! Hilfe! Komm' doch! Bin nochmal aus 'em Bett 'runtgefallen!"* And Ned would have to get up and light his lamp and go downstairs and nail the bed back together again.

Gramma told me she hadn't had one good sleep in that bed since Opa moved out to the milk house, where he still slept in a crawl space up in the attic. Every night he climbed up the narrow creaky steps and crawled through a small doorway into a loft in which all you could see were two pieces of furniture: a tall oak chest of drawers and an old birchbark bed.

I was told this bed had come from a slave cabin on a cotton plantation down in Mississippi. Abe Freundschaft, the one-legged trapper who later on lived in a shack in the woods out behind Opa's first farm up at Dee's Lake, took over the plantation as its company headquarters. Luke Everby, a Black man who was one of the slaves left behind to greet the company, became company cook, and when the company got orders to come back home, he chose to go along with them. He brought his bed with him, but got only as far as his first snowstorm and changed his mind and decided to go back to Mississippi. He gave the bed to Abe, who knew you couldn't look a gift bed in the mouth, and therefore brought it home. Thirty years later he died in it, and left a note saying he was going to give it to the only man who ever cared about him. Opa then had brought it along to The Place, where it lay in a pile above the rafters in the machine shed for the longest time, until at last Ned cut the legs off it, reassembled it in the milk house loft, and installed Opa in it.

In those days Ned had to sleep in the feed room above the granary. His bed was little more than a set of fir two-by-fours with short legs and a cornhusk mattress and goose-feather pillow. It didn't matter to Ned, he was asleep before his head hit the pillow and woke just before he had to get up to fetch the cows from the south forty. However, he told me he had to fight off granary mice, and sometimes it got pretty cold in the winter, so he was relieved at last to move into the house when they walled in a part of the attic to make a fourth bedroom. Ned's old bed was still up there in the granary, but now it was used to dry out gunnysacks. I used to go up and lie in the bed and pretend I was Uncle Ned looking for mice.

"What about Nettie then?" I asked. She was my last hope. I had run out of women. "I'm sure she wouldn't mind if I slept with her."

"No."

"Why?"

"Because."

"Because she's not all there, is that it?"

"No, that's not it. You know that."

"Why then?"

"It's a single bed. Anyways that bed belongs to Buck!"

"But he's not here. He's down in Texas flying secret airplanes."

She gasped when I said that. You weren't supposed to say anything about Buck and flying airplanes even when nobody was around to hear you. Even when we got together at Thanksgiving or Christmas everyone talked about cows and chickens and pigs and changing our German name, but nobody talked about Buck's flying secret airplanes. Buck himself got it all started when he hinted at it in a letter for the first time. He said he'd graduated from old yellow Harvards to a plane that could fly four hundred miles an hour and had two tails on it. Having heard that, we all huddled in the room whispering about it as if there were spies in the barn. When she first heard it, Nettie sat back and twiddled her fingers. "Nobody can't go four hundred miles an hour!" she guffawed. "Shhhh!" Uncle Jules growled. But they all had something to say about it, everybody that is but Uncle Ned. He just sat there half asleep. Ned never talked much if women were around. He was a silent man, a lone cowboy, he had spent his whole life in the fields by himself, planting, plowing and haying and harvesting, and then, soon as the snows came, he was deep in the woods hunting and trapping till that first thaw.

I came along and changed all that, breaking in on him.

So together, we spent that first summer, the two of us, working our way back and forth across the fields, plowing or cultivating corn, haying, harvesting, and at last, just before I went back to school in the fall, filling the two silos with corn silage. He became my summer father. He talked to me when we were together out in the fields. So far as he could manage anyways. I drove the tractor and pulled him as he worked the hay-wagon and loader up and down hills, never tipping over, back and forth across endless windrows of sweet-smelling dry timothy and alfalfa. Ned sweated mightily, stowing the dry hay coming off the loader about the wagon until the stack was twenty feet high and then he'd shout, "Whoa, Junior!" He'd walk around behind the wagon and unhitch the loader and come and sit on the tractor with me and wipe sweat off his face, and we'd drive the hayload back to the barn.

Often 'Whoa, Junior!' was all I'd get from him in a day.

But that Sunday when Vera kicked me out of her bed, he surprised me by coming to talk to me when we were pitching hay down the hay shute. I could see him looking for words, and finally, when he had them all lined up, he said, "Well, Junior, looks like you and me goin' to be bedmates."

"Looks like it. Don't know why though."

"Well . . . I guess you're too old to be sleepin' with women."

"I never had trouble sleeping with women before."

I had trouble sleeping with Ned that first night.

I lay there watching him take his clothes off. His long hairy pure-white arms and legs made him look like a spider. I moved over to the other side of the bed for fear of being bitten. The bed bounced around for a while when he got in, and then he lay there flat on his back with his arms cradling his head as he stared up into the ridgepole of the house. His lips moved once or twice, but he didn't say anything, and I thought, Oh no, he's talking to the spiders in the rafters. That wasn't good. But then he went straight to sleep and started to snore. Seemed however as if I had just got to sleep when the bed bounced around like a boat, and Ned lit a lamp and got up and dressed and went out to bring the forty-five Holsteins in from the back pasture.

He always left the lamp burning because he wanted me to get up and help with chores. I looked at his clock. It was four in the morning. I blew the lamp out and finally got some sleep, and woke just after seven when I heard everyone coming back to the house from milking and washing up for breakfast. I got dressed and went downstairs and sat at the table. Opa sat there looking at his lap, likely praying, and Gramma was watching him and speaking German. Ned came and sat down, but he didn't say a word to me, as if maybe he blamed me for all the snoring and tossing and turning and then not getting up at four o'clock. Esther came downstairs looking pale and frightened. She sat and scowled and then announced she had a dream about Uncle Buck dying in an airplane crash.

Nettie sat staring at Esther, her fingers flying, lips moving for a while and then said, "Why can't you dream about something good for a change?"

"Well, Nettie," Esther said angrily, "you think I can do anything about it? You can't plan out your dreams."

Vera came into the room toting a huge platter of steaming hotcakes, which she set right in front of Ned, and then slipped around the table and stood behind her chair.

"Nettie's going to move downstairs," she announced in a strained voice. "She's going to sleep with Ma till Junior goes home."

But it seemed she had forgot to tell Gramma, who looked up at her and exhaled sharply and said, "Why, that bed can't take two fat people!"

"I'm not fat as you are!" said Nettie, casting her words at her mother.

"Well, she sure can't move into my bed," said Esther. "I can't sleep with *anyone* any more."

"After breakfast," said Vera, looking at me, "you can move your stuff out of Ned's room and into Buck's, and Nettie, this morning you better move your stuff downstairs."

They all turned and looked at me as if it was some kind of a prize I had won. All but Nettie, who was stuck inside one of her ideas: "I don't know why *she* always says *I'm* fat. I'm not fat. She's fat. If I'm fat, she's even fatter."

Gramma looked to Opa for defense, but Opa didn't seem to be able to follow what was being said and sat there staring at us as if he'd discovered he was still sitting among cows.

"Oh, for goodness sakes, Nettie," said Vera, sitting at last, "we're not even talking about being fat!"

Buck's bed was plain and simple. It had a varnished wood frame and head and footboards, and the legs had been turned on a lathe and sprouted pointy spindle tops. "Store-bought sheets, they never fit the bed right," said Vera, making the bed before heading out to the chicken coop, "so Esther and me, we had to make all Buck's sheets on the sewing machine."

"That's because Buck built that bed at school," said Nettie, standing in the doorway twiddling and snapping her fingers. "He made it only to fit himself. He was five foot nine and one-half inches long and he made it that way, and then he wanted two foot out on the sides because he was tired of fallin' out of bed all the time –"

"Well, Nettie," barked Vera, "of course he didn't want to fall out of bed! You think people like falling out of bed?"

"But when he brought it home and set it up and then went to bed," said Nettie, giggling, ignoring her, "he fell right out of it onto the floor."

"Oh, Nettie, Buck didn't fall out of bed that night!"

"Yes, he did! He fell right out of bed."

"No, he didn't, Nettie. Now stop making up stories about falling out of bed!"

The bed faced the window looking toward town. It was the way Buck left it when he went off to war. In fact, everything in the room was just the way he left it. His clothes still hung in mothballs in the closet, the walls were covered with high school sports pennants, and there was a picture of an Indian princess kneeling before a wigwam. His school medals were all laid out on a shelf, and then there was a picture of Liz Stelter, his girl friend. She had signed it, it said, "I'll never forget you, Dear Bucky!"

That first night I blew out the lamp and lay perfectly still on my back in the middle of the bed. It seemed to fit me fine. It didn't curl or bounce the least. It didn't squeak. I knew I wasn't going to miss Vera's bed at all, and I was so happy to have escaped Ned's snoring.

The moon sifted its light through the dancing lace curtains. I sat up on my elbows and looked through the window. I wondered if Buck hadn't already done this too, looked out at the moon and the oak trees in the yard and the garden running down to No Nothin' Creek, where the cows lay chewing their cuds, and beyond all that, up across to the cornfields and the alfalfa pastures rising like incense in the night. I felt I had for the moment anyway eluded my father's grasp. I had my own bed. My own bedroom. I had my own Gramma and Opa and Ned and Vera and Nettie and Esther, and someday maybe I would have the whole farm. I slipped out of bed and went to the window, knelt and pushed back the lace curtains. I looked out across the fields at the cemetery and the trees that walled in the town.

Then I heard a train. It came hooting down through The Cut and I watched until it vanished, and all that was left then was the moon Uncle Ned must've looked at too.

5

Opa and Gramma, Uncle Ned and Aunt Esther and Aunt Vera and Aunt Nettie and then me. You got one king and queen, one prince, three princesses, and a pretender to the throne. What I mean to say is The Place was very like a medieval castle with its own towers and courtyards and walls and a deep moat of wheat and cornfields. Or maybe it was just plain old Opa, Gramma, Ned, Esther, Vera, Nettie, and me, all living out there in the countryside, surrounded by flocks and herds and even a pack of hunting dogs. They were stuck inside the farm and those four walls twenty-four hours a day – except for attending church Sunday mornings – every hour, every day, every month, every year. There were no vacations and very little truck with neighbors and the outer world. We had no radio, no telephone, no electricity, and we were hidden by corn stalks high as an elephant's eye in summer and in winter by high snowbanks.

Vera ran things, she made things go. Yet I found something odd about her that very first week I moved onto The Place. I noticed it was her custom when chores or meals were over and done with to walk into the parlour and stand twisting a tea towel behind her back while all the while gazing out one of the front windows into the gravel road that ran from town until it reached the front of the house. She would stand in the window without moving for ten minutes or more, barely breathing, as if under some kind of spell.

One time I slipped up behind her and saw her face reflected in the window. A long sad face, her eyes dark, something like defeat. It struck me she was gazing at something out there in the road that had happened a long time ago. I decided to ask her what she was looking at. "Oh, Junior!" she screamed, one hand to her heart, eyes full of terror. "Why, you scared me half to death!" Her face went white and she leaned back against the wall. "I didn't know you was in the house. What are you doing in the house, anyway? Thought you was helping Ned clean out the horse stalls."

I said, "I was just wondering what you were looking at out there in the road."

She thought about it a while and then said, "Who, me?" I nodded back. "Looking out at the road? Why, I wasn't looking out at the road. I wasn't looking at anything." She giggled and turned to look out at the road. "I was just . . . looking!" She turned to look at me, and now we were both laughing sadly. "Why, there's nothing out there to look at anyway."

She walked back into the dining room, and I looked out at the road to see if she was right. And she *was* right, there was nothing out there. But still, something was out there because the next day I found her back at the same window looking out at that same road, and so I started playing a game with her. I would say, "I caught you looking, what are you looking at?" and she would say, "I'm not looking at nothing." And then I would look out the window and say, "I don't see nothing out there." And she would say, "That's what I said," and I would say, "You're right," and she laughed sadly and would say, "There's nothing out there." And then we both would laugh. Sadly.

But I knew something was out there she didn't want to talk about. She could see what it was, but I couldn't.

Not yet anyways.

I went in to town on a weekend late in July because it was Bits' birthday, and I made up my mind to ask my mother about all this standing in the window and looking out at the road. Mom knew a lot about Vera. She told me once she had stayed at The Place for a month after she married my old man because she didn't have a place of her own.

She had baked a big birthday cake for Bits and spiked it with five candles, and now my old man sat at the table smiling and watching me carefully as if worried I was going to stumble and fall into the cake. I knew he knew he had lost control over me for the summer and was thinking up ways of getting it back again come fall. Most of that weekend I ignored him, and he ignored me. I kept looking for opportunities to get my mother aside and ask her about Vera. It didn't happen until Sunday, my old man being in the woods and Bits was away celebrating at a girlfriend's house.

I spelled out the story about the strange parlor game Vera and I were playing. "I'm sure there's something she sees out there in the road," I said. "She can see it, but I can't."

"Maybe you don't know what to look for."

"It's not like she's waiting for someone. It's more like she can't figure out where someone went."

"How did you know that?" she gasped, her hand to her heart. "Did she tell you all about him?"

"About who?"

"Did she say anything to you about Homer Brighton?" I shook my head, and she walked away from me and over to her own front window. "She's probably still thinking about Homer Brighton."

"Homer Brighton who?"

"A man she knew a long, long time ago. A man who shivered her heart into tiny little pieces. Homer Brighton left her . . . no, that's not right because she left *him.*" She looked down at me. "But that's not right either. You'd have to say she *dismissed* him. He had no choice in the matter. She sent him on his way. And she's never gotten over it." She turned around and fixed me with her large warm eyes. "Now, you don't really need to know any more than that." She went and sat down. "You go on out to the Place now, you'll be late for chores."

"It's because I'm too little, isn't it?"

"Too little?"

"I'll have to wait till I grow up."

"No, not that either. It's just . . . well, for one thing, it's taken *me* all this time to forget Homer Brighton. Why should I try to bring him back? We never talk about him any more. Nobody does. It's like he never existed. I don't even remember what he looked like now. I doubt she can either. And I don't even want to think about what he looked like." She smiled like a girl and looked out her own window for him. "Good-looking man, that he was. Tall man, curly dark, reddish hair. Always wore a hat with a tiny blue feather in it. He had this mole . . . right in the middle of his right cheek, and it sort of glowed when he talked!"

Since Bits was away, she decided to walk me back out to The Place that afternoon and while gathering wild asparagus out of the ditches along the road she told me the whole story.

It was already early November when he got to The Place, she said, and then he sat out in the road in that high old black car of his for three days and two nights.

Vera had seen him get out of it only that once. Early in the morning that second day. He took off his bowler and set it beside him on the horsehair seat and then stepped down into the road and walked over to the barbed-wire fence of a hayfield that ran down to No Nothing Creek. He bent over then and shoved a small black bag under the bottom wire, and, balancing himself with the grace of an acrobat, mounted the wires clear to the top and balanced there for a moment, his arms held out like wings and flew gracefully down to earth. She ran to the other window to see him strolling across the stubble of the field as if it was his own. The sun had come out at last, but you could still see his breath. She stood in the window hoping nobody would notice him. Half an hour later he came back from the creek. His beautiful broad forehead shone in the sunshine, the thick black hair combed close to his temples, the large, crisp jaw clean-shaven, the black pin-stripe suit, white shirt and red-striped tie neat and tidy, as if just back from a barber's shop. He climbed the fence again and got back into his high black car, sat over the wheel, and crowned himself with the hat. Without looking once back at her house, he drew the car blanket about him and lit a cigar.

All he lacked was the morning paper.

She knew – and had always admired – his pride and tenacity, but this business now, him sitting all day and all night in his car out at the road . . . Why, he seemed content just to sit there gazing straight ahead through the windshield of the car as if what he was doing was perfectly normal. Now and then he nibbled on a few salt peanuts or peeled and quartered a small green apple or an orange. Not once did he even bother to look over at the house. He didn't seem at all interested in the comings and goings and wasn't upset that while walking outside Vera hadn't paid any attention to him, not even on that very first day.

Shortly after he had arrived, Buck and tiny Esther disobeyed Vera's instructions and ran out to the car. Homer rolled down the window and with a boyish laugh tossed a handful of peanuts in the shell to them, but before they could run and collect them, Vera called them back to the house, and after a stern lecture, sent them to their rooms.

Homer had arrived around noon on a Saturday. He drove straight up from the highway (anyway, this is what Nettie told us, being as how she was out in the front yard raking leaves when they didn't even need raking) and turned around in the driveway, backed up and parked just off the driveway right in front of the house. Nettie also told us how she stood and waited for him to get out of the car and come to the house, and when he just sat there without moving, she called to him, "Ain't you comin' into the house, Homer?" Maybe he hadn't heard her. She walked out to the car and shouted again, and this time he shook his head. "Why not?" she asked, and then he rolled down the window and told her she should go ask her sister why not. Which is precisely what she did. "Vera," she asked, "why ain't Homer comin' into the house?" Vera herself might have known the answer, but she sure wasn't going to offer it to a dim-witted sister who couldn't keep her tongue in her mouth. She then issued the order she gave everyone else: "Now listen, Nettie, you stay away from that car, do you hear! If you go near that car, I'll lock you up in the chicken coop!"

Maybe Vera *did* know why he was there, maybe she didn't. But really, when you thought about it, whatever would possess a man to leave his family and friends way down in Chicago, walk out on his work, ignore the ultimatum in Vera's last letter, drive four hundred miles over patched roads though they predicted snowstorms, and then park right in front of her house and just sit there? She figured she had wiped the ledger clean when she told him weeks ago it was all over, that she had quit her job in his father's factory and moved back home because she had to, not because she wanted to, and that she was never coming back down there again because she couldn't come back down there, and that was that. She couldn't believe it when one week later she got a letter from him in which he said he was putting his business on hold and coming up to The Place to get her and take her back home. And he wasn't going to leave without her.

"It don't matter what you said in that letter," her tearful mother whispered as she looked past Vera's shoulder through the window at the man in the car, "the least you can do is go out there and invite him in to supper. He must be a block of ice by now, it hasn't been over fifty all day."

Maybe, thought Vera. But she knew that once Homer got his foot in the door, it was all over: she would have to pack her bags, climb into his car and ride back to Illinois with him and become his wife.

Which was, after all, what she so desperately wanted in the first place.

That night after chores, her father, bent over by rheumatoid osteoarthritis and pale with prostate cancer, walked out to the car and ordered Homer into the house. The man in the car smiled politely and said, "Albert, the only way I will vacate this car and come into your house is if Vera herself comes out here and tells me to do it."

They ate supper that night without Homer Brighton. Nobody said much until Nervous Nettie broke the ice: "How come he's sittin' out there like that? Why don't he come in and eat supper and talk to us?" Vera stared at her plate as if she had found a worm in her mashed potatoes. Ned, to save his sister from embarrassment, said, "Oh shut up, Nettie! This is none of your business!" Nettie picked up a spoon and threw it on the floor and then got up and stomped out of the house and into the woodshed. They sat for a while, and finally Ned had to go out there and tell Nettie as long as she was outside to go feed the dogs and then close up the chicken coop for the night.

Vera went to bed early but couldn't sleep.

Sometime around midnight she crept down the narrow steps in the dark and slipped over to a window. The moonlight enshrined his car, shimmered in his many windows, sparkled and cascaded across his glossy fenders and outrageous Phaeton hood ornament, but somehow failed to find Homer's glorious form. His love, she feared, was more durable than his high black car. What woman in the world wouldn't die for such everlasting love and devotion? Perhaps being so right, she was also so horribly wrong. Her resolve began to melt. She thought to go into the dining room and take a white linen napkin out of the drawer in the sideboard and then walk out to his car waving it over her head as a sign she was ready to surrender and be carried off, married, and made to live happily ever after down in Chicago.

"Oh, Homer," she cried to herself, pressing her forehead against the cold pane, "why don't you just go on home and forget me. There ain't no glass slipper in the world would fit me now."

But she knew he wouldn't leave, and that was what gave him the edge.

At first light the next day she came downstairs and walked to the window again, hoping to see an empty road out there. But the car was still there. It was again on Sunday, and so she dressed for church and then went and stood in the window while Ned brought the truck around to the house. Her mother and she went out and got into it, and then Ned drove them out the driveway. Homer sat like a stone idol while they, clutching their Bibles, moved around and past him down the road. Homer's eyes were fixed on a book he was reading, confident that in the end he would prevail. He didn't have to look at them to tell them that. He was there too when they returned. He was there all Sunday afternoon and Sunday night. That night she did not slip down to the window, but neither did she sleep.

Monday came and went, and he was still there.

This wasn't going to work, Vera said to herself. That night shortly after everyone had gone to bed, she made up her mind to go and have it out with him. She put on her coat and slipped out the kitchen door and walked across the white crusty lawn to the edge of the road. It was then she discovered that the wind was up, and there was the unmistakable smell of snow in the cold air.

She huddled in the dark and studied Homer Brighton's outline in the car. A window was lowered, and she said, "You can sit out here in front of this house as long as you want, Homer, I'm not going back down there with you."

There was no response, not at first.

"There's no way you can say that now," he finally said, his words forming mist in the frigid air. "You made too many promises. That was where you went wrong. You accepted the ring, you wore it on your finger for a year . . . the announcement was in all the papers, you became a part of my family. My mother, who isn't easily swayed by farmers' daughters in the first place, she made you her princess, and my father, who drove you all the way to Rockford that time and took you through his factory and then after you came back, he went out and bought us a honeymoon suite at Niagara Falls . . . my father is ready to make you rich." He turned and stared at the wretched little house behind her. "You can't just say it's over. A couple of words, a sentence or two, it means nothing to me. You're only one half of the whole, Vera. I'm the other half, and I haven't said it's over, and until we both say it's over, it's not over."

She tried to keep her voice steady, but it cracked in the middle and spilled out: "But you read my letter, Homer. I thought I explained myself very carefully, and so you know why I can't come back with you –"

"I read the letter," he said, snapping, "and I read the letter again and it still made no sense at all to me."

"Well, it made perfect sense to *me*!"

"You'll be twenty-five next May, Vera, I'll be thirty. We aren't children anymore. You left home four years ago because you didn't want to become an old maid spending the rest of her life collecting eggs. You said you wanted to make something of yourself. You said you wanted to use your talents. You came and you got yourself a good job at my father's mill, you met a man, a rich and loyal and honest man, and when he asked you to marry him, you accepted him at once, and then you made plans to spend the rest of your life with him . . ."

She looked past the car at the woods and the hills. For sure it would snow before morning. She would wake and find him and his car buried up to the fenders in a snowbank unless, somehow, she could convince him to leave tonight.

"This has nothing to do with you, Homer. It has nothing to do with me. It's The Place, that's all. This is my home. They need me more than you do. I'm the only one who can save them. My father has cancer and it's getting worse, he can't help around the farm, and Ned can't do it all by himself, and my sisters Doris and Ollie and Esther have already up and left and have their own families somewhere else, and now Ma fell on the porch and hurt herself, and she can't keep up the house and care for the family and help with chores, and then there's Nettie –"

He suddenly stuck his gloved hand through the window and pointed a finger at her. "I don't want to hear another goddamn word about Nettie!" She jumped at the size of his voice. "I'm sick and tired of hearing about Nettie!"

She stood for a moment and then turned away from the high black car in the road and limped back across the icy lawn toward the dark house. A car door opened somewhere, and she knew he had gotten out and was coming after her. She didn't know whether to run or maybe turn now and slap him in the face. She did neither. She kept on walking slowly and surely across the white crust until he put his hand on her shoulder and wheeled her about and then held her out before him at arm's length for examination.

"Just how will you face it, Vera?" His eyes blazed and she could smell his sour breath. "How will you ever live it down?" When it was clear she wasn't going to answer his questions, he exhaled sharply and said, "Maybe you think you can just quit and devote the rest of your life to the religion of cows and chickens and pigs."

"Yes, maybe I can do that," she said with surprising strength. "Maybe that's the one thing I can do."

She waited for him to find something more to say, something that would allow him to be a man and to climb back up into his car and drive it off down the highway.

He studied her. It took him a while, but at last he found the right words: "All right, Vera . . . you know there are other women waiting for you to quit on me." He huffed and puffed in clouds of mist and then said, "I guess . . . well, I guess I have to say then that it's over. You leave me no choice." He turned to go but changed his mind. "You needn't worry about me. I won't write you any more. I won't bother you. You're on your own now. I know that's the way you want it."

She put what little breath she had left into a smile: "No, not the way I want it, Homer. It's the way it has to be."

He returned the smile, turned, and walked out to the road, got out the iron crank and walked around to the front of the high car, leaned over and heaved the crank with those beautiful arms of his, the engine now gasping for life, and then when it recovered, he climbed up into the car, and without once looking back at her, drove off down the road.

Vera stood in the yard watching him until his red rear light was gone. Her tears turned to ice. She looked up at the leaden sky. She was right. It was starting to snow. She walked to the woodshed, got out the snow shovel and set it by the back door. She would need it first thing in the morning. She would shovel a path to the milk shed and the outhouse and then down to the barn. She went into the house and climbed the stairs to her bed. She slept soundly that night. In the morning she came downstairs again and looked through the window at the road. She almost expected to find Homer Brighton back again, sitting in his high black car to make one more attempt to try to make her happy.

But there was nothing out there in the road.

"No matter how hard she looked out that window," said my mother when we reached the grey thicket of Draeger tombstones, "there was nothing to look at out there. Nothing at all."

6

I was sound asleep and yet I heard someone calling my name. I sat up in bed and heard the rain hammering the roof and saw branches of pulsing light in the window, and the whole house shook when the hard fists of thunder struck the ground.

"Junior!" shouted Vera from the doorway, "get up, boy, get up! We're all going downstairs! It's going to be a bad one!"

Somewhere behind her, I heard Esther say, "Has Ned gone down?"

"Ned!" cried Vera, and there came a muffled sleepy voice out of Ned's bedroom. "You had better get up now and come on downstairs."

A kerosene lamp cast a yellow and frightened figure on the wallpaper. Vera and Esther wore shoes and clumped down the narrow, nearly vertical stairway, and then in another flash of light I saw Ned stumbling out of his room hitching up his overalls. He was barefoot. "I guess we should've brought in that hay today," he said to me. "Now it'll get good and wet, and we'll have to leave it out for a few days because we have to get those peas in first."

I followed him down to the parlour.

Gramma and Nettie were already there, settled deep into the sofa, arms folded across their big belly pajamas, staring out the windows at the forked lightning. They looked like they were waiting for a bus. Wearing only his undershirt and overalls Ned fell into a chair beside Oma and said, "That hay's gonna get good and soaked now. I told Junior we should've brought it in today." A little while later Vera came into the house with her arm around Opa. He was wearing pajama bottoms and a torn shirt and looking thoroughly disgusted with her for dragging him down the ladder and into the house. Vera parked him on a hard-back chair at the dining table and went and fetched him a glass of water, and then she came and sat beside Esther in the creaky rocker at the far side of the room. Me, I sat on the piano bench watching the rain plaster the windows. "If Amos'd only showed up like he was supposed to," grumbled Ned to himself, "why, we'd have that hay in the barn by now."

Opa looked at all of us and said something like, "*Mir hat's mein Schirm nicht mitgebracht.*" I recognized the word 'umbrella', but the rest of it was mere noodle noise.

Nobody said a word in either German or English for the next ten, fifteen minutes. It wasn't allowed. You had to concentrate hard. You had to be ready to jump. Everyone knew that. It was part of the plan. Before a storm hit, you had to get out of bed and come downstairs and sit around huddled together in the dark, ready to climb up onto the raft. You just never knew. In this part of the world you just never knew.

Summer thunderstorms always came on capricious and baleful, black-bellied, torrential, serpentine, sometimes hatching tornadoes that slid to the ground and then blew barns and sheds and houses into smithereens, all the while hurling down lightning bolts so white you couldn't look at them. You wouldn't have been surprised to see a big old oak tree chopped to kindling right in front of your eyes. And seconds after the blinding light, thunder so insistent, it could crack the old fieldstone foundations of the house and hurl to the floor pots of African violets from the what-nots. Often we'd come down the next morning and go through the house straightening pictures and sweeping up plants and soil.

We sat there in the room imagining barns and farmhouses blazing because they were too far from town for fire engines and volunteer firemen. Our house, like the others up and down the valley, was crowned with four tall lightning rods harnessed to a network of braided wires threaded through green crystal balls, and down along the spine and over the eves and cornices straight into an iron stake in the ground. If the gods were particularly angry and heaved a bolt of lightning our way, the charge would, God Willing, be carried off harmlessly into the sweet neutrality of terra firma. An even larger harness shrouded the barn, with seven or eight giant lightning rods spiking the roof, and several green glass balls high, and even thicker braided wire trailing off over the eaves and down.

Even if there *was* a system of safety high on the roof, the seven of us sat there white-knuckled at our lifeboat stations. The lightning sliced the air that night, a brilliance both blinding and revealing. I studied the midnight masks of Gramma and Opa and all my aunts and my one dear uncle, and thought how very odd they all looked. Nettie twiddling her fingers and thumbs in that nervous, silent ballet in which she found reflection and consolation. Esther, back home now that her husband had shot himself with the very same .22 his mother gave him on his 13th birthday, her head bobbing in an effort to stay awake, observing this family ritual, but only as a heretic. Opa's head now resting on his hands placed before him on the table. Gramma, her eyes closed in prayer to the God of vengeance and retribution, her feet planted firmly into the rug, ready to run. Uncle Ned was sleeping again, though sitting upright. Gramma punched him with her elbow. "*Du schnarrst* !" she explained, and he looked at his mother as if she were a stranger. And then there was Aunt Vera. She sat in her chair with the tears running down her cheeks, yet her face was like a rock. Maybe she was worried about that tall black car not sitting out in the road.

And so we sat as the storm blasted its way eastward. At one point I pulled my bench closer to the window and, leaning forward and pulling aside the lace curtains, gazed out into the night to make sure the storm had left the barn right where it was supposed to be.

"Junior," said Vera, "what are you doing? Stay out of that window!"

* * *

Too late. The whole night at that moment burst into white heat, and I smelled loud sulfur and saw the whole barn lighting up, a giant necklace of circus fire spinning out into a spiral of sparks, a carnival of phosphorescence and a torrent of magic light rocketing back and forth across the roof and shooting downward and exploding as it dove into the ground making night disappear into blinding noon. The next thing I knew I was lying on the floor, and Vera was leaning over me and running her hands across my forehead, and Gramma and Esther and Nettie floating above her like three moons.

"Is he electercuted!" screamed Nettie.

"Oh, Nettie!" Esther snapped, "he just slipped off the bench, didn't you, Junior?"

"Can he hear?" said Vera. "Can you hear us, Junior? You think he can hear?"

"Is there a black spot anywheres?" said Oma in the hollow of the room.

"I'm all right," I said, smiling and trying to get up. I looked up at my aunts and right then and there realized that I counted for something in that room. They looked like they'd have gone to hell for me, all I'd have to do is ask. "I just fell off the piano bench, that's all."

"He just got scared," said Vera, smiling at me. "He'll be all right. I know he'll be just fine."

Nettie said, "He just saw too much light all at once't."

"I could smell that one, it was too close," said Ned, seeing I was sitting up. He went to the window and looked at the barn. "What is that? Do I smell smoke? I better go out there and have a closer look."

"Where do you see smoke?" asked Esther, telescoping her eyes at the barn. "I don't see smoke anywhere."

"Well, I can smell it," said Ned.

Vera said, "Don't you go out there, Ned! You ain't wearing socks or shoes or nothing!"

"I'll get my boots on and just run out there and have a look," he said, walking out of the room, and then I heard him putting his boots on.

Vera led me over to her chair, sat down, and made me sit on her lap. We heard Ned going out the kitchen door. The rain got worse for a while and then fell away a little. Gramma went to the window and said, "Where's that Ned?" Everyone but Vera got up and stood and looked out the window. After a while Ned came back into the house soaking wet in his brief clothing and announced that the live-stock in the barn had gone back to sleep, and there weren't any fires anywhere. "It's all over now," he said and led Opa back out to the milkhouse and then went straight up the stairs and into his room, changed out of his wet underwear, and the rest of us sat down again and waited until the rain had completely stopped. Esther announced at last she was going back to bed, and Gramma and Nettie got up and went into their bedroom and drew the drapes across the doorway.

I went to go upstairs, but Vera stayed me with her hand. I saw her face, it was glowing in the dark. "Going out to the fields every day like you do," she said in a dark blue voice, "sitting on that tractor all day in the sun . . . helping with chores and working so hard seven days a week . . . my, but you must be getting sick and tired of living out here at The Place. So much easier in town . . . all your friends, they get to play all day and listen to the radio at night."

"Maybe."

"You don't miss your friends none?"

"No."

She touched me on the forehead in the same way they do in church. "You know you're the last one."

"Last one what?"

"The rest are just . . . girls. Dorothy, Fern, Veronica, Betty, Marjorie, why, they'll all just get married off one by one and have to stick on someone else's name. You're the last Draeger. You're stuck with that name. After you there's nobody coming along with that name. You can't avoid it. There's only you, and there's only The Place, and, well, after me and Ned and Esther there won't even be that."

"What about Nettie!"

"Nettie don't count."

"Yes, she does!"

"Ya, but what I mean, there aren't any more Draegers to run The Place. Nettie can't run it. After the war Buck will come home and marry Liz Stelter and move into town and get a job in Esther's bank." In a flash of lightning, I saw a face that scared me. "Then what do you think is going to happen to The Place?" She gave me time to come up with an answer, and when I wasn't able to do it, she came up with one. "Nothing's going to happen to it. The Place will die . . . just like an old cow. Why, they'll have to come out and bury it alongside me and Ned."

"How do you bury a farm?"

"You dig a big hole and you bury it in it."

Another flash of light, smaller this time, but enough for me to see she was mourning the death of the whole world.

"Don't you worry none, Vera," I said, desperately, falling to my knees and taking her hands in mine. She tried to pull away, but I held on. "I promise I won't let that happen . . . I promise! I'll even leave my folks and come out here and run The Place."

"Did you know I left The Place once?" she said, pulling away with a small laugh. "It was a long time ago . . . but it happened. I left The Place. Did you know that?"

I wasn't ready to admit that my mother had told me the whole story.

"I was eighteen," she said, getting up now and walking over to her window and gazing out into the road. The lightning was dim and far off now. "Ma and the others didn't want me to do it, but I went down to Chicago and got me a job in a fabric mill. I worked for two years down there, and I was making good money too, and then I met a man. He was the son of the owner. I don't know why but he took a fancy to me, and after a while we started going out. It wasn't more than a month and he came up with a ring! I didn't say a word to Ned or Ma or anyone. And after a while we made plans to get married . . . but before I could write home to tell them about it, I got a letter from

Esther begging me to come home to help out because Pa couldn't do much now. I knew there was nothing I could do, I couldn't just stay down there. I had to come back, and I . . . I never left again. Been here the whole rest of my life." The next thing I know, Vera was standing over me. "There was no way out of it," she said, "and maybe that's good too."

She started up the steps. She looked back and waited. I blew out the lamp and went up past her and back up to Buck's bed and lay there for some time looking out the window. The storm had swept everything away but a sky full of stars. I thought about what Vera said but couldn't make any sense out of it. No way out, I thought? What Vera said didn't make any sense. There was always a way out.

7

Gramma stepped across the narrow gutter between two cows, turned around, and then slid down the bony flank of the cow she called 'Dolly Madison' while Dolly turned and stared back at her. She dropped a troika stool directly below her, spun about at the very last moment, milk pail cinched between her legs. Then she sat and dusted off the cow's udder with her old bony hands. It took her maybe seven minutes to fill the milk pail, and then she grabbed the cow's tail and hauled herself back onto her feet.

Anybody else trying to fool around like that with Dolly would get a shitty foot in the face.

Gramma Draeger was short and round and looked exactly like what you would think a peasant looks like. Mother had instructed me not to say she was 'fat', I should say 'stocky' or maybe 'stout'. I knew she was more than the sum of her weight. She was tough, she was fearless. One morning in the spring of 1938, right after chores, Turk The Bull lowered his horned head and pawed the ground and blustered at her since he had happened to find her cornered in the barnyard. But before he could blink twice, Gramma came at him with a pitchfork and would have gored him good, but he dodged about and slunk off and then hid among his harem.

Gramma had wise, thick bones showing through her shanks, and her large coarse hands and feet performed rough rural patterns. But her pride was her long, thick grey hair worn in a big bun at the back of her head. Beautiful hair. Silver, shot with gold. I used to peer through the curtain that was her bedroom door while she sat on the bed combing it out. She looked like a fairy princess preparing to fling a braid or two over a railing to anybody out riding and looking for love in towers.

Her eyes were heavenly blue and grateful, and they radiated a love of humanity I have since seen only once or twice in my life.

I couldn't imagine how Grampa had been able to corner her. Quite likely it was the other way around since she was the man in the family. She was everything Opa was not. She was at any one time everywhere on The Place, but you had to settle for a mere glimpse of her as she slipped from shed to barn to the fields or maybe you chanced upon her out behind the chicken coop carving a stick in the crab apple orchard.

Grampa, on the other hand, was right where you could see him. Daytimes of course he was out plowing his little kingdom. He seemed never to recognize me when we crossed paths. "*Was machst du da?*" he would say, or "*Wo gehst du hin?*" He would draw up short and crank his wrinkled eyes at me as if waiting for me to get out of the way.

There definitely was something wrong with him.

I didn't know what it was so one day I decided to ask Gramma. I found her shelling corn, at her feet a gaggle of Leghorns, cackling and fussing. She sat on an upended rusty milkpail and leaned back against the red slats of the granary, a pail clamped between her knees. I walked over to her and said, "Oma, what's wrong with Opa? Why does he plow the same ground every day?" I knew she was a little hard of hearing so I leaned over her and said it louder: "Oma, I asked you a question!"

Her eyes flew open, she jumped and the pail dropped from her knees and washed the nuggets out onto the ground among the congregation of white hens.

"Eh?" she gasped. "*Was du gesagt?*"

"I asked you why Opa keeps on plowing the same patch everyday? Why does he do that?"

"Who?" I pointed across the yard at Opa, who at that very moment was harnessing MackandJack, a pair of giant chestnut Belgians, to an old bottom plow. "Opa, you mean?" she said, following my finger. "You mean Opa?"

"Why does he keep doing the same darn thing every day?"

Opa got up before dawn like everyone else and went out to the barn and milked three, maybe four cows, and came back to the house like everyone else and ate his breakfast staring at something just above the clock in the dining room like it was talking to him. And after breakfast he went out to the barn again and harnessed up MackandJack and led them over to the machine shed and coupled them to the old plow, and then, unlike everyone else, took them out to the same piece of ground he'd plowed the day before. And he did that six days a week. Sundays Gramma harnessed him to a black suit, white shirt, and black tie and made him climb into Esther's car and go with her and Vera to town for *Gottesdienst* at Grace Lutheran. But then Monday morning there he was back out there plowing it all over again. He had it all worked out ahead of time. He'd start fresh on the outside of the field in the morning, and by sundown have it all finished and ready for the next day.

Gramma said, "What same darn thing?"

"Going out there and plowing that same darn field every day. I don't think that's right."

She grunted and pulled her old ratty scarf about her big flabby ears as if it was a silly question. I studied her ears. My mother told me once she had some kind of disease that had inflated and reddened her ears and nose and lips. She said it was called Rosacea, but she said I wasn't ever to ask Gramma about it.

"Well . . . look at Vera," she said, shucking again. "She goes out to the chicken coop and collects eggs every day, and Nettie, she peels potatoes and mows the same lawn . . . well, not every day maybe. Ned, he throws down hay to the cows and cleans out the barn, and every day he goes out with the manure spreader. This is a farm, this is what we do."

She looked up at me with her laughing kind eyes, waiting for a sign that I understood her. Part of me did. I knew on a farm you were one of the animals. You never stopped to ask what you were doing here and how or why you were doing it, or whether you should or shouldn't be doing it. If you stopped to ask questions, nothing would ever get done. You did what had to be done. It maybe wasn't always fun, but you had to do it anyway.

"Oh, it's not the same thing, Gramma, and you know it."

She shucked for a while and then stopped and looked up at me. "*Doch!*" she growled. "*Doch, doch, doch!*" But then she shook her head and looked at the chickens. "No, maybe not the same thing. You are right. Opa . . . you see, well . . ." She turned and looked out at the fields in the west. "Well, when first we come to The Place," she said with a far-off voice. "You know what he did, your Opa? He cut down all the trees along the tracks. I asked him how come he cut down the trees along the railway tracks, and you know what he said to me? He said, 'So I can keep one eye on California.' That's what he said! He said, 'So I can keep one eye on California.' Oh, that man . . . that man could talk about California! He was always talking about California. 'Can't you see California?' he would ask. 'Why, it's just beyond the tracks there, see it?' That's what he'd say, and after a while I thought sure I could see it too." I looked west past the corncrib and out into the fields, but I didn't see any California out there. Just more barns and silos and cornfields and farms that make up Diamond Valley. "But, you know, after that stroke he had, he didn't talk no more about California. Maybe he give up on it. Maybe he couldn't see California no more after that stroke."

We both turned and watched Opa struggle up onto the iron seat of the plow and urge the team out the driveway toward the road. He sat bent way over, his head swinging back and forth like a pendulum, his old straw felt hat tied tight to his ears, the reins slack in his hands. It looked as if he had fallen asleep already.

"Where'd he come from?" I said, when he was out of sight. "Was it far off?"

"The Old Country . . . Germany, you know. That's where everybody come from when we come here."

She told me the Draegers were Mennonites way back when and owned a large farm that straddled three rivers and two islands near Posen, Germany. Opa was just a boy when his Uncle Hermann, who had come out in 1848, wrote to say he owned a huge dairy farm and would they please send someone to help him out. Opa was only thirteen at the time, but Hermann demanded they send him. Once on a visit to his Uncle Abel in Warsaw Opa had seen huge posters at a train station instructing everyone to come straight to California, where farmland was cheap and there were endless groves of orange and grapefruit trees, and there were these gold nuggets just lying out in open sight in the riverbeds, and, best of all, they had outlawed winter out there. The only thing California lacked was people, and why don't you volunteer to help out? Opa assumed his uncle's farm was in California, and so he demanded they send him to his uncle's farm at once, but his father laughed and ripped up his brother's letter and told Opa anyway he was needed at home. His mother spoke up for him, but his father finally took a stand: he said he would never sign any papers dealing with this. His son would have to wait until he was 21 if he wanted to go anywhere. It took Opa three years of dreaming about California and writing secret letters to his uncle until at last, Uncle Hermann devised a scheme. He sent his mother the money for the boy's passage. His father found out about it, and there was a fistfight. His mother took to her bed, and his father sent the money back to his brother, and that was that. Opa ran off to Warsaw the very next day and his uncle Abel hustled him out of the country, buying him passage to New York on the understanding he would pay him back someday.

To his utter disappointment Opa discovered that Uncle Hermann's farm wasn't anywhere near California, and there were neither rivers of gold nor groves of oranges, and the winters were far worse than the ones in Posen. Fortunately, he arrived at Uncle Hermann's farm on a hot July afternoon, and his first view of the countryside gladdened his heart, for it resembled the kind of paradise he had in mind: valleys of lush green gardens and hilltops of maple trees, valleys of small villages, church steeples, large red barns, cattle grazing alongside meandering streams. It was, he concluded, a good jumping off place for California.

Uncle Hermann told Opa that the land he saw wasn't at all like the land when he himself arrived. It was a quarter section of mammoth dead stumps – the land having already been logged off and the original trees milled into flat boards. It had taken him two years to root out all the stumps, pile them up and burn them, meanwhile erecting a small white house and a red cowbarn the size of a cathedral. Nowadays he was milking thirty head of purebred registered Holsteins and selling the milk for good money to the Schmoch's Corners Co-op Dairy Company, which manufactured the world's finest butter. It didn't take Opa long to learn how to be useful. He worked hard and asked little in return, but it didn't take his uncle long to discover something unnatural about the boy: a certain dark and dreamy reluctance, restlessness, a preoccupation with the setting sun. Uncle Hermann often caught him standing in the middle of a field, leaning against his pitchfork and staring west, or sometimes in the evening after chores halfway up the silo ladder staring at the setting sun, and when asked what he was doing up there, Opa would ask how far it was to California. If he asked it once, he asked it a dozen times.

"*Ach ya* !" Gramma said, "your grampa was a dreaming man, but such a handsome dreaming man! So straight, so tall, and he had a good voice, too! And now I remember, in those days he could play the violin! You know the Mennonites, they think music is like talking. Every night after chores back in Posen they sang, the whole family. The girls played the piano, the boys violins. If you don't learn violin when you are eight, it is too late. And in church . . . why, in church you could hear him above everybody. And oh, he loved songs about the sea! *Ya, der könnte ein Heldentenor sein!* He took me out in his buggy for long rides, and he sang me songs he knew. Sailor songs. They said the same thing. What you want is over on the other side of the water . . . the other side of the mountains, the other side of the world. He asked me why there wasn't no songs about California. At least there was no winter out there, he said, only orange trees and grapefruit trees and gold in the water, and he laughed and told me he had a map inside his head." She laughed when she remembered. "It showed him where all the gold was laying in the rocks in the creeks out there."

Opa spoke to Gramma's father and asked for her hand in marriage. That was about a year after he came to his Uncle Hermann's farm. He told his uncle he was going to get married and move to his own place. Hermann reminded him he had promised to work until he paid off his passage money and figured it would take him five years to do that. But Opa hadn't listened to his father, so why should he listen to a mere uncle? They argued, and Opa finally gave him back what little money he had and packed up and walked out while his uncle followed him out to the road and shouted at him till he was out of sight.

He married Oma and took her about twenty miles west of town, where he settled on a farm he called 'The First Place,' since he said there were going to be more of them as he worked his way out to California. The First Place was almost all sand, and the corn never got more than ankle-high by the fourth of July and by September bore only runty ears. The wheat and hay grew a little higher maybe, but was always only half a barn full.

Meanwhile, Gramma produced a rich annual harvest of robust children, eight in ten years. Half looked like her – round, stout, Slavic, peasant-like – and half like him – tall, gaunt, fox-eyed, Prussian. Eventually, he sold the farm and moved thirty miles west to 'The Second Place', a quarter-section farm in the heart of Sipping Valley. Less sand, more loam, but still unsatisfied, five years later he sailed thirty more miles west to 'The Third Place'. He'd moved fifty miles in fifteen years. At that rate it would take him around three hundred years to get to California.

Still, he knew you couldn't find better land anywhere between The First Place and California. It was a bottomland farm, its soil so purple and loamy and oozy that when you turned it over with a plow, the soil just glowed and glistened like a rainbow gone to ground.

Now it was simply called 'The Place'. Perhaps because Opa sensed there wasn't going to be a 'Fourth Place.' In the meantime he'd come down with a bad case of arthritis of the spine, which bent him over nearly double, and his children were starting to defect, just the way he had defected from his old man in The Old Country. The two oldest girls, Doris and Ollie, barely out of country school, sprinted off to the city and married the first pair of pants that stepped in front of them. Vera was different: she stayed on until she was twenty and *then* ran off to a fabric mill some four hundred miles to the south. First Esther and then Colvin – my old man – went to town and finished high school and found a way to stay there and not come back to do their fair share of the chores on The Place.

So, Opa was down to three - the half-wit Nettie and the two boys, Ned the Oldest and Buck the Baby Boy. Ned was steady and strong. Buck was quick and smart. He was the best athlete in school and class valedictorian and started to hang around town after school and find ways of getting out of evening chores, and then in his final years of high school took to hopping freights and going out to work at the wheat combines in Montana.

That left Ned.

And Vera.

Vera was recalled to The Place when it was clear Ned couldn't run it alone. Nettie was causing more and more problems, and Oma and Opa were all too often down and out with various ailments. And finally Esther came home when, as I've said too many times now, her husband went out to his mother's grave and joined her.

Now Ned and Vera ran the farm, and Esther made lots of money working in the bank. Gramma helped with milking and tending the pigs. But arthritis had doubled Opa over, and now prostate cancer and plain old nuttiness had him going around in circles. He slept in the attic of the milkhouse and spent his days in the field, appearing in the house only at mealtimes. He had lost his teeth and most of his hearing. He often stood stooped over and looked about at everything as if he wasn't quite sure where he was. He fascinated me still, not just because of what Gramma said about California and all, but I thought I would study him and maybe learn something about my own old man if I could figure him out.

But nothing came of it. It was like watching a corpse walking around his in own cemetery. Still, I knew my old man was inside Opa somewhere, locked up like a prisoner, but I couldn't figure a way to get him out.

One day Ned said he had to go in to town to get the mower sickle blade sharpened. It was the first week of September. I was going back into town in two days. I decided it was time to have it out with Opa. But Ned had the last word: "If you're looking for something to do, you can go and shock that field of oats we bindered yesterday." Ned had tried to show me how to shock. He said, "You pick up two bundles of oats and set them up against each other." It looked easy at that stage. "Then you go get four more, and you set them on either side of it. Now you got yourself a little house, and you get another bundle and splay it out over the tops of the others like a roof. That's to keep the rain out."

Nettie stood leaning against the handle of the lawnmower listening to us. She mopped her brow and laughed when Ned walked toward the barn. It was hot, and yet here she was wearing that old patched thick winter coat and a wool stocking cap pulled so tight you could scarcely see her wobbly eyes.

"They won't let me shock," she said, "Mama says don't even go and watch them shockin', she says." Her voice sped up at all once, and she blew anger into her words when she saw Vera come out onto the back porch to pump a pail of water. "And Vera, she helps shockin' but she can't shock either . . . leastwise not as good as Ned. Nobody can shock like Ned." Vera began to pump the iron handle. "Ned says Vera can't tell one end of the bundle from the other –"

"Oh, Nettie!" shouted Vera. "For goodness sake, why can't you leave Junior alone. He's got work to do!" Nettie swore at her and pushed her lawnmower off between two oak trees down toward the garden. Vera lifted the water pail when it was full and started for the back door. "If you're going out to shock," said Vera, "you better take a few of Gramma's rolls with butter and brown sugar along, and a thermos of cold water." We went into the kitchen. She filled the thermos, buttered and browned the rolls and wrapped them and stuck them in a paper sack. "That field you're going to shock, Junior, it's down toward the tracks, ain't it? I wonder if you would stop and have a look at Pa on your way?"

"What am I looking for?"

"You never know."

When I came outside, Nettie was grumbling away and pushing the lawn mower around the yard as if she figured she was cutting off everyone's head. "I know you can do it," I said to her when she stopped. "You're my good Aunt Nettie, and I depend on you to do something so's I can watch you do it and then learn it from you." She stared at me, and I wondered if she understood. "I won't never be mean to you, not in all the days to come."

I went out to the barn, where it was all cool and silent and full of buzzy flies, and then I crossed the barnyard to the straw stack and climbed it. From the top I could see Opa circling about his field. I jumped down and followed the lane over the top of the rise overlooking the creek. Opa sat on the iron seat of the plow, bobbing about like a puppet on a string, the reins loose in his hands and looping out over the tongue of the wagon and up through the rings in the harness to the brass bits in the slimy-green mouths of the team of horses. The plow blades were biting into the white sand and churning it up again soft and yellow. I climbed the fence and walked across a stubbled hayfield to the barbed wire fence that surrounded Opa's sandbox, climbed it, and crossed the fresh furrows. When Opa came around the first time, he ignored me altogether. The next time he tossed me a glance. Still, I wasn't sure he saw me. I waited until he made the third circuit of the field before I decided to make my move.

I walked out toward the oncoming horses and stood in the way. I figured he would have to run me down. As he came closer, I got a little worried and started windmilling my arms. He said something to MackandJack, and the team drew up about six feet off. I walked around and stood close to him. He sat for a while in his high iron seat and stared at me.

After a while, he said, "*Was machst du da*?"

I laughed to myself because I now understood what he was saying. I'd been on The Place for only three months, but I didn't know until that moment that a few words of German – the language of the Nazis, after all – had been planted and taken root like weeds in my English garden.

"Du muss' mir Englisch sprechen, Opa. Deutsch kann ich nicht."

MackandJack took a few steps forward as if they were going to interpret for Opa.

"Englisch?"

"Ja," I said, stepping closer, looking for more to say. "Can you speak English to me?"

Suddenly, he laughed and said, "I can speak English, *ja*."

"Tell me about California."

"California," he laughed. "Where oranges and grapefruit and lemons grow in trees and you can find gold in the creeks." That's all he said. His lips kept moving but nothing was coming out. Then he said it again, *"Kalifornien!"* He turned his head and looked across the tracks, and then back to me. He fixed his eyes on me and lifted the reins and shook them twice. "Tzk, tzk!" he announced, and MackandJack pushed off with their giant haunches and ferried Opa and his plow back onto their eternal rounds. I stood and waited, but each time he orbited past, he spent less time looking at me. Finally, he circled about without even looking my way. I felt like I had been there for him at first, but now I wasn't even there.

Just like my old man, I thought.

Now I see where he gets it.

8

That first summer at The Place was up and gone even before I had settled comfortably into it, but I had to go back to school. It was the end of August when Vera packed my old leather suitcase and, along with Nettie, came out to the edge of the lawn and stood watching me walk down the road, cross the bridge, and walk up through the silver gates into the cemetery. I climbed up onto great-grandmother's tombstone and waved back to the two of them still standing in the road. And then I walked away and looked behind every elm tree all the way down Main Street, expecting a homecoming party. After all, Ronnie and the other hoopsters had been deprived of my leadership all summer, surely they would be happy to see me again. Meanwhile, I nodded to the old ladies rocking a hot afternoon away deep inside their screened porches, fanning themselves with newspapers, and to old men pushing lawnmowers across their acres of dry bluegrass lawns.

"You'll be back at school, won't you, Junior," Mrs. Zempel sang to me. "Ned's going to miss you, I'll bet. He's going to have to keep Amos dry now till they silo."

"He'll have a hard time doing that," I said, waiting for Ronnie to ambush me when I turned my back. "Amos and Ned are up at Dremel's place today harvesting. Dremel's got a horse trough full of beer bottles floating around in it and waiting for them to come to lunch."

I turned the corner on Main Street at Stringer's Store and headed across the Iron Bridge. Still no sign of Ronnie and the gang.

Then I snuck through our landlady Mrs. Horton's garden, and came upon my mother sitting on the top step of the porch and pinching beans.

"Oh my goodness, boy, let me have a look at you!" I dropped my grip and flexed my new muscles. "Why, you must've put on a good twenty pounds!" she said, pushing away the tears and coming down and hugging me. "You go now and take you a good warm bath and then we'll go down to Stringer's and buy you some school supplies, tomorrow's the first day of school."

It didn't take me long to figure out how my mother had spent the summer. She had hatched plans that would see me spend more time working for Mrs. Horton's when my old man was in the house. She had me raking *her* yard and burning *her* leaves, sweeping off *her* sidewalks, stacking *her* wood in the shed and filling *her* woodboxes twice a day, shovelling *her* sidewalks, all for a measly ten cents a day. (Aunt Vera had folded a five-dollar bill into my hand on the way out the door, and that was going to have to tide me over for the winter.) That fall for some reason I could never figure out, my old man hung about the house more, even after supper, before heading downtown to Slim's for his pinochle games and stinky cigars.

So, more than usual I was sent packing across the hall to Mrs. Horton's rooms. Mrs. Horton usually stuck me in a straight-back chair across from her at a card table where she practiced Oriental torture in the way of Chinese Checkers and talked endlessly about *her* father and how mean *he* was to her. She told me the same stories over and over of how he'd built a feed mill and got himself elected mayor of the town, and how it was all because of him that we got all the iron bridges all over town, especially the big one across German Creek, and the brick streets and electric streetlights, and of course the fire hall and the library, and how he put all the taverns along one side of the street so drunks wouldn't get hit crossing the street.

She even called her father 'the FDR of Herring', which of course if you didn't know was our hometown.

* * *

But one night that fall I learned way more about the FDR of Herring than I wanted.

It was during a game that had gone wrong from the very first marble. I hadn't made more than four jumps across the board before she picked up one of her red marbles and hopped it clear across the board and all the way home. She stared at me with a smile sharp as a butcher knife. "Now it's your turn," she said. I leaned forward on my elbows and studied the blue and red marble maze. I saw one that could jump two holes. "No, no, no!" she stayed my hand. "Take this one, Junior . . . this one!" she said, pecking at one of my blue marbles with a long, crooked finger that had black veins scrawled across it. "Tiny little thing, all by its little lonesome, don't you feel sorry for him at all?" So I jumped him over three of her marbles and smiled thanks back at her. She leaned back in her chair as if I had farted. "What?" she said, poking her finger into an empty hole. "Why, you can take him all the way over *here!*"

So I moved him all the way over *there.*

Which was right where she wanted him. She cackled the same way she did when she showed me a mouse in one of her traps. "Watch this, Junior!" she said, picking up her red marble behind my tiny little lonesome blue one and hopping him clear across the board until he nestled up next to the first one she got home.

"That isn't fair, Mrs. Horton, and you know it!" I said, collapsing against the pillow and making a face while I kicked at the rungs of the chair. In those days I knew how to throw a tantrum even when my old man wasn't around.

"Everything's fair in love and war and Chinese Checkers!"

She leaned toward me and feasted her eyes upon the board, looking for more lonely blues. I wanted to quit and took to staring at the clock on the wall. Four, five minutes at most and I'd be in bed. I listened to a wedge of oak snapping away at us from her parlour stove and smelled butterscotch cookies and marmalade and ground coffee, furniture polish, bleach, and lots of other things stinky old and hidden and never moved. We sat deep in a forest of beige-fringed oil lamps and polished inlaid oak tables and elaborate pressed doilies covering every surface in the room. There was a bookcase of fat books shouldered together on shelves behind smoky glass, and the walls were crowded with oil paintings of Dutch boys skating past windmills, spiky cathedrals poking at black clouds, mountaintop castles, sailing ships on high seas, old men digging in potato patches.

And of course that photograph of a big old ugly Blackbeard in a shiny black suit. He glared down at me as if he'd like to come down there and give me a good boot in the keester. But what scared me most about him was the way he had clamped his fists onto the spindly shoulders of a small ugly woman who looked scared stiff while balancing a poker-faced young girl on her knee as if she was made of porcelain and might fall and break unless she held on tight.

"Who's that picture again?" I said, spitefully.

"I told you, it's nobody!" she growled. "And don't you go asking me about pictures. I don't want to talk about pictures." I pouted even more and kicked away at the rungs of my chair. She softened her voice and blew her nose. "You wouldn't know them anyways." I was going to pout some more but I could see she wasn't done. "That's my family, that's who . . . but they're all dead and gone, all but me."

"Figures," I said to myself.

Then for some reason she twisted around in her chair and looked at the picture for the longest time. "If you really want to know, that one up there's my father and my mother and me."

At that very moment the clock began clearing its throat but before it could say anything, my mother came into the room and turned and looked back out into the cold dark as if she thought someone had followed her across the hallway that separated our part of the house from Mrs. Horton's rooms.

She closed the door and walked to the table and said, "So who's winning, Lilah?"

"We both are, Missus," said Mrs. Horton. "Youth and Old Age. Innocence and Wisdom. We learn from each other."

The clock, having said its piece, moved on, and my mother placed a hand on my shoulder and said, "Time for Junior here to get ready for bed."

"Yes, Bonnie," said Mrs. Horton, powdering her words with arsenic. "You'll want him upstairs and safe in bed before his father gets home."

My mother folded me into her skirts and said in a false voice, "Why, Mrs. Horton, what an awful thing to say!"

"It's the truth and you know it." Mrs. Horton was going to play up her part as Wisdom Woman. "Things was awfully quiet over all summer, but soon's Junior comes home, the yelling starts up. Those two should be sat down and given a good talking to if you were to ask me."

"Well, I won't ask you then."

"No, you wouldn't."

"No, I definitely wouldn't."

My mother took hold of my left arm and dragged me out of the room without even thanking Mrs. Horton for the cookies and the Chinese Checkers lesson. I looked back at the old lady as I was being hauled through the hallway, and she looked at me as if she couldn't wait for me to come back again so she could teach me a lesson or two.

I stood at the window of my bedroom watching the snowstorm clawing at the narrow glass that stood between us. What chance did I have? The storm was a monster and where was my mother when I needed her? I turned and looked back at the orange light in the stovepipe collar. The stovepipe heated my bedroom during the day, and at night, when it was twenty below and I couldn't get to sleep, Sometime I'd get out of bed, spin the collar open so as to look down into our living room.

I walked over to the stovepipe, kneeled and peered down through it. Mother sat on the couch crying softly. I wanted to call down to her, but if I did so, she would only smile and wipe away the tears and say she was only pretending to cry and then tell me to get back into bed. Tonight something very sour had boiled over and scalded her. And then suddenly as I studied her, she got up and walked over to the stove and began shutting it down for the night. I figured she was going to bed early, so I jumped back into my own and drew the covers up over my head. She came upstairs, crept into the bedroom and checked my sister Bits' crib and then my bed, and left the room, crossed the hallway and up the two steps into her own bedroom. I got out of bed and cracked my door and waited a minute before crossing the arctic stretch of hallway.

I leaned against her door and, hearing her sobbing away, said, "Mama, is that you?"

I cracked the door open and peered into the room. My mother was sitting on the edge of the bed silently wiping away her tears. I stood watching her weigh what she wanted to say. At last she blew her nose and patted the bed beside her. "Come on over here then," she said, "but just for a minute, it's way past your bedtime." I ran to her, and she gathered me in and wound me way into her warm soft body. It was like the two of us sat together in a small boat in a gale. I was so scared that I began to cry along with her. "Hey now," she growled, "don't *you* start crying on me!" she said, trying to laugh. "You'll just make it all the worse."

"Make what worse?" I said.

"Everything," she said to herself. "Nothing."

She blew her nose and, withdrew and settled back against a pillow, and I said, "That doesn't make any sense."

She studied me for a while and then sat up and reached out and held me away from her at arm's length, and said, "Now, you listen to me, I'm only going to say this once. Okay? I want you to promise me something." She threw me that look she used whenever she lost her patience with me. "Will you promise me?"

I would have promised to take on the monster now attacking our house. "Huh?" I was scared now. "Sure, I promise."

She looked up into the dark ceiling for words. "All right," she said, "you have to promise me you'll always be good to your wife for all of your life. You won't treat her mean." Then she started to cry again. "And you won't go out night after night and leave her sitting all to herself at home."

"Okay."

"And you won't treat your son so bad." I thought, hell, this is easy! "You going to promise me that?" I was going to say yes when she seized me by the shoulders and shook me so hard I thought my teeth were going to come out. "You going to promise me that!"

"I promise," I said.

It was a good year for promises and easy to make.

My old man was a short, stout bully who always wore bib overalls, even on Sundays. He was a carpenter, about as good as they come. He had built most of the new houses in our town by the time he was forty. He could pound nails in a clever way, but that was just about it. Wait, say something nice! Okay, he wasn't just a carpenter. He had a special gift. He had to have everything perfect, all the finishing work, the cabinetry, the flooring, the moldings. People said you could always tell you were in one of Colvin Draeger's kitchens when everything was *ausgezeignet*: all the cabinets were true and perfect, the drawers ran as if on satin, the corners were all absolute, the grain tight and smooth. Nothing ever came apart or bent or broke, no matter how you mistreated it.

He hadn't learned this in school. He had barged through grade school and high school without ever cracking a book. He hadn't come to school to read books anyway. He had come to make more touchdowns than anyone else in school history. He had personally put this tiny town on the map in 1928 when he led the tiny town all the way to State. That he never learned to read or write in high school was a mere technicality. It did not prevent him from securing a football scholarship to Portage Point College. Unfortunately, his college career was history even before it was news. In the first game of the year, he got tackled hard and broke a leg and then had to attend classes while it mended. His teachers called in the Dean and handed him the astonishing news about the young football star. This student couldn't read or write. I don't know if they kicked him out at that point or he quit, but one thing I do know, I paid the price: he came home a bitter man who boiled up that bitterness again and again whenever he saw me.

I don't remember him being quite so handsome as he is in the huge murals that nowadays line the hallways of the new high school. You see him up there big as life and you think right away of Paul Newman or Gary Cooper. I stood looking up there just recently trying to find my face in his, but of course it wasn't there. He wasn't like me at all. He was an iron man. He never knew how to quit even when they quit on him. Until late in his life he continued playing baseball. He played on the city team and developed the nasty habit of breaking windows all up and down the street across from the baseball diamond.

People around town found him handsome, honest, sweet-tempered, hard-working, solid, sober. They loved him, and they loved me too because I was his son.

It snowed hard the first week of November. My old man was out in the woods trapping when one morning my mother bundled up my sister Bits and lashed her onto my Mars Rocket snow sled, and the two of them set off for groceries down at the Red and White Store. Of course I was sent packing over to Mrs. Horton's side of the house for another round of torture. I heard the old witch creeping about in her kitchen when I knocked and walked straight in without waiting for her to answer. As usual I pulled the card table out from behind the door and set it up, unfolded the checkerboard and loaded it with two sets of marbles, her red and my blue.

"Where are you?" I asked. "I got it all set up." She carried on digging something out of a cupboard. "Maybe I'll come back later."

To my surprise she walked into the room carrying a lighted coal oil lamp in one hand and a set of keys dangling from one of her skeleton fingers.

"I got ears, you know," she said and let out a wise smile. "I can even hear the two of you through three sets of walls."

"Who two?"

"You and him. What are you now, ten years old? You spent the whole summer out at The Place and didn't learn a thing?"

"I learned how to drive a tractor," I said. I wasn't afraid to talk back to Mrs. Horton. She had taught me how to talk back. "And I learned how to cultivate corn and how to shock and how to haul in the hay and –"

"That's neither here nor there. You didn't learn how to cultivate and shock your own father, did you?"

She had me there. Nothing had changed. In some ways it was worse. It was like my old man held it against me because I hadn't been able to kill one cow all summer and also hadn't succeeded in tipping over on the tractor and squishing myself to death.

"Come along with me upstairs. I got something I want to show you now you're ten years old."

"Upstairs?" I said, watching her cross to the hallway door. "Where upstairs?"

"Never you mind where upstairs."

I knew she wasn't talking about my room, and it sure wasn't my mother's bedroom.

She was talking about *that other* room.

I'd never been inside that room, and neither had my mother. "That's Mrs. Horton's store room," she told me. "We're not paying rent on it, so you stay out of there. You don't know what's in there, and I don't know what's in there, and you know what? Neither one of us wants to know what's in there." I didn't like the way she said that, but when I asked her what she meant, she refused to go into it. So naturally I had long ago begun to worry about what was in that room.

One night I cracked my bedroom door when I imagined I heard voices coming out of that room. It sounded to me like someone was in there walking around and talking. That very night I had a strange dream. I was lying in bed and heard a noise and snuck out into the hallway, and there was a hissing sound coming out of that room, and then the hissing got louder and smoke started seeping out from under the door, and I turned and ran back to my bedroom but my door was stuck or something, I couldn't open it, and then from behind me I heard the door of that room opening on its own, and I turned and saw what looked like a long red tongue sliding out through the smoke and across the hallway toward me.

But now, here we were, the two of us, walking up the stairs and going into *that* room. I was ready to bolt even before she turned the key in the lock.

"This used to be my bedroom when I was your age," she said and then stared at me. "I can see you're worried, but there's nothing in here now 'cept family junk."

She opened the door and walked across the dark room and set her lamp on a table covered with a white sheet. I stood just outside the door and looked in after her. Mrs. Horton was small, but in that room she looked as big as an elephant. The lamplight flicked its eyes into corners of a room stacked high with old steamer trunks and bony furniture covered up in sheets. Everything smelled dead. I took one step forward as she lifted the lid of one of the trunks and dove headfirst into it and then went swimming around in it until she found what she was looking for, a big cardboard box.

She took it out and set it on the table by the lamp and slipped the ribbon off it and lifted out a wood-framed picture with cobwebbed wires dangling from the back of it.

"Come on over here and look at this," she said, turning and holding it out to me. "Well, come on, boy, I haven't got all day!" I crept across the room, the floorboards disagreeing, and studied the picture. It was an old yellow picture of a tall bearded man, a small woman, a girl, maybe eight or nine, and a boy, older, maybe my age. The man stared down angrily at the woman, the woman stared down angrily at the girl straddling her knee, and the girl stared angrily over at the camera. The only one who didn't look angry was the boy, who sat off to one side, all by himself, as if he belonged to somebody else, a boy they borrowed to give the picture a larger symmetry. She gave me a while to look at it and then said, "You know who these people are?"

I said, "I don't see anyone I know."

"You've seen this picture before, of course."

I looked again. "Well, maybe the man . . . he might look a little like that man in the picture you got on your wall downstairs. And oh yeah, there's you when you were a little girl."

"Very good, Junior! But there's somebody in this picture that isn't in the one downstairs."

"The boy."

"That's my brother, and like the one downstairs, that man's my father and that woman's my mother and that girl's me. My father's name was Ebenezer Benjamin Hammond Horton." And I thought, here we go again. "He was born in London, England, and came over when he was a boy. He was one of the founding fathers of this town. When he got to be mayor, he brought in electricity so he could grind more grist at the mill and make more money faster than anyone else, and then he got the town to buy a fire truck just in case his mill caught fire. He went down to Chicago one time and got them to make the trains stop here so he could ship his grain around the country."

"You told me all that," I said, almost crying.

"Why, he even wanted the council to change the name of the town to 'Hortontown', but they wouldn't go that far. And then he built the biggest house in town – this one – and he insisted on calling it 'The White House.' He built it so's he could store me up inside it and make all the young men in town think twice before coming up here to ask for my hand in marriage.

"And that woman, that's my mother, Evelyn Mayberry Lewis. She died about a year or two after we moved into this house. My father was a hard man, but he never got over her dying on him. He loved her in the worst kind of way, and she was too scared of him to love him back. I was scared of him, too. But the one scared most was my little brother. The boy in the corner of the picture. My father was so hard on him! He used to hide when my father came home." She looked at me, studied me for a minute. "Remind you of someone you know?" She didn't wait for an answer. "My brother, he took my mother's death harder than my father. He started playing hooky and then quit school altogether. He left home and moved out to the Gustafson place up in Pleasant Valley. Old man Gustafson was old and bad off, he needed a hired man to help him with chores. He was also a drunk, and he got my brother drinking. People came and told my father about it. One Saturday night my father found my brother staggering down the street arm and arm with Gustafson and dragged him back home and told him to clear out his room, he didn't ever want to see him again, and moreover he was cutting him out of his will. My brother started sassing him back and then they got into a fistfight, and I tried to stop it, but my father took me and locked me into this room until my brother was gone."

She stopped as if that was all she was going to say, and I looked over at her. She gazed at the picture and little by little tears filled her eyes.

"Whatever happened to your brother?"

"Drank himself to death. Look at him carefully, Junior. He was about your age when that picture was taken." She dried her eyes and turned and stared at me. "And that's why I brought you up here. I wanted you to see this picture of my brother."

"Okay . . . now I've seen him, can I go?"

"Look," she said, raising her voice, "you don't think I don't know what's going on?"

"What's going on?"

"Your father and you?"

"What about it?"

She swallowed me up with her eyes and then turned around and put the picture back inside the box, closed it up, and re-tied the ribbon and nestled it down inside the trunk. Then she came at me and seized me by the shoulders with her claws. I was surprised by the strength in her hands. I felt like a Chinese Checkers marble, one of those lonely little blue lads she was going to jump across the board. "I'm going to tell you what I see in that picture," she said, her old grey eyes flashing. "I see you in that picture. I see my brother in you. You sit around and let your father bully you around just like he did. Your father is like my father. He has got the idea he can come home and pretty well do what he wants to do with you." She dug her claws deeper into me and her voice got louder. "Running out to The Place in the summertime won't help. You got to do something, and if you don't do something, pretty soon there won't be a *damn* thing you *can* do about it!"

"Mrs. Horton, should you use dirty words around children?"

"I can because you're not listening!" she growled, and I wondered what my chances were when she took to ordering me around the same way my old man did. "Are you listening to me now, boy!"

I went limp. "No."

"You sure don't look like it either."

But I was thinking about her brother. "Well, if it comes to that, I guess I can always take up drinking!"

The words came straight out of my mouth on their own. Scared me half to death, and I lit out across the hallway and straight into my room, slamming the door behind me. I dropped to the floor, put my head on the floor and peered out through the opening at the bottom of the door. It wasn't long before I saw her feet. She came out of the room and locked the door and then headed straight down the stairs. She was talking to herself all the way down.

I thought of Ned and Vera and Nettie. It wouldn't be too long now, and I'd be back with them, and then I wouldn't have to put up with this kind of Oriental torture day in and day out.

9

It was a warm December morning when Nettie saw MackandJack heading out to the sand patch without anyone sitting on the seat of the plow.

At the time Vera was in the henhouse collecting eggs, Ned was in the woods trapping, Gramma was in her bedroom combing out her silver mane. It was just after breakfast, the very time of the day Nettie knew her father always set out for the creek bottom. At first when she saw the horses from the window, she didn't think much about it. Maybe the team had decided they could do without him for a day. But no, that wasn't it! She ran to the mudroom and slipped on her ratty galoshes and hurried down to the barn and walked through the horse stalls and over into the cow barn. "Pa, you in here?" She lifted the chute into the haymow. "Pa, you up there? Hope not because MackandJack just drove off without you!" Clearly, her pa wasn't in the barn. She then went on to the machine shed and found him stretched out flat on his back, his eyes staring up into the rafters, as if there was something up there. "Pa?" she said and knelt down and shook him and then leaned over him. The eyes were blue yolks on white pie plates. "I'm going to go get Vera," she told him, "you stay where you are."

She hurried over to the chicken coop where Vera was scattering clean straw below the roost, a chorus of chickens complaining about it. She told Vera what she found on the floor of the machine shed, and the two of them hurried over there so Vera could prove once again that Nettie was ready to be trucked off to the nuthouse. Once again she was wrong: Opa was right there where Nettie said he was. Vera fell to her knees and put her head to her father's chest and then stared into his face. Then she sat back on her heels and began to sob as she reached forward and took one of his hands into hers. Vera said something so low Nettie couldn't hear and frankly did not want to hear and then looked up at her with the look that asked her whether it was all her fault.

"Well, don't just stand there!" Vera declared. "You won't get nothin' done just standin' there!"

"He's dead, ain't he? I know when somebody's dead."

"Well . . . then go get Mama!"

"You go get her. She won't listen to me."

"Oh, for goodness sake, Nettie!" Vera stumbled to her feet and ran up to the house. She had to tell her mother first and afterwards do something about it. She thought ahead. There was no phone though they said it was coming. Ned was deep in the woods looking after his traplines, and Esther was working at the bank. She herself would have to walk all the way into town to get old Doc Prill. She took her boots off and tiptoed into the bedroom where her mother sat up reading the Bible and combing out her long silver locks, which were washing down over her shoulders and collecting and then revealing winter's lights.

"Ma," Vera said, settling on the edge of the bed. It began to creak as she leaned over and put her arms around her mother's shoulders. "Ma . . . I don't know how to say it so I guess I'll come right out and say it. Yes, it's good if I come right out and say it. It'll be easier if I just come out and say it."

"Also, was sagst du?"

"It's Pa. He's laying out there in the machine shed on his back." Oma looked past her and tried to understand. "He's just laying out there in the machine shed –"

"Was gibt?" said Oma, her lips quivering. Nettie suddenly appeared in the doorway fiddling her fingers. *"Was meinst du?"*

Vera flung herself back and commenced sobbing on her own.

"Them horses," said Nettie, "they just got themself headed out into the road when I seen them and I seen he wasn't setting on the seat either and Vera was out in the chicken coop and Ned and Esther's gone so I went out to the barn to look for him but he wasn't there and then I run over to the machine shed and that's where I found him, he was just laying there on his back and all and I figured –"

"All right, Nettie, all right!" said Vera, talking through tears and turning and making a rotten face. "We don't need to know all that now!" She put all her irony into her voice. "You think we need to know all that now?"

The three women went out to the machine shed and loaded Opa into a wheelbarrow and trundled him up to the house and then dragged him inside and laid him out in his dirty overalls on the kitchen floor and covered him up with blankets as if they figured he would get cold on the floor, and then Gramma washed off his face and hands, and Nettie went and stood in the middle of the room, fingers flashing, watching, crying. "He's gone off to California," she announced. "And that's good . . . that's good, ain't it? That's where he wanted to go. Anyways, it's better than just goin' 'round in circles in the creek bottom."

"Nettie, please . . . just shut up!"

Vera got dressed and went out of the house and walked all the way to town and straight over to Dr. Prill's house. Prill, a small, owlish, bald man, excused himself from Mrs. Ladenour, who showed up with a squawky and sniveling cold, and took Vera into another room, where she told him about her father, and Prill went back and gave Mrs. Ladenour a free bottle of pills and sent her on her way, and then led Vera out to his brown Model-A car – it had chains on it as if he had already expected her – and drove her back out to The Place. There he confirmed by the miracle of modern science what Nettie knew the very moment she saw her father stretched out across the dirt floor of the machine shed: Albert Siegfried Draeger at the age of 85 had died and gone to California.

* * *

By one o'clock Christmas Day the Draegers and all their kith and kin were gathered around the silver curlicues on the upright woodstove in the parlor. Horse buggies and Tin Lizzies filled up the yard. They'd had a nasty snowstorm, but everyone came to The Place anyway. Oma sat like a holy icon on the chesterfield, her Bible open across her lap, Aunt Esther and Aunt Ollie each warming one of her hands and staring at the tree. As they did every Christmas, names had been drawn, and gifts were already nestled beneath a tree cut down from the woods that straggled along the creek bottom.

It was silent and smoky in the room – the men were smoking instead of talking. Even Great-Aunt Lizzy was smoking a cigar. The oldest uncles and aunts had the look of people knowing they were the next to go. Ned was the only one not wearing a shirt and tie. He didn't seem especially torn up by his father's sudden death. Maybe he was more worried about his traplines that went without him now that he had to stay home and mourn his old man. He leaned against the doorpost, as if he didn't know whether he was coming or going, arms folded, staring at the floor and when he got bored with that, he grinned at me as if we were sharing a private joke.

It was quiet for a long time before Aunt Ollie took it upon herself to speak up. "He was a damn fine man, was my father," she said, getting to her feet and waving her hands about to clear the cigar smoke. "He worked his fingers to the bone, never took one day off neither. Never drank, never smoked . . . didn't cuss more'n he had to. Went to *Gottesdienst* if someone told him to. Still, he was a God-fearing man!" She looked back at Oma and chose her words carefully. "And you know what, Mama, he loved you . . . he did, he really loved you."

"He knew his Holsteins, all right," said my Aunt Doris, who didn't like it when her sister tried to run everything, "and he knew how to survive the bad times we went through and not complain. But there was one thing I never understood: he never talked to anyone unless he had to."

"Well, he wasn't a man of many words," interjected Aunt Esther, who had more of an education that either of her sisters had and knew it was her business to give the final word on family matters. "Pa was a man of disappointment and anger, and maybe he just couldn't find the words to measure that out when he should've, so people figured he was just a quiet man or maybe even stuck up."

Esther had stirred up the pot now, and her sisters could only stand by and wait to see what floated to the surface.

"He never said nothin' hurtful to me," said Gramma, who finally looked up at the faces around her. "Me and your Pa, we was together for more'n sixty years, and we never had no problems."

"Maybe he had a few disappointments, but he took care of his family and all his friends and neighbours," said Aunt Ollie, fighting back, "and helped out whenever somebody needed help."

"You can say that again," said Leonard Newstead, the neighbor who lived just south of The Place and always came over to Christmas dinners because he lived alone on his farm. "Albert was one of the most helpfulest fellas I ever knew. When Arnold Braemer got sick that time, Albert, he went over there and did chores for him for two weeks all by hisself, he didn't even wait to be asked! He helped me put that roof on the barn when it got too late and it was snowing so hard."

"He's going to be missed," said Aunt Ollie, getting back into it. "You could set your clock by him and that team of his going out to that same field every morning."

"That's so," said Uncle Jules when he realized the sand patch was maybe going to be a tricky subject. "Regular as deer ticks in July."

Aunt Ollie thought of something else and was about to say it when Vera turned at her station in the front window and walked into the middle of the room with the look of someone who had seen a great light. She said, "The Lord could see him all bent over and burning with pain, and took pity on him at last and come and got him." Then said in a darker voice than the others. "He was getting worse and worse and worse, why he couldn't hardly get up out of bed toward the end. Ned, he had to move him out of the milkhouse into his own bed. Pa couldn't get up the steps no more. But then he wouldn't eat nothing. He was down to a hundred pounds. He couldn't understand why he was still alive. He kept saying over and over, '*Was soll ich machen? Ich bin hier, aber was soll ich machen?*' Oh, he was quite ready to go, couldn't really wait to go."

Vera looked disgusted with life itself. "And Dr. Prill? His name should be 'Pill' because that's all he ever gave Pa." And here her voice broke down.

She looked so sad that heads fell and throats were cleared.

Aunt Nettie came to the rescue. "I saw MackandJack and that ol' gangplow going out to the road that morning," she shot across the room as her fingers flew into classical ballet, "and the road was full of snow and then I see he wasn't on the seat or anything –"

"Oh for goodness sakes, Nettie!" said Vera. "We know all about that, you don't have to keep saying it over and over."

" – so I went out into the barn –"

My old man growled and then spat his words across the room: "Can't someone shut her up!"

At that Nettie stormed out of the house, slamming the door behind her. A cold silence moved into the room. Nobody seemed to know what to say now. I was making preliminary moves to join Nettie in the woodshed when Uncle Jules cleared his throat and spoke up. "Well, somebody's got to tell Buck, don't they?" he said, looking over at Aunt Esther. "He's got a heck of a long way to come if he's going to make it in time for the funeral."

Esther got up and stood in front of her chair for a moment, balancing herself, and then said, "Why I never thought of it before . . . never once thought it was possible for him to come. The war's got to wait a while. I'll go in town to the telephone office right now and send him a telegram. You know, Buck lives in airplanes, surely he can get one to fly him up here in time for the funeral."

One day later we got a telegram from Captain G. F. Draeger saying he was flying to Chicago and taking a train that would bring him home the day before the funeral.

Three days later Esther came to our house in town and picked up my mother and me and drove us down to the train station to meet the two o'clock local. We left Bits with Mrs. Horton and parked behind the station, and Mother and Esther took me into the station and stood at the pot-bellied stove getting warm. His girlfriend Liz Stelter was already in there. She wore all black and had red eyes and sported a crinkly hankie, but the excitement of seeing Buck again kept bubbling up through her tears. I got bored listening to them talk and went out to the tracks and looked to the north. The sun was reflected on the twin steel tracks like magical wands to conjure up Uncle Buck, and I wondered where the rails eventually went and what it looked like when they got there. I looked south too, and saw how the tracks kept on going straight as an arrow until they vanished, and I imagined them to be steel rainbows with pots of gold out along the horizon.

Then I saw smoke and heard the whistle. Mother and Esther came out of the station and stood beside me on the platform as the train drew up and stopped, and then Buck, carrying a canvas bag and wearing that neat and pressed uniform and the little hat cocked off to one side – just as he looked in the pictures he mailed home – stepped off the train, his gold buttons flashing in the sun, his pantlegs tucked into high, brilliant boots. I remembered the pictures of knights that I'd seen in a book about King Arthur. Buck was tan and taller than I had remembered, and the pock marks on his cheeks seemed to have been scrubbed off by flying fast secret airplanes, his high cheek bones sharper, his eyes bluer too, maybe because he spent so much time up in the sky. His chin was thrust forward, but there were tears in his eyes, and he looked sad and bereft and maybe even a little homesick.

He kissed Liz first, and she cried, and then everyone got a kiss and a hug, and a few words of greeting, and then Buck leaned down to me and said, "You going to the funeral, Junior?"

"Yup," I bragged. But that wasn't what I wanted to talk about, so I said, "Uncle Buck, did you fly up here in a secret airplane?"

He laughed for the first time and whispered, "No, how could it be a secret then?" Everyone laughed foolishly, and Liz said she had to get back to work now and would see Buck at the funeral. They hugged again and went down the track a fair bit to be together for a little while. Esther and Mother and I walked out back to the car, and then Buck came and said he had been sitting a long time and wanted to walk out to The Place. Then he looked at me. "You want to keep me company, Junior?"

The women took off, and Buck and I walked out along the snowy road toward The Place. I spent all my time trying to keep up with him. He seemed strong and sure-footed and every inch a hero. I was sure now we would win the war. "Tell me about your secret airplane," I said. "How fast does it go?"

Buck said it had two engines and two tails and was the fastest airplane in the world, way over 500 miles an hour. He looked worried when he said that and said, "It's got a real kick to it, and it still has a few kinks left over. It's way too fast. Tails and the wings, sometimes they flutter 'cause you're going too fast. I think they need some kind of rake to them. We've had a few accidents. I've been working on things. I think I've got it all in hand now. The plane's so fast the Japs won't be able to catch up with it."

I looked up at Buck and felt good. I thought about after the war and how, when he came back, maybe *he* would take over The Place, and then Ned and Buck and I, we could all farm it together.

With Buck home again, the family seemed to have forgotten all about Opa.

After all, we hadn't none of us seen Buck for over a year. He had enlisted in the army back in 1941, the summer before Pearl Harbour, and then became a pilot right out of boot camp. Buck told us last time he was home on furlough that he had graduated from flight school and was training to fly fighter airplanes. One time he wrote to say they had returned one of his letters because he had said too much about airplanes, and that left him with only the weather to talk about. And once he let out that lots of foreign pilots had moved to his base, and he was teaching *them* how to fly airplanes. Anyway, I couldn't wait to get him aside the first time I saw him and ask him more about that secret airplane.

Uncle Buck stood before the chesterfield in the sitting room when we arrived at The Place, and we all lined up in the dining room and filed slowly past him one at a time – the Draegers and Kirkhams, Stuebbens and Schoenhofs and Schimmelpfennigs, his old high school friends and all the farmers up and down the valley – maybe fifty of them, all crowded into that small farmhouse. We were thrilled to see our hero again, and yet we knew why Buck had come home and why we were all gathered there in the parlor, and we had to smile and cry about Opa at the same time. It was hushed and sanctimonious in the room, and Buck stood shaking hands like a preacher as he would when you come out of church.

When I came and stood beside him, he crouched and let a small smile sleeve through his lips, said, "Well, Junior, are you going to have a chance to show me how to drive that new tractor of yours?"

Two hours, and we had our coats back on and all of the mourners filed out into a light snow and climbed back into the cars. A parade of black and brown Model A Fords – except of course for Esther's yellow one – drove slowly out into the white road and down over the iron bridge and then past the graveyard Opa would be buried in. I looked out the side window of my old man's car and saw a mound of ugly brown earth and three men fitting a metal frame over a hole in the ground. Something about it made my stomach turn. I turned quickly and snuggled down deeper under the blanket and stared at Bits and wondered what it was like going down into that hole. You die and they put you into a hole and you're going to be in that hole forever. You are going to be down there dead and moldy. There is no second chance. Once and that's it. Times like this they always talked about Heaven and all, and it sounded nice, but the truth of the matter was when you're dead, you're dead, and they put you into a hole, and you're down there forever. No matter what they say, you don't come back up, you don't ever come back up, you just stay down there in that hole.

Forever and ever. Amen.

I was suddenly conscious my mother was shaking me and calling me to get out of the car. We were parked at the church. I told her I didn't want to get out. "Get out of the car!" growled my father. "I tell you, I don't know what's wrong with that kid!" I got out of the car to avoid his coming after me and walked between my mother and my sister Bits into the church and down to the second row. Captain Buck Draeger was sitting in the first row beside his mother. The light was flashing off him and shooting around the church. Ned sat between Esther and Vera. They had left Nettie under a blanket in the cab of Ned's truck. I rested my eyes on the back of Buck's head. During the service the sun came out and fell directly through the windows and across his shoulders as if to remind everyone that Buck was the chosen one.

People cried to the left and right of him, but Buck sat there upright, stern-faced and serene. His father was dead, but he knew it was going to be all right. He didn't seem at all worried that when you're dead, that's it, they put you into a dark hole forever.

Pastor List and the choir went on and on; the rest of us just sat there and took it all in. Buck then got up and made a short speech about his father. He said Opa was a pioneer who left the old country and found freedom and enterprise in the new. He broke ground and moved the frontier back and helped his country grow strong. At the moment he himself was busy trying to keep it that way, and as soon as the Nazis and the Nips were put into their place and the war was over, he would hurry home and help to set things straight again.

You could see people really wanted to applaud him, but this was church, wasn't it?

The minister followed with a long sermon that made Opa look less like a farmer and more like a saint. By the look of his crops,

Reverend List sang, God had shown his acceptance and had reserved a place for him on His own heavenly farm in the sky. We sang more hymns and then got up and filed one by one slowly past Opa's casket. Gramma broke down looking at him and had to be shouldered back to her pew. When I got up there, I looked in at Opa, and though his eyes were closed, I imagined them flicking open and him saying, "*Wer bist du?*" Holding my hand, my mother leaned down and whispered into my ear, "My, doesn't he look like he could just get right up and walk on out of here!" I didn't think so. But one thing I did know: he didn't have to get up and go out there and plow that sandy bottomland day after day. All he had to do now was lie down in that black hole forever.

The last hymn, and we went out to our cars and got into a line of twelve black and one yellow Model-A, and followed the hearse across town and out to the cemetery. It was no longer snowing, and the sun stood once more and looked down across the glassy fields around the cemetery. It was a warm December this year. Buck stood beside his sobbing mother up front at the edge of the grave. Reverend List wore a heavy fur coat and stood at the other side on the snowbank. "Old Albert," he said, "was one of the best farmers in this country. The Place is a sign of his reward for a long and productive life. He will not be forgotten. On the contrary, he will be remembered as a man who worked long and hard and loved his family and knew he was but a child to his God."

That did it. The casket was lowered into the dark. We began to cry out loud once more. Then Mr. List gave the benediction, and Buck turned to grab a shovel but slipped and nearly fell into the grave. We all screamed and caught hold of him. He tossed the first spade of dirt into the grave, and then Ned and my old man did the same, and after a while we headed back to our cars lined up over the hill.

I saw Nettie sitting in Ned's truck and staring out the window at me. I threw open the door and said, "How come they're keeping you here all to yourself, Nettie?"

Her eyes were red, and she held a small handkerchief to her face. She said, “Vera said I cry too loud.”

“You should’ve heard *her* crying!” I smiled at her, and then gave her a chance to say what she had to say about everything. “Did you love Opa a whole lot?”

She looked crazy for a moment. “Silly!” she growled at me. “Everybody loves their pa. Don’t you love your pa?”

I turned and looked back at my old man. He was still standing at the grave watching them remove all the machinery from the graveside, and I could see he was crying along with the rest of them.

I said, “Maybe.”

All that day I watched Buck to see whether he was going to take us kids up to the haymow and do his circus tricks.

My cousin Dottie finally went and tugged at his sleeve and said, “Uncle Buck, will you take us kids up to the haymow and do some tricks?” And Vera said, “Dottie, this is not a good time for that. Everybody’s thinking about Opa and we’re going to eat soon.” Uncle Buck shushed Vera and whispered something into Dottie’s ear, and she laughed and jumped up and down, so I knew it was going to happen eventually.

Buck’s haymow show for the kids was a family tradition. During family gatherings, he would wait until there was a break in the action and then gather up all the kids and take us up to the haymow, where we’d sit around on the hay as he skinnied his way up a pole to the rafters and then get up onto one and stand balanced just like they do in the circus, and then he’d walk barefooted across it to the other side of the haymow. We’d cheer and applaud him, and he’d perform stunts like sitting on one leg, and that had us screaming. We’d sit hugging each other, holding our breaths, until his last act, which was grabbing the hay rope and swinging through the air, back and forth, his feet wrapped around it, until he pumped himself up into the highest arc he could, and then he’d let go and plummet through the air thirty feet or more and land in the haymow and then catapult down in front of us and laugh his head off and bow and do clown-like things as we jumped up and down and applauded his show.

As usual, the menfolk left the women and kids and got together on the sun porch just off the kitchen. Being as how it was in December, it was cold out there, but the porch gave the men a place to guzzle beer and smoke cigars and listen to their hunting stories. Ned, of course, was the bard. My way of getting out to the porch in time to hear Ned's hunting stories was to sit with the girls in the living room playing a card game called 'Authors', but as usual, since I didn't know any authors and losing three straight, I would slip out to go look for Buck and the other menfolk. I walked straight through the women in the big kitchen and opened the porch door and was swatted in the face by the cigar smoke and the cold.

But this time it was Buck already regaling the assembled. "Why," he said, "she can climb to twenty thousand feet in just a little over three minutes and fly somewheres at five hundred miles an hour for damn near two hours and then come home again. Pressurized cockpit, glass as strong as steel, fluorescent controls glow in the dark. And she's got one big 50 millimeter cannon and four 20 millimeter machine guns, and they're strapping a ton of bombs onto her belly too."

"What's this airplane look like?" said Uncle Arnold. "Is it a secret?"

"Not exactly a secret, no . . . she's got these two engines and two tails, and a main fuselage where the pilot sits. That way, you see, you don't have to fire through the props, and you're sitting right behind the guns, so you get a better look at what you're shooting at. She's all sleek stainless steel, and the rivets don't stick out and slow you down. They're smoothed off and slick. Got tricycle landing gear, with a wheel in the nose, makes it easy to taxi." Suddenly, he darkened and looked at me just as I tried to hide. "As I told Junior, she's a little hard to handle sometimes. So damn fast, you know! Like a colt. She wants to get up and go, doesn't like you holding her back. The trouble is it's hard to pull her out of a steep dive. When you get her up to 500 miles-an-hour or so, she doesn't always respond to controls."

"Then what do you do?"

"Talk to her," laughed Buck.

"What do you say?"

"'Come on, girl! You can do it!'"

Everyone laughed, and Jules Stubs asked, "When you going to war, Buck?"

Buck leaned forward and whispered, "Well, you know the Japs have landed in Alaska."

"I hear we're next."

"If I have anything to say about it, Jules, that just won't happen."

Before supper, the men went out to the barn and helped Ned with the milking, and the women went to the chicken coop and the pig shed with Vera and Gramma, and then, after washing up, the whole bunch of them went to the table in the dining room. Us kids all sat at two card tables in the parlour.

Great-Aunt Doris, who considered herself the spiritual leader, looked around the table and then dropped her head and started praying. "Dear Father," she said, and I stood up and looked over at Buck. He was sitting there and staring straight ahead during the prayer like a prisoner listening to a verdict. He wasn't thinking about Our Father. He was thinking about his airplane, and he looked worried, too. He must've sensed I was watching him from the parlour because he turned and winked at me and broke out of his darkness. "Amen," he said, along with everyone else when Doris got to the end of her long prayer. Buck told everyone about living these days where every day was sunny and nobody had ever seen snow.

After supper when everyone got to washing up or sitting around and talking. Uncle Buck got me aside and said, "How old are you now, Junior?" he said. "Twelve, isn't it?"

"Thirteen," I said, flinging down my trump card.

"Thirteen! Isn't it an unlucky number?"

"How do I know?"

"They avoid it in the army. Airplanes are ten, eleven, twelve, fourteen, no thirteen."

"What's the number of your airplane?"

"Four seventeen," he said, as if it were a statistic he'd rather not think about.

"Do you like flying? You said so in your letters."

"Oh, I do, I do!" He laughed in a dismissive way and right away changed the subject. "Vera tells me you're a big help. Someday Ned can turn The Place over to you."

"No, he's going to turn it over to you."

"Oh, I don't know, Junior." He smiled sadly and looked away. "I . . . well, I've been thinking about things." He studied me for a moment as if wondering whether he should say anything else and then said, "I'm thinking after the war I might go off to college. I already have a college scholarship, you know . . . being valedictorian and all, but my folks couldn't afford to send me at the time, and so I just lazed about, working in the pea factory and riding the freights out to Montana, and then I joined the CCC and worked in the woods till I got drafted. Now, I got some time on my hands, and I've been reading some books and thinking about . . . things." Then Uncle Buck did a strange thing with his eyes: they were warm and smiling one minute and cold and frightened the next. "I've been thinking about what's going on in the war. They fill you up with lots of big words. They tell you how God's on your side and all that, and how you have to go over there and defend your country by getting your brains blown out and how those Germans are all a bunch of monsters and how you have to go and kill them all off."

"But it's true, isn't it? That's what Mrs. Bennett says. She's our teacher, she says the Nazis are planning to take over the whole world. She says look at what they're doing to the Jews –"

"Sure, sure!" he growled, "All right! I know all about what they're doing over there. I know we've got to try and stop them from coming over here, I know all that. Opa lived in Germany way back, and he told us how they came before he was born and burned down his uncle's barn and stole all his cattle. That sort of thing's been going on for thousands of years, Junior, and I guess it's our turn now." He looked at me then. "But a lot of things have changed since then. I'm flying this machine, see? It's a beautiful machine. It can shoot down anything. You know, I had a choice . . . well, it wasn't much of a choice. I chose to become a fighter pilot. It was the lesser of two evils. I could have been a bomber pilot. That's what they wanted me to be. They wanted me to fly 'The Flying Fortress'. I thought about it. I thought about what I would have to do. I'd have to fly over German cities and drop firebombs and blockbusters on people. Okay, I thought, they're just Germans and Japs, they're our enemies, they aren't really people." He closed his eyes. "But me personally? I can't think of it that way. They said you have only this one job. You go over there, you drop your bombs, and then you get to hell out of there. Simple. But then I think, Hey, wait a minute, what about all the kids and Omas and Opas you just killed down there? You going to run away and forget about them? You go over there and kill them and leave a terrible mess, and you don't have to clean up afterwards? Sure, they're Krauts and all, but, look, they're human beings, aren't they? I'm a Kraut too, and I'm a human being." He flicked his eyes open and fixed them upon me. "Think about that, Junior! Maybe there's something that can be done after the war."

I didn't know what it would be. I was scared because of the look on his face. It wasn't my Buck. I'd read the newspapers. I'd seen enough. I knew all about Hitler. I knew how the Japs treated everybody. But I was just a kid. I just couldn't hold two ideas in my mind at the same time. We were in big trouble. If something wasn't done now, maybe we'd be the ones they'd come and drop their bombs on.

Finally, I came up with something, I said, "Do you think the Germans think the same way you do?"

"No, they don't," he said confidently, wrinkling his brow and booking out of the thought. "They're not allowed to think. But maybe if they think like me, someone comes and shoots them for thinking that way." Then he smiled, but he used all his teeth to do it. "But you understand now how *I'm* thinking, don't you?"

"How?"

"That something's got to change. I mean real change. The people I see around me, the only change they see now is destroying the Nazis and then taking over the world for themselves. Well, I'm not going to help them do it. That's not the world I have in my mind."

He didn't seem to be able to describe what kind of a world he had in mind. He looked off and shook his head. I got up and walked away because I didn't like the way hc was talking.

Buck went to visit Liz Stelter several times and then left us in the first week of the new year. It was a brilliant cold day. My old man drove us down to the train station. We were the first ones there. We went into the waiting room and stood around until we heard Esther's car. I ran to a window and saw Gramma and Esther climbing out, and then Buck got out. Gramma and Esther walked beside Buck and held tight to his arms as if he was a balloon that would fly off if they let him go. Vera walked two steps back, staring at the ground and carrying Buck's dufflebag. I asked where Nettie was. "We didn't bring her," Vera said. "She was acting funny and saying goofy things and carrying on. She wouldn't even say goodbye to Buck, and when I said something to her, she ran out to the woodshed, and that's where we left her."

Uncle Buck wasn't talking either. He looked worried. His pockmarks had come back. He had lost his tan. His buttons were showing only the clouds. We all stood around the stove in the waiting room, the women wiping away tears, whispering to each other. My father looked at the floor and tried to pretend everything was normal. I went and stood beside Buck, and he poked me in the ribs and smiled. "We never got around to that tractor," he said. "We'll do it next time." He went over to my mother and held Bits in his arms until the train arrived, and then we all went out into the cold, and Gramma and Esther once again walked beside Buck to the little stool thrown down by the conductor. And then one by one we let him go, and he climbed up onto the steps and turned around and waved like you see in the movies. The conductor blew his little whistle, Buck laughed for no reason, and then everyone began to shout and reach out for him. "Bye, Buck! Bye-bye!" we screamed. "Write soon as you get back to camp! Don't forget to go to church! Don't gamble all your money away! Keep safe! Don't take no chances! The war'll be over in no time and you'll be back home safe and sound!"

He took a seat halfway down the coach car and leaned into the window to wave again to us. I wanted to jump onto the train and kidnap him and take him back out to The Place and never let anyone get near him. No, he was going off to war, and the war wasn't going to be over without him, I knew that. Maybe we'd never see him again. Buck was flying an airplane he couldn't handle. It was way too fast for him. Maybe the Japs had their own secret airplanes that went even faster than Buck's. Maybe they'd shoot him down, and he'd come home in a box.

The train shuddered and began to crawl, and I ran alongside it down the platform. The train gathered itself. I kept up for a while. Buck sat in the window and waved to me and then mouthed something. He said the same words over and over as if maybe he thought I could hear them. But I couldn't hear anything and ran off the end of the platform and fell headfirst into a snowbank. I lay on my elbows and watched as the train cleared the pea factory and the co-op feed mill, and then it was only a cloud of black smoke that hovered for a while before it too vanished.

I have spent my life trying to figure out what Buck was trying to tell me.

PART TWO

The Alto Saxophone

10

School was closed for two weeks that winter because the buses couldn't get out to fetch the farm kids there and back again. So I went out and stayed at The Place.

I set out Monday morning. The snow was blowing sideways. It was dark as a grave till noon, and then the temperature began dropping. Later that day Esther brought home a bug from the bank. She showed up and went straight to bed, and before you could count to ten, Vera joined her, the two of them lying up there in the same room and not even talking. They would be down for three days. And then Gramma woke Tuesday morning and found she couldn't get out of bed, and so the only ones up were Nettie and I and Ned, who did all the farm chores and kept both stoves in the house going while Nettie and I played a hundred games of double solitaire at the dining room table when we weren't ferrying food from my mother and hot tea around the house, and then Wednesday Ned came down sick, and my mother and my old man had to come out to The Place to do all the chores Nettie and I couldn't do.

By Friday Vera felt better and came downstairs and stood at her window looking out at her road. She asked, "Is it the end of the world?" It was like living in a snow cave, so dark in the house we had to walk around carrying oil lamps all day. Saturday was the worst; the day came up grey and went dark by ten o'clock. Ned got up and helped me dig trenches out to the milkhouse, the chicken coop, the barn, and finally out to the dog kennel, where we found Loud, the head bloodhound, and Lady and Clarence, all three hunkered down inside blankets inside their doghouses, and we fed them hot pork slop, and they cheered us on our way back to the house by howling and jumping up against the chicken-wire fence. "They like it cold," said Ned. "It makes them want to get their claws into something."

Then we dug our way to the Outhouse and stocked it with an old Sears and Roebuck catalogue since fortunately the new one had come in the mail long before the Earth lost its way.

Days I had the barn all to myself because Ned was too weak to do much more than chores. I had to feed the cows and the horses, clean out all the stalls and the whole barn, free up the water fountains. It was silent in the barn, and warm too, because it had animals to heat it up. I'd go up into the haymow at ten in the morning and toss timothy hay down the chute and fill the cow troughs with mash and then the horse mangers with corn mash and cobs, which they ate with gusto as if the corn cobs were ice cream cones. And when I was done, I put on a show for the cows. I'd walk back and forth in front of them and belt out the new songs from the Hit Parade on the radio. "Kiss me once and kiss me twice," I'd swoon, leaning over the long snout of a cow, "and kiss me once again, it's been a moo moo time." She'd pucker up and blow me a kiss. "Never felt like this before since Heaven only knows when." I imagined I sounded like Frankie and Bing and Perry Como all rolled into one. The cows were all busy chawing away, smiling with big fat pink lips and staring up at me with their marble eyes, and I'd strut up and down entertaining them at their own nightclub. I hung about the warm barn until Mom called me up to the house for meals. It was so peaceful walking around the barn and I thought how perfect farm life was and how I could go on forever living like this!

Ned had gone down last but had come back first, and then one by one the others came around, until at last Esther was able to return to the bank. I went back to school and discovered the teachers were desperate to make up for lost time by piling on the homework and sending you to the principal's office if you said the least thing.

February was sunny and frigid, but by March winter released the thumbscrews a little, we thawed out, and then before you could see it coming, everything turned to mud. The mud froze in April, and it snowed as hard as it did in February. We froze, and then thawed out again. Mud and then snow, mud and snow. I went out one warm morning in May to spend the day helping Gramma clean out the pig pens, and my mother drove out in the afternoon while I was there. I watched her go out to the chicken coop to have a long conversation with Vera. They came to the chicken coop door and looked over at Gramma and me, and I could hear my mother talking. She was telling Vera that my teacher had put me in the front row in the classroom because I was not doing too well and she thought maybe the reason was I needed eyeglasses.

Uncle Buck wrote home once a week that spring, but he said the same thing over and over in his letters. It was always about the weather. "We don't have too much weather down here but the last week has been very cold." Well, I thought, we could tell *him* a thing or two about cold weather. But Esther had another interpretation, she said, "He's not really talking about the weather," she said, tears welling up in her eyes. "He's trying to tell us where they're sending him. That's code language he's using to tell us they're shipping overseas."

In his next letter Buck wrote, "The weather down here has warmed up a lot." Esther read it and said, "He's already left."

"Had a light rain last night," he wrote. "Don't worry about me, folks, I'm fine. There's not much to do. But they've got a big library here at the base, and I've been reading books I've always wanted to read, books I never had the time for. I've read *Great Expectations* and *The House of Seven Gables* and *Adam Bede*." Esther said, "They're all English novels, aren't they? So he's trying to tell us he's being sent to England."

A few weeks later Buck wrote again. "The weather's turned cold again," he said. "Junior will be out of school soon and back on that tractor. He'll be taking my place again this summer. Tell him I'm just doing my job to make sure he lives in a country where, now that spring has sprung, he can go out into the field riding a tractor and not being shot down just because he's a Jew or a Frenchman. This is a turning point in history, and I'm lucky to be part of it."

"He's going to France," said Esther.

"He's not going anywhere," I said. "Every letter's been mailed from the camp he's been living in for the past year."

But Buck was right about the tractor. Three days after school ended, I lit out for The Place for my second summer.

That day it was hot, and No Nothin' Creek was now Somethin', high up, bubbling, and dark brown, carrying tree branches, roots, and grass, wearing away its own banks. The water was high, almost to the roadway over the iron bridge. I stood for a while and admired it. Nettie came out to the ditch in front of the house and escorted me into the house, and Vera made her carry my bag up to Buck's bedroom. Gramma hugged me and said, "Isn't the creek high?" Vera said Ned had gone out to Uncle Jules' place to help him fix fences and would be back later in the day, and so I had a few hours to kill. Nettie and I drifted out to the barn and talked to MackandJack and fed them a few cobs of corn, walked out to the barnyard, sat on the seat of the manure spreader to talk, and then climbed the straw stack to survey the fields of fawn-green shoots of corn and oats and timothy.

I started to feel something was about to happen that would change my life forever.

I left Nettie behind and walked down to Opa's bottomland, which didn't know what to do now that it wasn't being plowed to within an inch of its life. Strange sharp weeds had sprung up and bragged about it and plotted an invasion of the rest of the farm. I walked to the fence along the train track and gazed west. "Opa," I said out loud, in case he was listening, "you were dead wrong, you know. There's no California over there . . . just plain old Thompson Valley. If you wanted California, you should've climbed over the fence and hitched a ride on The 400."

Which turned out to be prophetic.

I heard the express coming and climbed the wire fence and held on to a post to get a better view down the tracks. Suddenly a blinding headlamp came roving around the bend and the long series of blaring trumpets announced an intention to slice right on through town without so much as a sideways glance. I waited for it to come barreling past me, but it came on slower than usual and then a whole lot slower, and by the time the last car reached me, The 400 had stopped altogether.

I looked east along the track and saw the signals cocked halfway, the lights red. I climbed up a fence post and waved, but no one seemed to notice. They were too busy laughing and chatting and smoking cigarettes and drinking bright things in tall sparkling glasses. All of them wore jackets and ties and fedoras and bonnets. They looked like movie stars. Some leaned in close to tell secrets. So beautiful, so confident they seemed, yet so restless. I imagined them carrying on some kind of romantic adventure, and yet were curiously unsatisfied and wanting more. The upper half of the door at the front of the car suddenly opened inward, and a man in uniform leaned out through it. Then he stepped back, and another man took his place, and then a woman came and leaned against him. The two were holding tall glasses with something green in it. They chatted quietly and laughed as if they hadn't a care in the world, and then they did a little dance to the music behind them.

And what music! I had never heard anything like it.

"Hey, kid!" the woman shouted. "You speak English?" At that moment I regretted saying yes. "Where in hell are we anyways?"

"That's the town of Herring over there," I said, pointing proudly to a paltry few white houses showing through the trees. I looked over at town and the silver water tower as if through new eyes.

It turned out to be an embarrassment.

* * *

Then I heard trumpets and trombones and saxophones, but it wasn't the kind of music we had in this town. The man lifted his glass to the woman. "Well then, here's to Herring!" They drank and laughed. "It looks like a nice little place, doesn't it, Betty?" But she only giggled.

I noticed the way the two of them had been working on their hair, and as they talked, how they played with it as if tempting each other to do more. I had my own Humphrey Bogart and Lauren Bacall. They talked to one another as if they liked what they were saying. Words came naturally to them. They didn't have to think about words before they said them. The woman wore a red dress and lots of jewelry. The man sported a dark pinstriped suit studded with bright things in it, and his shining wavy hair was reflected in the window. They had large plans, they had worlds to conquer. The war was going to reduce Europe and Asia to ashes, and they had plans to build it up again. The whole world was going to be bigger and better after they got ahold of it. These were people who knew they were destined never to die, but at the same time a little surprised by their mortality. They knew too they had to get somewhere fast to accomplish all the miracles they had been called upon to complete before they went down into that black hole like Opa did.

I worked up my nerve at last and shouted, "What kind of music is that?"

"Why that's big band music, boy . . . don't you get big band music in Herring? That is Glenn Miller's 'In the Mood.' Don't you even have radios?" I didn't want to admit we had radios, sure, but of course all we ever got on them were The Six Fat Dutchmen and Whoopee John Wilfahrt and the Grand Ol' Opry. Then the two of them seemed to have forgotten all about me before I could ask another question. They left me suddenly. The door slammed shut. The train began to move. The woman and the man appeared again sitting in one of the windows and smiling out at me and waving goodbye.

I waved back, but a big part of me was already sitting there on the seat beside them.

* * *

Esther came home from the bank that week with another letter from Buck. "You won't believe how this letter got to us," she said. She held onto the letter until we sat down to supper. We had new seating arrangements now: Vera had me sitting at one end of the table where Opa used to sit.

Esther finally opened Buck's letter and read it to us:

"I found a way to write you that would take me around the boys with the scissors," he said. "I dropped this letter off at a country post office. You'll see the name on it isn't mine. I'm going to take a chance the letter doesn't come back to me. Anyway, just to tell you I'm about to ship out. I don't know where but I'm guessing Alaska. We've got some foreign pilots now and we're training them. Last week I met a fellow from Russia. Sasha is his first name. His second name is so long it would take me the rest of the war to say it. He speaks broken English, hard to understand. Says he's a Communist. I asked him what that was, and he said it means he runs his own country. I said I was a democrat, and we did the same thing here. He grabbed me and hugged me like a woman and said together we would make peace last forever."

"Russia!" shouted Nettie. "He's going to Russia!"

"Oh Nettie!" said Vera. "For goodness sakes . . . he's not going to Russia. Whoever goes to Russia?"

Ned ignored her and said, "Won't he be able to come home before he flies away?"

"He's definitely going to Russia," said Nettie, flipping fingers.

"He just might," said Esther, ignoring Nettie. "You look at the map and you'll see what I mean. If he's way down South and he's got to fly north by northwest to get up to Alaska, maybe they'll let him land his airplane somewhere nearby and come home for a day or two."

"You and me," said Vera, "we won't know when or why, that's for sure. Whichever way he goes, it'll be a big secret."

Nettie laughed out loud and shouted out, "Maybe he'll land his airplane right out there in the pasture!"

"Nettie, stop it!" said Vera, giving her a dirty look and making her voice into an instrument of torture. "Land in the pasture! What do you know about landing in a pasture? Those airplanes are way too big to land in a pasture!"

Nettie then gave me one of those looks she reserved for times she knew more than the others what was going to happen. I followed her outside over to the outhouse. She slammed the door and began to talk to herself. I slipped over to it and leaned my head against the door.

"Just leave me alonc!" she screamed. "Leave me alone!"

I went out and looked at the pastures and asked myself whether Buck could land in a pasture.

A week slipped past, and then another. One day out in the south forty cultivating corn, I decided to get out of the sun for a while and dove for the water jug I kept below the old oak at the edge of the field. I sprawled in the shade and then I heard an airplane. It turned out to be a silly little yellow Piper Cub. Another time I heard what sounded like thunder a long way off. I searched the sky for a squadron of B-17s or P-38s, but couldn't see anything, and then there was lightning all along the northern tree line, and I knew it was only the weather.

Once I saw a plane way up in the sky, then maybe two or three, but they all went away without coming anywhere near The Place.

Middle of July it was. A Tuesday, I think. Just past noon. We'd had dinner, and they'd all gone down for naps. Ned had fallen into his newspaper. Gramma was flat on her back across her bed, snoring, an open Bible beside her. Vera's head was thrown way back as she slept in the rocker, Nettie folded up into the fetal position on the couch. I lay on my belly on the carpet in the parlour reading the funny papers. Li'l Abner finally was going to marry Daisy, and Dick Tracy had cornered Ace Eyes. I needed to get out of the house and down to the creek on such a day as this.

I searched the sky for signs of fighter aircraft as I raced across the burnt hayfield and down through the cool bearded grass and through the trees to the creek and tore off all my clothes and waded over to a swimming hole nestled in the high bank at the roots of a giant elm, stood for a moment watching the sunfish scatter, and then dove to the bottom.

I hung there in the zebra halflight.

I was eleven years old now, going on twelve. Five-five or six, ninety, maybe a hundred pounds. Something was happening I couldn't explain. During the past school year I found myself looking at other guys soaping themselves down after basketball in the school showers to see if they had any hair. Most of them had a ring of bright kinky hair and large puds, but I was bald as Old Man Jacobsen. We stood around laughing at Arnie Schalinske's dirty knock-knock jokes and pretending we understood them. Most of the jokes had to do with tits and twats. I myself had been thinking more and more about tits since the girls in our class were beginning to sprout them.

I wasn't supposed to know anything about tits, or if I knew, I wasn't supposed to tell anyone I knew. It was all hush-hush and made girls even more interesting and at the same time more dangerous. At recess we still played jail games. The boys chased the girls, and when we caught them, we towed them back to 'jail', and when they were all caught and in jail, then someone shouted, "Girls chase the boys!" I always went after Marlene Benson, the class athlete, and she paid me back when it was her turn. There was something going on between us, but neither of us knew what it was. At the time all we could do was try to outrun and outhustle the other. When I caught her, I'd hold onto her and then try to feel her up. There wasn't much to feel. Little bumps is all. Not tits. I knew what tits were. Ronnie Lighthouse owned a stack of magazines with pictures of naked women with tits. The magazines were stuffed into the floorboards above his garage, and we used to slip up there and look at tits. We'd sit and stare at the pictures without saying much. "Look at *that* muff!" Ronnie would say, or "Holy Lollapalooza, get a load of *those* tubes!"

We couldn't even call things by their real names.

Just before school had let out for the summer, I worked up enough nerve to ask Marlene out. We went to Richard's Milk Bar first and had chocolate malts and then headed for The Opry House for the seven o'clock movie. There was a newsreel mostly about the war and then a Looney Tunes and previews and a Tom Mix serial and a travelogue about Mexico, before *The Courtship of Andy Hardy* came on. We sat in the back row away from people, and during the movie I reached across the armrest and down into her lap and cradled one of her hands in mine. Our hands rested on her left thigh, which I imagined to be more interesting than the movie. I inched the hands down her leg, something warm washed over me, and I had trouble breathing. I let her hand go and moved mine slowly up her leg. She sat there chewing away at the popcorn and watching the movie as if unaware what I was doing. I kept moving closer to my target, feeling the softness, and after a while, without looking at me, she reached down and pushed my hand away.

I told her I was going back out to The Place for the summer when I was walking her home after the movie. "I'm sleeping in Uncle Buck's room now," I said, to impress her. "Buck's in the army air force and flies secret airplanes. He's off to war soon. Me, I drive the tractor all day all by myself out in the field. I'm cultivating corn right now." Then I told her about my secret swimming hole, walled in by elm trees where nobody could see you. I told her exactly where and when I went swimming. "Why don't you come out next week and go swimming with me?" She smiled and sucked in her breath and her eyes got really wide, and eventually I got her to promise she'd come out when it got good and hot. "I usually go swimming around twelve-thirty for a half hour or so every day. Everyone up at the house is sound asleep, so nobody's around. What do you say you come out and we'll go swimming together?"

She said, "I don't even own a swimming suit."

"Oh, you don't have to wear a swimming suit out there!" I said, shocked at my own audacity. "As I said, everybody's up in the house asleep, nobody around. Me, I don't wear a swimming suit, I swim in the skinny." She drew in her breath and widened her eyes with disapproval, and I thought I could smell sex coming out of her. "But of course I'd probably wear one if you were there." Then she looked at me up and down as if trying to imagine what I looked like without a swimming suit, and giggled and walked up the curved walkway to her house.

"Promise you'll come?" I said. She stopped and looked back at me. "Promise?"

"We'll see!"

"Pretty promise?"

"All right, pretty promise . . . but only if it's good and hot out."

She went into her house, and I stood for a moment and something rose up inside and breathed all over me.

It was good and hot as I swam to the surface of the swimming hole and looked up and saw the light dancing down through the leaves. I smelled the sticky, ripening elderberries and felt the soft fingers of the creek on my shoulders and lay back on the cool sandy bottom and closed my eyes and listened to the suck and slither of the waters feeling their way along the shore. I walked down the creek and dropped to my knees and toppled forward onto the sandy bottom and lay there embracing the creek and thrusting my hips into the warm sand, rolled over and over in the water, and then jumping up and running up onto the shore, I fell into the fine, sharp bristles of the wild grasses, letting them sting and whip me.

I lay on my back in the sunlight with my eyes closed. Marlene had pretty promised she would come if it was good and hot out. Well, it had been good and hot Sunday and Monday and she hadn't come, so maybe she was waiting for today. I imagined her coming along the shore and finding me naked. She'd undress, of course, or maybe she had on a swimsuit I could talk her out of. I imagined her naked . . .

But after a while I knew I was kidding myself. Marlene wasn't coming, or if she did come, she would bring her younger sister or that awful Jean Colbright, and then it wouldn't work. I didn't mind Marlene seeing me naked, but if there was someone else with her it would probably scare me off. So I decided I to go put on my underwear. I got up and walked back to my strewn clothes, and as I reached for them I heard a noise in the bushes.

Footsteps.

Someone was coming up the creek through the elderberry brambles.

I got the wrong leg through my briefs and tried several different moves, but at last fell on my keester and looked up just in time to see someone standing on the opposite shore.

Only it wasn't Marlene Benson.

It was Nettie.

11

I got up and ran across the creek to my old swimming hole and plunged to the bottom and lay there till my lungs gave out, and when I came up for air, Nettie was pointing her finger at me and laughing like a little girl.

"That water's good and cold, I'll bet."

I screamed, "Nettie! What are you doing here?" She couldn't stop laughing. "You aren't even supposed to be here!"

"Who says?"

I added a little injury to my complaint and cried, "You shouldn't be here. I didn't hear you coming, where did you come from, why did you sneak up on me like that?" She looked away off across the fields as if questions had nothing to do with it. "How'd you know I was down here anyways?"

"I saw you leave the house, silly."

At which, a dangerous thought coiled itself around my brain and shook its rattle. Okay, it wasn't Marlene, but it was a girl. I was twelve years old. There had to be a first time to face each other without clothes on. So slowly I lifted myself out of my waterhole and walked and stood facing her. Nettie smiled and didn't seem at all impressed with my little noodle.

"All right, all right then!" I worked up a little anger. "As long as you're here, you might as well come and join me!"

Her smile vanished. "No, no, no . . . I can't swim."

"Swim? You don't swim in No Nothin' Creek, it's way too shallow."

"Know why they call it 'No Nothin'?"

"No, and I don't care."

"Because it don't amount to nothin'."

I'd seen Ronnie's pictures, but I'd never seen a real woman naked, not even my own mother, who always closed the door behind her when she got undressed. I just wanted to see what Nettie looked like. Even if she was just an aunt, even if she was old and fat. Fat aunts are better than nothing.

"Look, are you coming in?"

"I can't come in, I got my clothes on."

"Well, take them off then!" I said, even before I planned to say it. She sucked in her breath and stared at me as if I had told her to stop twisting her fingers. "Oh, Nettie, for cripe's sake I won't even look!"

Vera didn't go so far as to say Nettie was 'crazy' or 'missing a few cards in her deck.' If that were the case Nettie would already have been logged into the County Insane Asylum. No, she just said Nettie wasn't *all* there. I knew she was *different* of course. She spoke English but it was a child's kind of English. Short and square she was, like an Eskimo, and she had the small round face of a grown-up child. Except for the eyes. They were large and blue and saw through and around things. She had stored up everything that had ever happened to her in her own lifetime, and when Vera or Gramma forgot a name or a place or got something mixed up with something, they heard from Nettie.

My old man was fond of saying, "We can put her away," but Nettie had no real conception of being *put away*. Likely she figured she was just another piece of furniture. And in a way it was true. She was stored in various bedrooms when nobody else was using them, or when neighbors or Dr. Prill or Adolf Scheer, the Watkins man, or Pastor List came calling. She was our Cinderella. But we knew it was unlikely some prince would ever come along with a glass slipper in hand since Nettie never went anywhere, certainly not out to a ball-room, and her feet were bigger than even Ned's.

Her world was flat, and she worshipped the law of gravity. She knew if she stepped beyond the ditch in front of the house, she'd fall over the edge and keep on falling. She could inventory her entire world on her fingers: three drawers containing four or five pairs of patched underwear to be re-patched whenever she got mad and hid out in her room, an apron or two, two or three flour-sack dresses Vera made for her for Christmases and Thanksgivings and Easters, one pair of overshoes, two pairs of town shoes, black and brown, worn in case of funerals. And in the cellar, one bin of white potatoes that had to be peeled and soaked before meals. There was also one farmhouse, four bedrooms, one sitting room, one dining room, one kitchen, one pantry, one mud room, one back porch with a water pump, one massive lawn to be mowed and re-mowed, one wire cage with three bloodhounds howling at the moon and waiting always to be fed, one outhouse moved from time to time when the hole filled up, one granary, one big red barn, two concrete silos, two tall iron windmills – only one of which worked – one machine shed, one milk house, one woodshed to hide in, one stinky old chicken house, three yucky pig pens and four pigs, fifty-three head of Holstein, two ugly bulls, one of which Gramma fought off with a pitchfork, four Belgian workhorses – make that three, one having developed thrush and later, worse, strangles, and then sold for mink food – one rusty skeleton of the old Model-T in which Ned used to drive the family to church and then his sister Esther back and forth to business school in Red Wing, now only a skeleton buried among ten other rusty corpses of antiquated farm implements, all hidden by the crab apple orchard above the chicken house, and of course way out beyond the house and barn, one hundred and sixty acres of corn and wheat and clover and alfalfa and peas.

In the middle of everything, her apple orchard. Down below the pigpen and barnyard, it consisted of seven apple trees, all in a row. Golden Harvests, Red Delicious, Winthrops. Like Eve, when the woodshed was not far enough to get away from the human species, she found shelter out there and communicated with the devil. She'd sprawl below a tree and go at the apples and carry on a conversation you could hear all the way up to the pigpens, and if you peered through the high weeds around the fence, you could see her rehearsing those intricate finger ballets that she'd eventually perform in front of the whole family.

Just as surely as she knew the season had turned when the first robin hopped across the yard, Nettie knew when I crossed Iron Bridge the day after Decoration Day, that summer had finally come. I was the herald of summer. She would wave to me and jump up and down and thrust her arms out toward me, and when I reached her, gather me up and transport me across the lawn toward the house talking so fast I could barely understand her as she reconstructed everything that had happened since I left the day after Labour Day.

Not all there? It might be more correct to say Nettie wasn't all *here* because she was all *there*, all those events locked up in her own mind, her own Lilliput. A country with its own language. Her mouth always ran away with itself. Each word rushing out bumped into the next as they ran past each other. She was always in a hurry to finish what she was saying, like a teacher who heard the bell ring and hadn't finished explaining Vermeer and still had Rembrandt to go even as the class rose and headed for the door.

Vera was always there, waiting for me in the kitchen. She got as close to a laugh as she could get as I put my arms around her fat frame. "It seems you just left and here you come again, wherever does the time go?" she would say. "Why, you look like you put on thirty pounds over winter. Your Ma must be feeding you whale meat!" And then I would have to remind her I'd been out to The Place during the winter now and then, sliding down the hill and playing around in the barn, helping Ned. "Oh yes, I remember now." And the three of them – Nettie, Vera, and Gramma – would start in on me as I sat in a chair by the stove. "Is your mother over her cold yet? I just got over mine. Is she still helping out at The Quality Store? Your dad still out at Delbert Schwock's, putting on that roof? How's Bits? She's going to start school next fall, isn't she? That's Miss Schoffer's class, isn't it? How tall are you now?"

* * *

Gramma was there too. She always pulled a pan of Parkerhouse Rolls out of the oven when I got there and set it on the stove water tank to cool. And then Vera said, "Ned's out in the machine shed. I think he wants you to go out and cultivate the corn. It's just tall enough now. You go see him, and then you come back to the house before you head out, and we'll have one roll with butter and brown sugar on it for you."

Nettie kept trying to get a word in edgewise, but Vera wanted the floor. As soon as she stopped talking, Nettie jumped right in. "Vera found a double yolk egg last week in the hen house," she said, "and Ned dug up a dead cat in the silage last month, the one that went missing? and you remember that cow that had the five teats, well, they decided that –"

That was enough for Vera. Vera waved her off and stepped in between us. "Oh for goodness sake, Nettie, Junior just got here. You can tell him your stories after supper!" And then she turned to me: "Do you remember what we paid you last summer?"

"Fifty cents a week."

"See?" she said, turning to Gramma, "that's what I told you. Well, anyway, Ned says we should pay you fifty cents a day this summer."

"A day!" I cried, pennies from heaven raining all about me and I thought of an endless supply of movies and malted milks with my new girlfriend Marlene.

"You should see how big the peas are this year!" Nettie began again, one word somersaulting over the next. "Ned wants to start in on them peas early, he's got 40 acres this year, you came by the pea viner up by the cemetery, did you see it, they're opening it up already, why Jim Hadorn has 80 acres, the peas is real good this year, such big pods, so sweet, and the oats is already showing, Ned says the alfalfa the other side of the creek is clear up past your knees –"

"Nettie, Nettie!" said Vera, washing off the oilcloth, "go find something to do."

"– and we had to sell old King, he got worser and worser, he had strangles, you know, but when they come to get him, King wouldn't get into the truck, he kicked Jerry Randall and it took Ned and Jimmy Randall and . . . and who else was it –"

"Slow down," I said.

"Can't you make her stop, Vera?" grumbled Gramma.

"You talk to Junior all the time," said Nettie, turning on Gramma, "why can't I too? Only you and Vera can talk? I got a job to do. Junior has to know what's happened over winter! I have to catch him up!"

"Your job is to take Junior's suitcase up to Buck's room," said Vera, patiently. "Ned is waiting for him, and you can talk to him later!" Nettie thought about it, looked at me and realized she didn't want to make trouble now that I was at The Place. She left the room with my suitcase, and Vera shook her head and said, "She's not all there, you know. Some people think we should put her away."

"You're talking about my dad," I said, remembering a winter of regimentation. "Don't listen to him. Me, I never listen to him."

I have only one photograph of Nettie as a child. It was taken in September 1911. She's six years old. Must be Sunday. Her brother Ned stands behind her in a long-sleeved white shirt, suspenders, knickers, clodhoppers. Her sister Vera, in a flour-sack print dress, leans down over her and tries to hold her still for the camera. Nettie's puffy white dress is a blur of motion. She is a cute little blond nymph, willful, sassy, restless, prettied up for her first day of school. In a few moments the three of them will walk down the long sandy road to the schoolhouse, about a mile away at the intersection with a road that runs south to the river.

I wish I had a photograph of her four years later, when her mother harnessed up the team in the late afternoon and drove to the school. She had waited until all the children came home and then told them she was going to a neighbor's house. They were too busy with their afternoon chores to see her leave. When she arrived at the school, she found the door standing open and the teacher writing away feverishly at her desk.

* * *

"Why, the children've all gone home, Missus," Miss Lehmann said as Gramma walked into the room. "Did you not see them?"

"Of course, I saw them," she said, "but I come to speak to you about one of them." She stood anxiously in front of the first bench. "I come to speak about Nettie."

"Nettie Amelia," said Miss Lehmann, being precise as a good teacher should be. "Well, what is it you wanted to say about her?"

Gramma didn't really know what she wanted to say. No, that's not it: she knew what to say, but she didn't know how to say it in English. She wished the teacher could speak German. "We must do something. It cannot go on like this. Yesterday, the boys, they locked her in the outhouse when school let out, and they left her in there. She did not come home. I had to come and get her out."

Miss Lehmann dismissed it all with a polite laugh: "Yes, well, you know, boys will be boys."

"It happens and happens, Mrs. Lehmann."

The teacher folded her arms and leaned across her desk to deliver her thoughts. "You see, Nettie Amelia, well, there's not much I can do for her, I must tell you that. She's ten years old, but she's still in the second grade."

"They make fun of her all the time."

"Yes, and I talk to them about it. But there's precious little I can do when they leave the school grounds."

"The Horel boys, one time they take . . . took her clothes off."

"Yes, and when I heard about that, I punished them proper."

"They follow her home and call her terrible names on the way."

"I'll be honest with you," the teacher said as she got to her feet, and Gramma noticed when she walked, she hobbled a bit. "There's something . . . wrong with her."

"This I know!"

"She's slow. She can't put two and two together. She remembers everything – names, dates, places – but she can't make anything out of it. She can't relate anything to . . . well, just about everything."

Gramma leaned back against a desk to keep from falling down. "I didn't come here you should tell me what I already know," she said. "You must find a special school."

"Perhaps so. I had the district nurse look at her one day. She talked to her for an hour. Did she ever tell you that? Afterwards, the nurse told me Nettie was . . . well, the word she used was 'retarded.'"

"What does this word mean?"

Miss Lehmann came and stood right in front of her as if she were trying to teach her something. "It means there's precious little we can do for Nettie. I'm afraid she won't ever graduate from country school." Gramma must have flinched or started crying because the teacher went back and stood behind the desk again. "Why don't you get Doris and Vera to teach her at home after school? It would be easier that way. And you yourself, you can teach her how to cook and do housework . . ."

Afterward, when Gramma came home, she called Nettie into the house and told her tomorrow she wouldn't have to go to school and face those horrid Horel boys. Or the day after that. In fact, she wasn't ever going to have to go and face them.

"I will be your teacher from now on," she said, "and this," pointing at the kitchen stove, "this is your new schoolhouse."

But the following morning Nettie slipped out of the house, and Gramma had to go to school and fetch her home again. Nettie screamed and fought her all the way home in the buggy, and Opa had to come and help steer the screaming child into her room. Later, when Gramma went to hang out the washing, she saw Nettie running down the road toward the school.

It was almost noon when Miss Lehmann drove her buggy into the yard. She climbed out holding the sobbing child and walked her into the house. Gramma went and got Opa, and they all sat down in the parlour. The teacher said, "Nettie, I want to talk to your mother and father." Her mother told her to go outside and play. Nettie hid behind the pine tree in the front yard. In time the teacher came out and called Nettie over and smiled as she placed her hands on her shoulders. Gramma and Grampa came and stood in the doorway. "Close your eyes," the teacher said, "and hold out your hands." She then laid something in Nettie's hand and closed her fingers over it. "Now, don't you open your hand and look at what's in it until I'm gone." She kissed the top of the child's head, climbed up into her buggy, and drove off down the driveway in a cloud of dust.

When Nettie opened her hand and saw the gold locket, she looked over at her mother and father. She knew now she hated them as much as she hated Miss Lehmann. She ran out to the far pasture fence and threw the locket at the buggy driving off. Then she went into the barn to see if she couldn't find some cats to throw a pitchfork at.

So now I walked back into the water and said, "I promise I won't look, Nettie. I'll close my eyes."

I dove back into my dark hole and slipped under, to give Nettie time to undress. I held my breath as long as I could, and when I came up, I saw she had succeeded in dismantling her patched green apron but was now carrying on an argument with her patched brown gunnysack dress as she jerked at strings and buttons that wouldn't come away.

"You said you wouldn't look!" she hissed when she saw me.

"Okay, okay . . . Jeez!"

I slid down under the water again and held my breath. When I came up again, I could see she was in big trouble. The dress was at her feet, but even though it was high summer she had to fight her way through two thick beige-colored petticoats that somehow had been stitched together, and she was muttering away at something and looking thoroughly defeated. She was a bank robber spinning various combinations on a safe and finding none worked.

She turned to look at me and muttered, "You're looking again!"

I pretended to go under this time but settled just below the water, like a crocodile. I watched her wrestle her way out past the two petticoats, but now she faced an amazing patchwork quilt of pink garter belts and woolen, shredded brown stockings safety-pinned to a belt. She grunted and growled trying to extricate herself, and I decided I couldn't bear to watch. I dropped to the bottom of the swimming hole and stayed there as long as I could. When I came back up, she stood in front of a mound of clothing absolutely stark naked.

She was staring at the water, her round jelly face turning pink and then red, her gray eyes darting about suspiciously, her superwhite arms wrapped about her superwhite pendulous tits. They were so round and huge! It looked like she was carrying a basket of pillow-cases and sheets. She didn't look at all like the women in Ronnie's gallery. They were nude, Nettie was naked!

I felt suddenly sick. Was this how real women looked? I had made a serious mistake. This was all wrong. I was about to tell her to get dressed and go back to the house when she waded out into the middle of the creek.

"I hate swimming!" she groused. "I can't swim anyway!"

Without warning, she plopped down into the water and sat splashing about like a baby in a bath water. After a while she turned to look at me and cried, "You're looking! You said you wouldn't look, and now you're looking!" She seemed to be having the time of her life. I crawled out of my swimming hole and on my hands and knees and slipped up behind her with my hands scudding some water at her. She screamed and turned and laughed and scudded back.

"Hey, that's a declaration of war, Nettie!" I said, sitting and kicking water at her. She got slowly to her knees and began scuffing water back at me, and I turned away uttering a mock cry of fear and ran splashing down the creek and laughing like a child.

Then.

Something . . . what?

I looked up. Something way up in the sky. A flash! It came out of nowhere and just as quickly vanished, leaving behind a roar such as I had never heard in my life. A kind of scream. Something was up there and yet it wasn't. It sucked in all the air along with it and you couldn't breathe afterward. A scream and then silence, but for just a moment, and then the oak trees around the house swirled and danced in the aftershock of wind, and every animal on the farm started clucking and neighing and barking and squealing and mooing. The Place was struck down by an invisible tornado.

Then I saw it.

Climbing straight up into the sky. A speck up there maybe but then it came back down and roared straight over the farm so close you could read the numbers on the fuselage and wings.

Number Four Seventeen.

12

I yelled, "It's Buck!"

Nettie was standing ankle deep in No Nothin' and pointing at the silver arrow now tearing across town. "Watch out you don't hit the water tower," she shouted. "Don't hit that water tower!"

I had to get up and out of the creek and away so I could keep an eye on him. I had to get up onto the flat field so Buck could see me. I ran to the fence but remembered I was naked and ran back and pulled on my shirt and pants while Nettie stood in the creek following the airplane with her finger as it circled over town. I was following Buck and just cinching my belt tight when I happened to look down along the creek and saw someone standing on the far bank.

It was Marlene Benson.

She was wearing that tiny red dress I told her I liked. Standing at a bend in the creek, her mouth a perfect O, staring at the two of us.

"Oh my gosh!" I couldn't believe my eyes. "Marlene, oh my gosh!" I ran toward her. "Look, I can explain! Oh my gosh! I can explain everything!" She had a yellow striped bag hooked over her shoulder and was staring hard at Nettie. "Marlene, now I know what you're thinking but it isn't . . . well, what I mean to say, it doesn't look like it looks!" But I didn't get to tell her what it looked like. She had already turned and was pummeling her way back through the elderberry brambles toward the road just as Buck came roaring back across town just above the barn. "Marlene!" I called, splashing down the creek after her. "Wait up, Marlene! I can explain everything!" But it seemed like maybe she had already got too much of an explanation.

I watched her pushing her way through the bushes toward the road.

And looked back at Nettie still standing pointing up at the sky, and then I turned and ran up onto the field above the creek. Buck had disappeared from view now. But all hell had broken out on the farm. The chickens were scuttling about the yard, squawking hysterically, flying to the lower branches of the crabapple trees and perching there and bitching, the horses had broken loose in their stalls and Mack had bolted from the barn and was already halfway out the driveway, and the pigs were heaving themselves up against the wire fence, squealing and snorting and waiting to be saved.

Then I saw Vera and Gramma and Ned. They had come running out of the house and were standing now in the yard, hands to their foreheads, scanning the sky.

"It's Buck all right!" I shouted, running toward them. "He's come home to show us that . . . that secret airplane!"

"Buck?" I heard Vera say. "That Buck up there?" Gramma couldn't turn her head high enough to see airplanes, so she just kept talking to Vera, confused.

"Well, of course, it's Buck!" I said, "Who else would it be?"

Suddenly, Buck came out of nowhere and once more roared close to the ground. More animals squawking and squealing away. We all stood and waved to him as he shot overhead and went up straight into the sky.

"Where did it go?" shouted Vera, thinking maybe I was the specialist now.

He was going straight up and up. "Now he's going to do the loop-the-loop," I called out, having read a comic book about loop-the-loops. "He'll go way up and then come back down and come right over us again, you wait and see."

"Will we be able to see Buck?" said Gramma.

"No, he won't let us see anything, it's secret," explained Ned.

"Oh, I don't think that's Buck," said Vera trying to find the airplane.

"It's Buck all right," I said.

"It's not Buck," said Gramma.

"It's Buck, I read the number on the side of the airplane."

Except for the consternation in the barnyard, it was now eerily silent. Barely a breeze. The sky cobalt blue. A lazy cloud here and there. Ned and Vera kept searching the sky, hands shielding their eyes, and then Gramma held onto Vera as if she expected her to rise up like a balloon all by herself and take her along. "I don't think that's Buck," said Vera. "It can't be Buck."

I was about to run into the yard and join them when out of the corner of my eye I saw Nettie strolling up from the creek bottom, her eyes to the sky. She didn't have a stitch of clothing on. I looked over at Gramma and Ned and Vera, staring at the sky and for some reason drifting out the driveway toward the road. I pushed Nettie into the house and closed the door, and all of a sudden I felt something, some pressure in the air, something wicked coming. I looked up and saw the black speck spinning out of its high loop and flashing down out of the sky, beginning to level out, heading straight toward us, the sun shattering off its bright wings. The sound hadn't caught up to the plane yet, and so it flew absolutely through a vacuum. At last I could see the engines and tails and gradually the large round middle section, and the glass canopy in which Buck would be sitting. Then he was here. Engines whining and screaming as if in great pain.

He was still coming out of the loop. He was coming in . . . too low. Way too low. Something was wrong.

"No, Buck!" I said, remembering what he told me when he was home on leave. I ran toward the airplane, my arms warding him off. "Don't do it!" Still coming out of the loop. "Don't do it, Buck!" I sank to my knees and prayed to him. "Pleeeeez don't do it!"

But it was too late. The airplane clipped some of the roof off the barn and then roared straight across the highway and over the creek and straight into the hillside.

* * *

The ground shook and Vera and Gramma screamed and began running back toward the house, stumbling up against one another. Vera was yelling, Gramma swearing in German. Smoke rose in one huge black cloud from the woods on the hill. Another still louder explosion. Tracers of white shooting into the sky. You could smell burning metal. My ears were ringing. I looked at Vera and Gramma holding hands to their heads as if to keep them upright on their shoulders. Then I saw Ned, he was running down the road toward the highway. Vera dropped to her knees and fell forward onto her stomach. Gramma stopped and turned to look back at Vera lying in the road, but she didn't seem to know what to do about it. You could hear the fire seizing the trees and exploding the rocks up on the hillside and see the plume of smoke rising still higher and beginning to warp toward us, as if coming now to consume us too.

I reached Gramma just as she fell to her knees and collapsed, sprawling backward, her arms flung out, hands shaking wildly.

Another explosion. A devilish ball of flames spoke inside the smoke and then went upwards. There was nothing I could do for Gramma and Vera. I left them flat out in the road and took out after Ned. I saw him climbing the barbed wire fence on the other side of the highway and heading for the cow path that led across the swamp to the swinging bridge over German Creek and the hillside that burned away.

I ran down to the highway and climbed the fence and fell and hurt my arm and then got up and followed the path through the bushes and had almost reached the bridge when I saw Ned coming back. His face was red as if scorched, not by the fire, but knowing something he didn't want to. His eyes seemed twice their normal size, and his voice was low and broken.

"Go on back, Junior . . . it's no use . . . you can't even get to the bridge!" He took me by the shoulders and held me before him as if to teach me a lesson. The fire was now raging across the hill. "There's nothing to look at up there . . . everything's gone, that airplane and Buck, they didn't have no chance." He began to cry. "Come on, we got to get back to the house and drive into town and get the fire department out, I think that airplane crashed into Amos Victory's house!"

He released me and hurried off, but I couldn't move. I stood watching the fire eating up trees and the smoke funneling up into the blue sky, and I remembered Buck coming down too low and taking off the top of the barn. I was thinking he had done it on purpose just to make me uncomfortable, coming that close, like he used to do in the rafters in the barn like a circus star, trying to scare us. I remembered too what he had told me in the haymow after Opa's funeral, how he hated the war and the people carrying it on. Things were not right, he said. He was sick and tired of everything. He couldn't talk about the war in his letters. But what had he been thinking now that he was on his way toward it? It wasn't like Buck to do this on purpose. No, I had to fight off that idea. I looked at the fire and thought of Buck as maybe a mystery I had been chosen to solve my own way.

His fire was leaping out of the woods and coming after me.

When I got back to the yard, Ned had already driven off into town. I found Gramma and Vera in the parlour. No sign of Nettie. Gramma was stretched out across the couch, lying on her back, moaning, a cold washcloth across her face, her chest heaving, and Vera sat beside her reading the Bible, struggling through her tears. She stopped and looked up when she heard me come into the room and held out one hand. I went to her, and she gathered me into her. The three of us cried together, holding one another. Then I heard the siren in town lift its hysterical whine. Vera got up when she heard it and went to the window and stood looking into the road, and I went and stood beside her.

I said, "Where's Nettie?"

"Oh, that Nettie!" Vera grumbled, crying, and I figured now there was going to be hell to pay. "She's never around when you want her."

"I'll go look for her," I said.

I wandered outside and went up onto the knoll by the barn to look at the fire. The black smoke had turned to grey now. Then I heard another airplane. It came in low across town from the northwest. Another airplane like Buck's. This one had '419' written on the side of it. It circled the burning woods twice before flying off the way it had come. I knew it was one of Buck's friends coming to have a look.

I went down to the creek and picked up the pile of debris that was Nettie's clothing. I looked down along the creek where Marlene Benson had fled and knew when I went back to town I would have to pay the price for this. What would I say? There would be hell to pay. I carried Nettie's clothes back to the house and hid them in the woodshed and slipped past the Bible reading in the parlour and up to Buck's bedroom. I wanted to lock myself in my room and never come out again, but the door was already closed. And locked. I heard someone in the room sobbing and leaned against the door.

"Nettie," I whispered, and tried the door handle again.

"Go away!" she growled. "I'm busy!"

I went out to the woodshed and got her clothes and laid them on the ground below the window and went and got a ladder. I tilted it up against the house just below the bedroom window, took her clothing in one arm and climbed up. I could see Nettie sitting on the bed sewing on an old patched pair of underwear. She was wearing a winter housecoat. I tapped on the window and smiled seductively, but she ignored me. I tapped again and held out her clothing. She got up and opened the window, grabbed the clothing without looking at me, and was about to close the window again when I said, "Nettie, didn't you see what happened? Didn't you see Buck's airplane crash?"

"I don't have to tell you what I seen," she growled. "I seen enough for one day."

She slammed the window on my hand and went back and sat on the bed. I watched her for a while. She wasn't going to leave the room for the rest of the day, that's for sure. I climbed down and put the ladder away and went to watch the fire in the woods.

Two days later a khaki Chevrolet coupe drove into the yard.

There was a white star on the front door. Two men in army uniforms climbed out and marched to the house. One had a package under his arm. Vera had been standing in her favorite window all morning looking at the road and waiting, but it was Esther who went to the door.

"Are we at the right place?" one of them said. "We're looking for a Miss Esther Draeger."

"Esther Pabst. I'm Buck's sister."

"Well, ma'am, I'm Major Bedford and this," he said, nodding to the other man, "this is Captain Jim Schedler." She shook hands with them. "Captain Schedler was your brother's flying partner." Esther tried to smile at him, but began to cry and look away. "I wonder if we could have a few words with you."

"Won't you come in and meet my mother and my sister?" Esther said, pointing toward a sitting room that was empty at that moment because Vera and Gramma had already fled to the bedroom. Ned was out in the fields, and Nettie still hadn't come out of the bedroom except for running to the outhouse once or twice. I had taken food up to her, but she wouldn't eat it. The two men walked into the dining room. "You want to just go in and sit down, and I'll bring some coffee."

"No coffee, ma'am, we have to get along."

Esther went and got Vera and Gramma out of the bedroom. The two of them came out wearing their black church dresses and stood together, their faces drained and rinsed, as if on their way to the guillotine. The two officers rose and introduced themselves, again some forced smiles, and everyone shook hands.

"Look, good folks, we're sorry we have to be here today, and let me just speak for the two of us by offering our deepest sympathy," said the Major. "We want you to know we share your shock and your grief, much more than you can possibly imagine. Now, Captain Draeger was a fine pilot . . . the best we had . . . a real credit to the army air corps and to his country." What had started out as genuine grief became scripted and chiseled into formal rhetoric. "What happened was a tragedy of major proportion . . . an accident that should never have happened. We face a deadly enemy up there in the Aleutians, and we know Captain Draeger would have made all the difference in getting those Japs out of there." He handed Gramma the package he had been carrying. "We wanted you to have this, Mrs. Draeger. I can't think of anything I'd rather not have to give you, but there it is anyway." Gramma had no idea what it was and handed it to Vera, who opened it and took something out of it and held it up for all to see. "It's a Gold Flag, ma'am. You heard about the Gold Flag? You hang it in your window and let everyone know Captain Draeger gave his life for his country."

"Oh, thank you very much," said Esther, when it seemed neither Vera nor Gramma had the presence of mind to say anything. She took the flag to the front window and tried to hang it from something, but there was nothing to hang it from, and so she draped it over the piano and sat down again. Vera and Gramma huddled on the couch, bereft and lost, looking up now and then and trying to smile just to be nice. Esther was able to keep the conversation going. "You can imagine what a shock it was for the family, looking up and seeing . . . of course, I was working at the bank so I wasn't here when it happened . . ."

"Yes, it must've been . . ."

Vera said, "How did it happen?"

The Major turned to his companion. "Captain Schedler," he said, "perhaps you would explain."

"Well, you see, we were on our way to . . . to Alaska. Just before we took off, Buck asked if when he got up here, he couldn't maybe drop in on you . . . just fly over the farm, and I had to inform him it was against army regulations." He looked to the Major for help, but that officer merely stared at the carpet as if it was all news to him. "I told Captain Draeger that several times, but he kept insisting. We talked about it, the Major and me," he said, looking back at Esther, "and of course, your farm wasn't more than two or three minutes out of the way, so Captain Draeger left the formation and flew over to . . . to say goodbye to you good folks."

He stopped at that, and for some time nobody spoke, nobody seemed to know what to say. Then the Major himself cleared his throat and said, “Now, folks, I wonder if I could ask you whether Captain Draeger was specially close to his father. I mean, I know he passed just recently, and I know the Captain came home for his funeral.”

“Yes,” said Esther, “he came to it.”

“Was he very upset about it?” They nodded. “Did you notice whether he was unduly remorseful?”

“Unduly?” Esther said and looked over at Vera and Gramma. “How can you tell? We were all very sad, but Captain Draeger’s father wasn’t well. Why do you ask?”

“Well, was he maybe upset about something else? I know he has a fiancée here in town.”

“Elizabeth Stelter,” said Esther.

“Were they having any problems?”

“I don’t think so, no.”

“Can you describe what happened that day he flew over?”

“I was working at the bank downtown, but Vera and Mother were both here, and also my brother Ned.”

Vera thought about it for a long time and said she and her mother were in the kitchen at the time and heard an airplane flying very low, it came over just above the barn and by the time they went outside to look for it, the plane was way up in the sky and then before too long coming back down and clipping the roof off the barn and crashing into the hill the other side of the road.

When she got to the end of her confession, she stopped and gazed deeply into the floor as if there were more words written down there she couldn’t make out.

The two officers looked at each other for a while and then the Major smiled and said, “This all comes as a surprise because Captain Draeger knew all about stalls coming out of a loop, so it’s strange he was unable to pull out of this one, that’s what’s bothering us, you see?” Everyone went on nodding for a while. “It was something he did every day of his life . . . so I was hoping you saw something . . . unusual.”

No one spoke for some time, and Vera furrowed her brow and said, "Something must've gone wrong with the airplane."

"Of course, of course," said the Major, but hedged his words by consulting the Captain. "We figure that something went wrong, so Captain Schedler left formation at once and came over here and had a good look. The rest of us landed at a nearby airfield before he re-joined us, and then he told us what he had seen. We wrote it up as an accident. But the Army wants to have a look for themselves, you see? Just before we came over here to see you folks, us two went out and visited the hillside with your fire chief Mr. Bradshaw. We walked around and looked at the debris, and while we were looking around up there we met an old gentleman who lives up there . . . what was his name, Captain?"

"I forget his name."

"Amos Victory," supplied Esther.

"Yes, ma'am, Amos Victory. Well, Mr. Victory told us he was out in his garden when Buck flew over the first time and said he was watching as he went up into a high loop and then coming back down out of it right over your farm he came in too low, hitting the barn and then the hillside. He said the engines were going full out, nothing skipping or missing. Nothing falling off. He thought something had gone wrong with the controls, and that Captain Draeger must have realized it as he came out of the loop . . . but he refused to bail out until he was clear of your place."

It was quiet for a while because they all broke down again when they thought about how Buck had steered clear of The Place. Then Esther asked, "What could've gone wrong?"

"We don't know, ma'am," said the Captain. "This airplane is very airworthy . . . but it has its problems. I won't go into details. Technical stuff, you know. But we knew Captain Draeger was familiar with all that. He was a pilot who finally had it all figured out, and we know he wouldn't take any unnecessary risks coming down over your place especially."

"He was the best," said the Major. "The very, very best." He cleared his throat and went on. "I have to inform you that one day soon the Army will send a truck over here and collect the wreckage, and maybe we can piece together what might've gone wrong." He put his cap back on. "It all happened so fast Captain Draeger, well, at least he didn't suffer. I doubt he felt anything when he hit that hillside."

I was just as happy not to be interviewed because I didn't know whether I would keep my mouth shut about what might have going on in Buck's mind at the time.

Nettie wouldn't come out of her room the day of Buck's funeral either. We were all dressed and ready to go, and Nettie had gotten dressed but was still in the room. She had locked the door. Ned, dressed up in a suit and tie, went and tried to talk to her. But she refused to come out. "I'm not going to no funeral!" she said through the door. "Sit there and cry your eyes out and say your prayers, nothing's going to bring him back, so why go and do that anyways?"

It was of course our second funeral that year. When Opa died, there was a write-up in the paper and letters of condolence. Some people came out to the house. Everyone was sad. The church was packed for his funeral, and they said nice things about him, but that was it. People in town along the street stopped and looked at the big black limo and said, Who died now?

But this time it was different. Everyone knew who had died. The big city newspapers sent down some reporters, who interviewed Esther at the bank and went back and wrote up the story about the crash. It was on the radio. The town had lost one of its patriotic sons. Flags flapped in the wind up and down Main Street, the canning factory closed for two days, store windows were cleaned out and pictures of Buck stood proudly in the centre, black-framed, flags draped over them. Fatty Cameron, the police chief, set up a roadblock below the church and like everyone else wore a black armband. The postman brought a pouch full of cards addressed to Gramma. There was also a letter from the war department, and a telegram too. The morning of the funeral, a truckload of soldiers arrived and set up a tent in the field below the water tower. The funeral was to begin at noon. Esther had planned the whole thing. She said she wanted it to be what Buck might have wanted it to be. I heard her telling Ned she was going to use one of his hay wagons to carry the casket from the church to the cemetery.

"I know Buck would like you to drive the tractor," she said to me. "He was so proud of you. Why, he told me once he was going out to fight the Japs so you wouldn't have to."

Then, at eleven o'clock Ned hooked the wagon to the tractor and climbed up onto the rack and sat down on the edge of it like a well-dressed scarecrow. I drove the tractor through town and over to the church, and I don't think Ned blinked once all the way. The soldiers were standing on guard at the vestry. One saluted me and showed me where to park the rig. Ned and I climbed down and walked away, and then the soldiers began to string flags over it. The church was packed, people standing up against the walls, and those who came late and couldn't get into the church had to stand outside in the hot sun. Buck's casket, draped with a flag and guarded by six soldiers at attention, rested at the altar. I wondered how much of Buck was inside it. I sat and couldn't take my eyes off the casket and imagined a few burnt bones . . . but they were still Buck and would always be Buck.

I got around to remembering Opa in the hole and tried listening to Pastor List but couldn't lift my mind out of that hole. Opa had died just in time, I told myself. He wouldn't have liked seeing Buck hit the barn. Still, I wondered how much he would understand of it. Of course, if it was true that you died and went to Heaven, then Opa was up there watching all this and knowing about Buck and all. It would be difficult watching Earth when you were dead and seeing everything that happened afterward. What good was that? I wondered if they had thought that completely through. It would be better if you died, and that was it, you wouldn't have to lie around on clouds watching your sons dying in airplane crashes.

I was punched in the side, looked up and saw a dark look on my mother's face. "Wake up!" she whispered. "You going to sleep on us?" My old man leaned over her and glared at the toad sitting beside her. Mother waited for a while, and then added, "What would Buck think if he knew you were going to sleep on him?"

My old man shushed her, and I sat back and listened to the choir and thought maybe that was the answer. You had to stay awake thinking of what you owed the ones who died around you. You had to remember them, and in that way they lived forever inside of you, or something like that. That kind of thinking came hard. Better, I thought, to leave it all to Reverend List.

Afterward, we filed out of the church, our heads bowed, awash with grief, and Ned and I walked to the flag-draped hay wagon and stood watching them march Buck out of the church and place him on the wagon. The honor guard assembled in front of us and fell into formation. We drove down the hill and across the highway bridge, and then down Main Street. A long procession of cars and soldiers and people just walking along behind us. The curbs were lined with people, some from out of town. They had read in the paper how this army air force man flew his airplane home to say farewell to his folks and had trouble and crashed into a hill so's it didn't hit the barn.

When we got to the east side of town, we turned in at the gates of the cemetery and up the hill and then down to the lower end, where the Draegers all slept in their deep dark holes. One thing and another, I tried to look away, and before long they lowered Buck's casket into the newest deep hole, half the cemetery full of people who came to stand quietly and watch soldiers firing blanks at the sky.

The Gold Star was in the window when we got back to The Place, and it would stay there for three or four more years, till the gold had powdered into silver, the silver into grey, and then one day, many years later, Vera heard it fall to the floor and went and got it and put it away in a trunk nobody ever opened after that.

13

Ronnie Lighthouse laid the flashlight upon an old railroad trunk and then dug through the asbestos pellets between the rafters and pulled out a stack of yellow pictures. He placed them out on top of the trunk like a deck of playing cards. He said there were six new pictures to look at. I decided not to look. My heart just wasn't in it. It was because of Buck. Ronnie could see that. He looked at the pictures until he saw I wasn't looking and said, "I know what you want to do, you want to go up to Amos's woods and have a good look round."

"What's there to see?" I said, trying to cheer up. "They went up there with that army truck and took everything away. The only thing left up there is Amos."

"Maybe find some clues?"

"Clues for what?"

"What caused the crash."

That made me mad. I said, "We *know* what caused it!"

"So what caused it?" He was trying to be difficult. "You're so piss-head smart, Junior, what caused it?"

"Uncle Buck flew that damn airplane into the hill!"

"Now why would he do that?"

It was the question I'd been asking myself, and to hear it coming from Ronnie sounded like an answer.

"Something went wrong."

"What went wrong?"

"How would I know?"

"That's what I said, we should go up there and find out."

Now that made sense. I went home and told my mother we were going up Amos' hill to have a look around, and she told me to fill the woodbox in case I wasn't around when my old man came home. I filled about a half of it and went out and waited for Ronnie, and then we walked up the street. "Let's take the short cut up through the woods," I said, tossing my hoop into the bushes when we reached Old Lady Hatch's house.

"You know where it is?"

"It's back the other side of her mink cages."

"I hate mink."

"They don't like you either."

Amos Victory had cut a trail from his house up on the hill down through the woods to the back fence of Mrs. Hatch's mink farm. He designed it so he could make a beeline for town Saturday nights instead of having to walk that extra half-mile that it took to come down Jimcrack Road. I told Ronnie how Amos liked to stop and feed the mink while they zoomed back and forth in their pens. He told me he thought the mink were like people being penned up like that and going nuts going back and forth with nothing to do in their life but going back and forth.

Amos always cut across Mrs. Hatch's lawn to the street and then walked straight down the middle of it. Cars slowed and wove around him. They knew he wasn't one to compromise. Dogs around the neighborhood greeted him with a special nippy laugh because sometimes he reached into his little bag and tossed them bones with a little squirrel meat left on them. "There's Amos shaking the woods out of his shoes," my mother always said when she saw him going past the house. "You wonder he don't trip over his bootlaces and fall flat on his nose." Amos always stopped when he reached our house, turned and bowed low like an actor at the J. B. Rottner Shows that pitched their tents in Herring every summer, and then he crossed himself like the Catholics do. When he saw my mother in the window, he always smiled and waved to her. "Going down to Slim's," she would add, "since he's already sucked the Buckhorn dry."

Amos Victory lived in a tarpaper shack way up Solie's Road and in around and back of huge sandstone rocks sticking out of a drumlin hill crowned with a stand of Norway pine. The shack was just above German Creek. Sometimes, when Ronnie and I went skinny-dipping in the swimming hole right where it meets No Nothin' Creek we would come upon Amos, snoring loudly and sprawled across the bank, an empty bottle at his feet, his cane pole bobbing, a sunfish hooked and darting back and forth in the brown water. Other times we heard him in the woods up behind Mrs. Hatch's shooting squirrels. Mrs. Horton told me once Amos survived on sunfish, squirrel meat, and whisky, but Ned, who sometimes went and collected him at his house during hay season, knew him better than Mrs. Horton. "Oh, Amos, he eats real good," he said. "Why, out behind his barn is a great big garden full of corn and tomatoes and peas and pumpkins, squash as big as a cow's udder."

Townspeople always had a lot to say about Amos, probably because they didn't know anything whatsoever about him, and he wasn't one of those who cared what people said about him, no matter the weather.

"Our town drunk," they would say with a teaspoon of pride, "a no-good ne'er-do-well, a tramp, a cropper, but, anyways, you know, he don't cause nobody no trouble." The old retired farmers who got up early and walked down to Dolly's Cup and Saucer, filled up all the booths early and nursed their mug of coffee for an hour and a half complaining about milk prices, the war, the absence of legal muskies at the lake, and they especially liked to have a go at Amos, and Nate Hadorn liked to say, "He ain't always been that way, you know. He come from some good folks way back." Dolly herself, patrolling the tables with a topped-up coffee urn, snickered every time she heard him say that. She was the best thing about coffee at Dolly's but today she looked sour because she couldn't find any place to seat the two tourists who just came in the door on their way to fishing up at Lake Makwonago. "Yeah, but which good folks?" she growled. "Only they know, and they ain't talking." Doc Zempel, who at least bought more than a cup of coffee and a donut, leaned over his scrambled eggs and growled, "Amos Victory? Why, he ain't from around here. He's our *auslander*, never got no closer to town than that old shack of his'n above the creek." Dean Staats was sitting alone, taking up the whole booth and trying to be inconspicuous, finally broke down and said, "No, his old man was Mem Victory . . . used to own a drug store, why everybody knows that." Dolly came over and looked at his empty cup. "You about done, Dean?" she says. He looked at the couple in the doorway and got up and went and sat with Jake Dickenson, and Dolly finally got to seat her newcomers.

Nate Hadorn got up and went out to the door and then stopped and stared back at the strangers. "Amos, he once had money and lots of it," he barked, "but he drunk it all up, and that's something the rest of you boys ought to think real hard about!"

Amos Victory always showed up suddenly at The Place when you got around to starting a haying season.

He was a tiny, toothless elf. He had a wrinkled, sunburnt and tiny wizard's face and a soapy-white, shiny dimpled bald pate from always wearing a cap outdoors. He worked hard when he was sober, sweated profusely, and you could smell the alcohol boiling up out of him in the hot sun. In his pocket he carried a small, round cardboard tin of Copenhagen, into which on the way out to the field he hooked a finger and stowed a wad into his toothless mouth. I'd spend the next hour dodging brown globules as he hocked it into the wind. Still, he was always good-natured, giggled like a child, and when we sprawled together in the shade of the oak tree out in the field, he liked to tell stories about drunken Indians and train wrecks and spring floods, and his favourite, Al Capone.

He had several versions of it, but the one I liked best was the one about the big black Buick pulling up in front of the McLellan

Restaurant – my mom's father was running it at the time and my mother was a waitress. Around ten one night two men came in, according to him, and checked out the men's and the women's toilets, while another two walked up and down the street examining all the closed stores, and another one sat behind the wheel and kept the motor running, and then out bounced Capone. He went straight into the restaurant and sat down to his favourite rabbit stew and then gave my mother a five-dollar bill as a tip. That was like a million dollars today. Meanwhile, Amos, who'd been sitting out in front of Slim's, stopped one of the thugs and talked him into giving him a slug of whisky out of his canteen. He gave the man a chaw of Copenhagen, and then tossed him a five-dollar bill as a tip.

That was another million dollars for the local economy.

Ronnie and I searched all around the scorched hilltop looking for whatever we could find.

The spiky, black tree trunks had all been bulldozed into stacks to be burnt, and the forest lawn had been swept clean. Nothing was left but cinders. Ronnie was easily discouraged, and we were just about to go home when I spotted something shining from under a rock. I dropped to my knees and pulled it out. It was a small piece of steel fused into the shape of a small heart. The deadly heart of that P-38! Or maybe it was aluminum. Whatever it was, now it became *my* heart. I shoved it into the pocket over my own beating heart and felt tears welling up in my eyes. I brushed them away. I wasn't going to say anything about it to Ronnie. It was my secret. Buck had left it to me. I stood for a moment and surveyed the woods. What had really happened here? Was it an accident? I had to make up my mind before I left. I walked around for a while and forgot about Ronnie, and when I decided I couldn't decide, I went to look for him, I couldn't find him anywhere. I called his name a few times and heard a voice coming from the rocks above Amos' house.

"I'm going home now," I shouted. He didn't say anything. "Are you coming?"

"No, I'm going to look in on Amos."

"What for?"

"They say he's got a still."

I went over to him. "Who told you that?"

"Anybody!"

He kept on climbing down and then disappeared over the edge. I found him sitting on the edge of a flat rock jammed like a big diving board into the side of the hill.

"No smoke," Ronnie said, looking down at the house. "He ain't to home right now, that's what I'm thinkin'."

"So let's go home."

"Don't see no dogs neither."

"Amos doesn't own a dog."

He turned and gave me a dirty look. "I know that!" he said. He got to his feet and leaned over and picked up a small stone. "We'll just make sure he's not to home." He stepped back and launched the rock into the air. "If he's home, he'll come out like a mole when you pour water down the hole."

"Nobody's home," I said.

"How'd you know?"

"Ned paid him off at the funeral. He's away somewhere catching up on his drinking."

The stone struck the roof and bounced across it and fell into the trees. A bunch of chickens exploded out from under the shack, squawking and heading for cover in the high grass.

Ronnie waited a while and then stood up. "I'm going down to look for that still," he growled. "You don't have to come if you don't want."

"And what'll you do if you find it?"

"Get good and pissed!"

He slid off the rock on his backside without worrying whether I was going to follow him. I thought of going home again. I didn't want to mess around at Amos' place. I'd been there once or twice with Ned, but I always waited behind in the truck. Besides, my mother would have had a conniption fit if she knew I had gone to Amos's place when I knew he wasn't to home. It wasn't right. I really didn't want to go, but I dropped down off the rocks and scooted along behind Ronnie and down through the bushes. We walked along a broken red wooden snow fence until we came to the garden. Four rows of corn, cabbages, tomatoes, and, yep, squash as big as a cow's udder. It was all so neat and tidy.

"I wonder if that's where he keeps it," said Ronnie, pointing to an old barn with a badly bowed roof and a few orphan shingles.

Alongside the barn was a chicken house, and in front, a cemetery of rusty old plows and cultivators, and, out where the driveway runs out to the road, Amos' shack. It sat up off the ground on wooden hips and above an open crawl space. The door was closed, the windows curtained. I waited in the trees while Ronnie ran across the yard and up the three or four steps to the porch. He opened the front door. It creaked as it gave inwards. He stepped into the shack and turned and signaled to me, and I ran across the yard and up the steps.

Amos' kitchen was neat as a pin. A nice spindled wooden table stood against one wall, and a clean and pressed olive print tablecloth was laid over it, a setting for one. Two forks on one side of the yellow chinaware, two spoons and a knife on the other, a napkin folded and pushed through a ring, a sparkling water glass in front of the plate. The counters were as slick as Vera's, and everything was shipshape. The floor was hardwood and so clean and waxy it nearly blinded me, and the wallpaper was a bright yellow pattern with sky-blue Dutch windmills. A calendar and several paintings adorned the kitchen walls. The cabinets were stacked high with old white bone china with bluish patterns. Two loaves of freshly baked bread sat cooling on racks beside the woodstove and filling the kitchen with an aroma as wonderful as Gramma's house.

Ronnie opened some of the drawers and then walked into the front room, and I followed him. There was a brown overstuffed chair, a grey sofa with soft yellow-fringed pillows, two shiny brass oil lamps, a thick brown carpet, and old paintings and photographs covered the walls.

Ronnie laid his fingers across his lips, pointed to a closed door, and slipped across the room as he'd seen them do in the movies and unlatched the door and peered carefully around it. "Just as I thought," he said. I was thinking maybe he'd come upon the still as I crept up behind him, but it was only Amos' bedroom. One low-slung, narrow bed, tidy, made up neatly and covered with a frayed green and blue quilt. A door in one wall, probably a closet. Thank God, there was only one more door for Ronnie to open, and we'd be out of there. He walked to the door and paused before it. I knew what Ronnie was thinking: here at last was that still.

"If I was you, I'd try the barn," I said. "Nobody keeps a still in a bedroom closet."

He opened the closet anyway, took a quick look around and turned and walked past me and out to the kitchen with a disgusted look on his face.

I went over to shut the closet door and couldn't help looking inside.

Amos had a shelf of books. I had no idea he could even read. I studied the broken spines of the books. *Scarlet Letter*, *Red Badge of Courage*, *The Last of the Mohicans*, *Tales of Edgar Allan Poe*, *Arrowsmith*, and lying flat, a photograph album. I took the album down and laid it on the bed and began flipping through its yellowing pages. Someone had carefully noted the names of the people in the pictures. It was in a large, loopy, and old-fashioned hand. I had no idea Amos could write. Maybe he found this book somewhere. Old pictures of the town mostly, when the streets were just pools of mud and black horse buggies and farm wagons parked along Main Street. A train wreck, an old bridge broken in half and fallen into the creek, the engine tipped over and half under water. Old geezers in swollen beards, ladies top-heavy with peacock feathers and hats . . .

I hurried through the book, thinking I better go out and help Ronnie find the still, when I came upon a picture that punched me a good one in the guts. A ferocious black-bearded man stood behind a tiny woman perched in a chair, and two children kneeled at her feet on the floor, a girl leaning back against her knees, and a boy leaning away, off to one side.

I had seen that picture before at Mrs. Horton's house. She had showed it to me the time she dragged me upstairs to her storeroom. She told me it was a picture of her family, and it was the one with her brother in it. Her *dead* brother, or so she said! She showed it to me because she said he looked a lot like me. She said her old man treated her brother the same way my old man treated me, and in the end her old man had kicked her brother out of the house, and this led to his death. Above the heads of the grown-ups, someone had written out their names: 'Ebenezer Benjamin Hammond Horton' and 'Evelyn Mayberry Horton', and below the knees of the little girl, "Lilah Evelyn Horton."

And then I looked at the little boy. And just below his knees the name 'Amos Horton'!

Amos Horton? Why would Amos Victory keep a picture of Mrs. Horton's dead brother? Wasn't he dead? She said he was dead. And then for some reason I remembered how Amos always stopped and made the sign of the cross every time he walked past Mrs. Horton's house on his way to the tavern on Saturday night.

Maybe he wasn't doing that for my mother, maybe it was meant for his sister.

I heard someone shouting and ran to the bedroom window.

It was Ronnie, and he was in full flight, pedaling across the yard as fast as he could and heading for the back fence. And right behind him, Amos Victory, a pitchfork held high over his head. Ronnie scaled the fence and vanished into the trees, and then Amos threw down the pitchfork and came toward the house. The way he walked I could tell he was drunk as a skunk in a bunk.

There was a window looking up the driveway on the backside of the bedroom. I ran and tried opening it, but it wouldn't budge. There was no other way out of the house except back through the kitchen, and that would take me straight up against Amos. I heard him mounting the steps now and coming into the kitchen. It was all over for me. I thought about diving under the bed or hiding in the closet, but there wasn't time for it.

I'd just have to stand there and face him. I went out into the sitting room and stood. He came into the kitchen and saw me through the doorway.

"Hello, Amos," I said, trying to make it look as if I had been appointed a committee of one to welcome him to his own house. He stood and stared at me as if he couldn't remember me. Or maybe he was too drunk to make any sense out of my being in his house. In my mind I cycled through excuses. I had just walked up from The Place because Ned was wondering if he could maybe come haying tomorrow. I was out for a walk but got lost . . . But Amos had a look on his face that told me I wasn't going to get away with anything fancy. "All right then," I said more to myself, "coming into the house was not my idea, it was Ronnie's idea. I didn't want to come in but, well, we were up the hill looking around for souvenirs of Buck's airplane, and then Ronnie, he decided to come over and look for . . . well, he said you had a still, and you weren't home, so we . . . I mean Ronnie, he . . ."

"That Ronnie Lighthouse is a skunk," he said, slurring words. I could see he wasn't maybe so drunk as he was angry. "You shouldn't run around with the likes of him."

"I . . . I know that."

He staggered past me through the door and into the bedroom, and then I knew things were going to go from bad to worse. He saw the photo album lying open on the bed and turned around narrowing his eyes. He said, "You was in here going through my stuff?"

"No!" I shouted, but I knew how it looked. "Well . . . yes, I mean no. Ronnie, he . . . well, I was just putting it back when you came into the house."

"These is *my* pitchurs," he said in a hurt voice, going over and closing the album and dropping his voice into anger. "I don't mind you busting into my house and all . . . but my pitchurs . . ."

I felt as low as I had ever felt in my life. "Okay, okay, look, Amos," I said, coming closer, "I promise . . . I promise I won't tell nobody about . . . well, you know, about that picture."

"What pitchur?"

"You and . . . you know, Mrs. Horton."

He thought about it for a moment and said, "What about it?"

"Nothing . . . about it."

"You looked at it."

"Mrs. Horton's got the same pitchur over at her house."

"I know that!"

I nodded again. "She said it was a picture of her family and that includes her brother . . . who was dead."

"Well of course he's dead." He turned and looked out the window, his eyes darting about as if he had heard Ronnie coming back to the house. "He's deader'n a doornail."

14

Amos told me to sit down just to get me out of the way as he boiled up some coffee and set out two cups and saucers. I looked at the flower motif and decided right then and there I was going to China to study how to paint chinaware when I grew up. Amos and I avoided talking to each other for the moment because there was no way either of us could say what we were thinking.

He came at last with a steaming pot and filled my cup and told me to drink it so I could help him sober up. Mother had informed me coffee stunts your growth, but right at that minute I would've dropped down to an inch tall if Amos asked me to. I shoveled two tablespoons of sugar into the cup and filled it with milk. It tasted sour and sweet at the same time. Amos seemed to forget he was consorting with a juvenile delinquent who broke into his house and found his secret picture. We had jam and toast too, and soon he looked more like the old Amos stretched out and spinning stories beneath that big old scrub oak alongside the hayfield on The Place.

"Now, about those pitchurs in that album in there," he said in a crackly voice. "That's not –"

"Amos," I said, "you don't have to tell me nothing about those pitchurs if you don't want to. I'm not going to tell anyone."

But he wanted to talk about them anyway, and so he sat back with his eyes fixed upon something way beyond the room and the house.

"My old man," he said, "figured hisself ever' bit as good as Honest Abe because he was born in a log cabin too, but he wasn't poor and dreamy like Abraham Lincoln. Oh no! he had money and so he built hisself that great big house you're rooming in now. He called it 'The White House' to lay one on Honest Abe. But my mama – oh, she was a sweetheart, I tell you! She never had one good night sleep in that house because she knew the reason he built it was so's he could lock my sister up in it and throw away the key."

"I guess you're talking about Mrs. Horton," I said, a little heady and confident because of the caffeine.

"But she took good and sick when my sister was just six years old and spent the rest of her life in her bed. My old man, he could care less, he never paid no heed to her. She was just another piece of furniture he owned. One day my mama told him, she said, 'Ever'body can see what you're doing? You're using your own daughter to show everybody in town how you think you're better than they are.' I jumped right in and let him know I was on my mother's side, and then he give me a good hiding for it. We had two camps in that family. One was me and my mama, and the other, him and my sister. Only she was too little to know which side she was on.

"I was thirteen when Mama finally had enough. She went out and got herself a case of pneumonia and up and died. She wasn't in the grave three days but what my old man went and fetched my aunt back to the house. Gwenny, that was her name. Gwenny, she liked to quote the Bible about this and that while she slapped me around. She'd break down and cry and hug me and tell me my old man made her do it. Oh, she was a bad one, was that Gwenny! She wanted to scrub me down Saturday nights when I took my bath. She had her hands all over me every chance she got. One time she climbed into bed with me and I didn't know what to do. I went up to my sister afterwards and told her about it. She cried and said I shouldn't tell my old man because he'd just slap me even harder. That was when I called it quits. I started playing hooky from school and hung around the old man's livery stables, picking up spare change, and then praise be to God the war came along and I took off."

Amos spent two years in the trenches and finally inherited a good case of dysentery and grew some kind of stomach tumor, and they sent him back to England, where he spent the rest of the war.

"I come back home the fall of 1919," he said, "but I wasn't the same fella that left. I seen enough over there to last me the rest of my life. I seen good old boys gassed, I seen them puke out and turn green, I seen them when they couldn't breathe without gagging, snot running down their face, eyes turning over to look through the back of their heads, pissing, shitting their pants . . . I remember this one fellow, Alfred Johnson, he bunked next to me in the trench, nice fella too, had a couple of handsome daughters and a pretty wife – glued her picture to the butt of his gun – owned a dry goods store somewheres, sang with the voice of an angel. He gets up one foggy morning and says he thinks it's time to shave, climbs on a stool with his razor in his hand, and next thing . . . no shot, no sound . . . quiet as a church . . . and I look over and here come his head flying through the air toward me, and I catch it like it's a football or something." Amos shut his eyes and his jaw trembled for a while. "There ain't been a day gone by since that morning I haven't seen that damn head flying at me." He turned and rammed his eyes at me. "I'm stuck, Junior, carrying that damn head around with me all my life. I ain't been able to find a place to set it down. Only way I can get used to it is get good and drunk." He looked around the room. "Where's that bottle now . . ."

"But Mrs. Hiller," the coffee speaking up in me, "she's my teacher, she told us that that was a good war. She said it was the war to end all wars."

He sat back and roared with laughter and then stared at me. "There ain't no such thing, Junior," he snarled. "All a war does is start up another one like we're in right now. They make up sayings so young fellas like you and me can get all fired up about it and want to go over there and kill a bunch of boys all fired up to kill you." He waited for me to contradict him, but I was too full of gas now and couldn't think straight. "Everything is always falling apart, and so the big money men say, Hey this is a good way to get out of the red and even make some money doing it. You know there's a lot of money in war for the big boys, don't you?" He waited, and I was able to nod, perhaps not too convincingly, because he looked so angry. "The way they do it is get a bunch of young boys together on both sides and tell them to go blow each others' heads off. It costs them a little to do it, but they'll get it all back in the end. That's all it is, it's a business. It's a bunch of silly boys blowing ever'body's heads off so they can get rich."

"That so?" I said, thinking about Uncle Buck. "That what you think?"

"I didn't tell nobody I was coming back home," Amos said, quieter now, having made his point, "and anyways nobody would've recognized me. I was skin and bones, and my face was all cut up. When I got off the train it was dark, and I took my suitcase and slipped over to Mem Victory's drug store and told him I didn't want nobody in town to know I was back. He took me home and told his wife and kids about me, and we sat down and et and had a long talk. I told them I couldn't just pick up where I left off, and I sure couldn't go home and face my old man and my sister. I had to go away and try to put myself back together and maybe I could come back later. Mem, he give me a bath and put me up for a week, and then he told me about his hunting shack back there in the woods. Nobody'd lived in it for some time and it needed a lot of work, but if I was to fix it up, I could probably stay until I knew what I was going to do.

"I come out here and patched it up a bit, and after a year I decided there wasn't no way Jimmy Horton could go home. I told Mem how it was, and he said he had a lot of relatives back East nobody knew about and didn't care if I borried one of their names for a while. Mem spread the word around town I was some nutty relative from out East. I grew a beard, it come in grey in places and made me look way different. I went into town acting nutty, so's nobody'd get up close enough to me to see who I was. Not too long afterwards my old man up and died, and a few years went by and people forgot all about Jimmy Horton. Most people figured I died in the war. I finally worked up enough nerve to go call on Lilah. I told her who I was … and she wasn't surprised. She knew all about me anyways because she'd written the government and got all the information from them saying I was discharged and sent home at a certain time. She said she went along with the idea I'd died over there in France, and she didn't see any reason to change her mind. She's stayed all locked up in that house by herself even though the old man wasn't around no more. Once she broke down when I was walking past, and called me into the house. She said she wanted to give me some money, but I told her, I says, I don't need it, I don't need you, I don't need nobody.'"

And then he started to cry.

I got to my feet at that. His goddamn story, the coffee boiling up inside of me, and seeing him crying like that, I felt sick. I knew I was going to throw up. I got to my feet and ran out the door and without a word to Amos, I headed home. Amos didn't come after me, and I didn't look back once. When I got home, my mother could see something was up. I told her I'd been out to see Amos, and said he had given me a cup of coffee. She told me she would have a talk with him about it and gave me some soup and sent me to bed before my old man came home.

And I lay there thinking, here was a man who went to war to save the world but lost himself instead. A man who believed the only way he could leave home was to stay. The only way to stay was to go away.

After Buck died, The Place was like a haunted house. We walked past each other as if we weren't even there. Nettie was a ghost. I could put up with Gramma and Vera being ghosts, but not Nettie. One day Gramma was out with the pigs, and Vera in the chicken coop. The house was empty and hollow. I heard Nettie in her bedroom talking to herself and went in and held out my hand, upside down and closed. She looked at it and then at me, and I turned it upright and opened the palm.

"This is for you, Nettie," I said. "I found it up there in the woods where Buck crashed. There's nothing else up there but this. The army took everything away. It's a part of the airplane that burned up." She plucked it out of my hand and examined it. "And look, I'm sorry about what happened down at the creek . . . it's all my fault." She looked at the little scrap of metal from all sides and then got up and walked over to the chest of drawers. And I said, "It looks like a little baby heart."

"You want to see where I'll put it?" she whispered, trusting, without looking back at me. "Nobody, not Ma nor Vera, nobody knows where I keep my things." She opened her top drawer. There, under layers of recycled underwear and patched socks, lay three small boxes. One was wood, one shiny tin, and the last was gold-embossed porcelain. She took the boxes out and set them on top of the dresser. First, she opened the tin box. It was full of buttons and hairpins, snaps, bits of old lace, toothpicks, pins with pearl heads, safety pins, flint arrowheads. Each item she placed alongside the other and then stepped back to admire them. "They don't mean nothing to you, but they mean something to me!" She laughed but didn't seem to think she needed to explain as she carefully returned everything to the box, closed it, and then opened the wood one. Scraps of paper, the nib of a pen, a belt buckle, a torn joker from a pack of cards, a shoelace, a lens from a pair of eyeglasses. "These are special, but I can't figure out why neither," she said. "Maybe I just like to look at them." We looked at them for a while, her eyes blinking as though she were still trying to penetrate their mysteries.

Then, after tucking it away, she looked over at me with a naughty smile on her face and fingered the gold box.

"This one's chinaware. It's worth a whole lot of money, you know. Mama give it to me. She said it's 22-karat gold. She's right too, because it says so on the bottom!" She tipped it over holding the lid closed. "I keep my real precious things in it, things maybe everyone knows about but nobody knows about." On the lid was a hand-painted portrait of a gallant gentleman and a fine lady, elegantly coiffeured and draped in silken finery, openly flirting together in a small garden. She took the lid off and handed me a brass button. "Now, this here's a button off Buck's army uniform. Remember that real nice wool uniform he wore when he come home? Well, when he went back, that's when I found the button. It was stuck in the lint under the bed. I found it, but I didn't tell Vera."

She then handed me a torn and faded photograph of a man panning for gold along a small creek.

"I found this in the milkhouse attic under the feather tick after they brought Pa into the house when he got sick. It was his keepsake. He wanted to go to California so bad, but he never got there. Ma never wanted to go. Vera and Ned wanted to go but Esther didn't. Me neither. See what he wrote on the back?" She turned it over. "He wrote . . . *'findet das Gold irgendwo.'* You know what it means?"

"Something about finding gold."

She threaded a ring onto her finger. "And this's Ma's wedding ring," she smiled. "Her fingers is all swelled up now and bunched. She can't wear it, so she give it to me. Don't tell Vera. I'm not supposed to tell. She'd get mad. She give it to me when Vera came home that time. She knew it was safe with me, nobody's ever going to come looking for me. Pa told her one time he would give her ten gold rings when they got to California." She held out her finger and studied it. "You want to marry me, Junior?" I laughed, and I said maybe it wasn't such a bad idea. Then suddenly her eyes went red, and she started to sniff as she yanked it off and looked at it. "Someday you'll get married," she said, reconsidered the ring and then held it out to me. "I'll give it to you then."

"Me?" I said. "Naw! I'm never going to get married."

She picked out another thing. She fastened it, a tarnished silver locket and chain, around her neck.

"I went to country school when I was little, and I had this teacher, her name was Miss Lehmann, and she give it to me the day she come out to the house and told me I couldn't go back to school. I got so mad at her I took it and threw it as far away as I could . . . way out into the field, and then Ned, he found it one time when he was plowing. He brought it back to the house and give it to me."

I turned the locket over and said, "It says on it, 'I Love You' and . . . look, it has her name on it too. 'From Miss L. Lehmann.' Why, this is real nice, Nettie." I was surprised to see her big gray eyes in a soup of tears. It was, of course, the custom in our family never to use words like 'love' or 'hate' or anything that showed how you really felt about someone. But I couldn't stand it any longer, I looked at her and said, "Your teacher loved you, Nettie! Miss Lehmann loved you." She began to shake her head slowly. "You know something else? We all love you too, Nettie, especially me." I put my arms around her waist. "I love you, Nettie. You're my sweetheart!"

She wiped off her tears and pushed me away and took off the locket and laid it back into the box.

Then she held out a broken peanut shell.

"Homer Brighton," she said. "He set out there in front of the house in his car that time for three whole days, and it snowed and snowed, and he et nothing but peanuts. He wouldn't leave neither. I used to go out and just stand and look at him even when Vera told me not to. Vera, she wouldn't get into his car and go back with him, and so he finally give up on her and drove off. I went out to the road after he left and found this peanut shell in the snow."

She began putting things back into the box.

Afterwards, she looked again at the iron heart of Buck's airplane. "Add it to your museum, Nettie. Buck deserves something better than a measly old button."

"No, not him," she said. "This will always remind me of you."

She tucked it away inside the gold box. Then she stashed all the boxes away in the drawer and stood looking like she was going to pray, or something. I learned a lot that day. I learned my first lesson about love. I realized right then and there that I loved Nettie. She was different, and I was going to love people who were different because they were different.

15

We wore black armbands that summer. Nettie wore two. "Oh, silly, whatever for?" asks Vera. "One for Buck and one for Pa," says Nettie. Vera sewed only one, and Nettie made another for herself, but since Vera had used up all the black cloth, Nettie had to make one out of feed sack cloth, and it had yellow butterflies flying around in it.

Esther laid her armband aside after a week and said it was depressing to wear it around the bank, in spite of Pastor List having told her it should be uplifting. He made Gramma, Vera, and Esther sit in the front pew the first few weeks so he could look down at them when he prayed for Buck's soul, and after the service, when he and the choir came down the aisle, he stopped and held his arm out to Gramma and then told Esther and Vera and me to follow him into the foyer and line up like the Holy Family. Everyone stopped and shook hands and confessed that maybe Uncle Buck didn't come regularly to church, he was nonetheless a fine young man who died for his country.

Sunday suppers at the farm became a formal affair. Ned wore clean overalls, the women white collars and pressed dresses, and Vera stood up and said long prayers, and then she made me read something she picked out of the Bible. "Man," I said, stumbling through the text, "that is born of a woman has few days but is full of trouble. He cometh forth like a flower and is cut down: he fleeth also as a shadow and continueth not." After chores and before bed, we had to go and sit in chairs in the parlor and think about Uncle Buck. I couldn't think much and tried playing the easier songs from the church hymnal at the piano, and sometimes Esther and Gramma sang along.

Riding the tractor back and forth and sitting out there in the hot July sun, I often came upon the ghost of Uncle Buck standing like a scarecrow in the patch, and I stopped and asked him whether he hit the barn on purpose, but I never did get a satisfactory answer. All I had left to do now was drive the little grey tractor round and round in ever-smaller circles. I thought about Opa one day and worried that I had inherited his insanity, and here I was just twelve. I tried to think about Marlene Benson and wondered whether there was still a chance, but with my inner eye all I could still see was her coming upon Nettie sitting naked in the creek.

One day I got off the tractor and walked over to the train tracks. I knew the "400" was coming. You barely heard it before it was there. The sleek yellow train roared past me right at four in the afternoon each day of the week, its human cargo flying off to gay places, where they'd go dancing in the moonlight to the music of the Glenn Miller Orchestra. I waved to the high spirits in the windows, but going that fast, they really never had a chance to wave back. They saw me, but didn't, really. I'd hug the fencepost standing on the second rung of barbed wire watching the golden train disappear westward, feeling abandoned.

Amos came the day after Ned and I cut the corn and helped us to shock it. And a week later all the neighbors came with their wagons and teams to help fill silo. At the supper table the first night Amos told us how that particular day he was in his barn when he thought he heard an airplane and ran outside and then climbed up onto a bluff to watch as it flew straight up into the sky. "Gosh darn it," he said, his eyes fixed on his plate as if he couldn't look up or he'd cry, "I knew right then it was Buck. There wasn't no other explanation to it." He stopped and cleared his throat. "And then when he come back down out of the sky, I see he was coming too low, but before I could get out of the way, he come straight into the hill. I didn't have no time, I just jumped behind some trees and, well, after that, all I could hear was nothing. I was deaf as an earthworm, and I run back to my house and got out some pails and started throwing water up over the roofs."

"You poor man!" said Vera. "But you were lucky. It happened just that one time for you, but for Ma and me, we look up everyday at that airplane coming in at the barn and then try to change what happens afterwards."

The doom and gloom darkened late in August when they came for MackandJack.

Ned said keeping a team of horses around another winter made no sense, and so he sold them to a fox farm. Mack couldn't see out of one eye, and Jack was lame. The rendering truck came one morning while we were still in the barn milking, and Vera and Gramma and I, we stopped milking and went outside and watched Ned lead the two Belgians up the ramp and into the truck. We went up to the ramp and watched Ned leaning close to each of them and running his hand like a currycomb across the tops of their heads. He was saying something in horse talk. It was close to German, maybe even Belgian, because the two old Belgians looked at him as if they understood. But they didn't say anything back, just stood there, listening, their heads bowed as if praying. They knew there was nothing they could do about it. Ned had red eyes when he came back down the ramp. I looked over at Gramma, and she looked back at me. She was like one of those old Dutch women you saw in the newspapers watching the Nazis load Jews onto cattle cars. When the truck left, Ned disappeared. I don't know where he went, I looked everywhere, and when he came back in time for dinner, he just stared at his plate. He wouldn't eat anything.

The last week of August Amos went home to stay, and there wasn't a lot for me to do either. Ned was busy oiling the springs on his beaver traps and visiting the bloodhounds in the kennel, picking up feet and looking for ticks and broken blood vessels, and I sat watching him, knowing it was coming up on hunting season. I got the feeling I was crowding him, so I went up to the house and listened to the radio.

"Can you maybe come out Saturdays and help Gramma with the pigs?" said Vera in the doorway to my bedroom the day I packed my suitcase, feeling like it was the end of the world. "She's finding it harder to get down on her knees. Oh, and don't forget we have to do the slaughtering in two weeks. We could sure use an extra hand for that. We'll have to give you fifty cents a day as usual, of course. We're down to our last packages of pork in the freezer box at Kohnke's, and it'll be a while before hunting season starts up."

Vera and Nettie walked me out to the road and stood there as I went down the hill toward the iron bridge and up to the cemetery. I stopped to look at the two new headstones, and it occurred to me I didn't really want to go back to town. I wondered whether I could convince my folks to let me move out to The Place the year around. Gramma was getting on, as Vera said, and they needed a pig person, there being no point either in Gramma going out to help with the milking every night. It was only a mile or so for me to get to school from The Place. I could walk in the winter and ride bicycle in the fall and spring. Why, I could start my apprenticeship with Ned that very fall and in a few years maybe take over The Place.

That was the way it was meant to be, the way history had written it down, like the Bible, the way everyone wanted it to be.

When I got home, I found the back door locked. That door so far as I knew had *never* been locked. Even when we went out somewhere, no one ever locked it. I walked around to the front door. It was wide open. "Mama!" I shouted, stepping inside the house, "Mama, how come the back door's locked?"

"Why, I didn't see you come home!" she shouted from the kitchen, dropping a heavy spoon into the sink. "Now, don't look anywhere, make sure you don't look!"

"Look at what?" I said, giving the living room a good looking over. "I don't see anything." Except for that strange black box on the couch. It looked like a small coffin, and I thought, *Now* who's dead?

My mother came running into the room, wiping her hands on a towel and smiling the way she did when you sat around the tree opening Christmas presents.

"How come the back door's locked?"

"Well . . . because I wanted you to come around to the front door!" She came and lassoed me with her arm and steered me across the room toward that black box. "Bet you don't know what that thing is, do you?" I gazed down at it and shook my head. "Well, why don't you open it and find out!"

A summer of black boxes and black holes, I really didn't like my chances with this one, and so I said, "I don't like the way it looks."

"How do you know how it looks? You haven't seen it yet. You'll have to open the case up to see what it looks like, and then you can tell me whether you like what it looks like."

"I don't want to know what it looks like."

"How do you know?" I could feel the knuckles in her words. "You won't know till you see it."

I knew it was no use. Once she got her hands on me, there was nothing I could do. She could make me walk on the ceiling. So I leaned over and touched the little silver buckles on the front of the box. They snapped up like Uncle Archie's fox traps. I jumped back and my mother went and slowly lifted the lid. The darkness vanished and something . . . an odour. It rose out of the darkness and filled my nostrils. Something nasty about it. It smelled like my fingers after touching the inside of Marlene Benson's leg that night at the movies.

Curled up sound asleep on a purple velvet pillow, a silver body with a golden open throat. And all along its spine a bracelet of pearls. It looked like it wanted to be gathered up in my arms. I leaned over and lifted it out of its bed. It wanted to be held in a certain way, and it seemed I knew how to hold it, and when I held it, the coldness grew warm under my fingertips.

My mother then announced, "It's an alto saxophone! You know what a saxophone is?"

"What did you say?" I swooned.

Frankly, I had forgotten my mother was even in the room.

"I wanted to buy a piano, but Esther told me I'd have to come up with a hundred dollars, and so I figured I'd start you out on something simple . . . something you can get started on and then go on to the piano." I looked into my mother's eyes to see what she was up to. It was as plain as a potato that she was arming me against my old man. "I bought that saxophone off Mrs. Schiefelbein. It was Doris Mae's, she played it in senior band until she graduated and went off to college. Anyways, it's been sitting around up in the attic and Mrs. Schiefelbein wanted to get rid of it."

"You know *he* won't let me play it," I said, bitching. "Soon as he comes home and hears it, he'll take it away from me."

She knew that too, but she laughed and shook her head at my naiveté. "You let me handle your father," she said, placing a hand on my arm. "He doesn't have to hear it. You can play it right after school before he gets home, and he won't be working much longer this year and then he's out in the woods all day every day. It won't take long for you to learn to play it, and then what can he do?"

"Oh yeah?"

"There's absolutely nothing he can do then." A small tear slipped into the corner of her eye, and she brushed it away with another laugh. "Look, why don't we just put the saxophone together and try it once? Mrs. Schiefelbein said it's real easy to put together."

"Isn't it together?"

"She said it wasn't."

"Well, I don't know how to put it together."

"You don't?"

"No." I felt suddenly very crabby. "How am I supposed to know?"

She pushed me aside and grabbed the horn and opened a small drawer fitted into a corner of the box, and pulled out a curved silver piece that looked like a duck's neck. "This has to go onto it somewhere," she said, turning the saxophone around different ways and trying to fit it into openings. Finally, she inserted it into a small hole at the top and, pleased with herself, reached once more into the drawer and brought out a round black thing with a silver cover. It looked like a beak, so she pushed it onto the cork and then handed the horn to me.

"Okay, play it!"

I slipped the silver cover off the beak and ran my hands down over the body, growing erect, and then I inserted the beak into my mouth. I blew once. Twice. Nothing. I blew harder. Still nothing. Pure air. Undocumented.

My mother fell into a chair and looked up at me as if maybe it wasn't my fault. "It's no good, no wonder she charged me only $25 for it! Maybe she'll give me my money back."

"It probably sat around too long."

"I'll just take it back."

I cupped my left hand over the top and laid my fingers over the top three pearls, and my right hand over the bottom ones. That felt good. Then I held the horn close and blew into it once more. Still nothing. I pawed about inside the little drawer until I found a leather strap with a hook on it, and I hooked it to the saxophone and noosed it up over my neck, and then found a small flat paper sleeve with a stick of wood in it. It was flat on one side and round on the other. My mother was still thinking up excuses for Mrs. Schiefelbein, but I wasn't listening now. I placed the wooden thing flush up against flat edge of the black piece so the parts meshed and then screwed everything tight.

"Maybe I'll look at that piano again."

I blew into the horn again . . . and out came this large round squally fart. It filled the room and echoed through the house. My mother jumped to her feet and stared at me like it was all my fault. And I blew once more, moving my fingers, and something . . . something different came out of it. A rhapsody of one note. I tried three notes. I ran my fingers across the horn as she stared at me. Then I slipped the saxophone off and laid it on the couch and looked at my mother, and she looked at me. It was a very different world now. We were not the same people. I had finally found a voice that would take me wherever I wanted to go and give me everything I ever wanted in life.

All that fall, as soon as my old man left in the morning, I got out the alto saxophone and played scales and then hurried home from school in the afternoon to do it all over again for two hours till the old man came home.

It turned out too that the saxophone brought Marlene Benson and me closer together.

We were both in Mrs. Fenske's seventh grade classroom this year. Mrs. Fenske was the teacher for grades seven and eight, a gateway between elementary and high school. She couldn't have been over five feet, but she ruled over us kids a foot taller just as Napoleon had done, by shouting upwards. She arranged the classroom seating according to the alphabet, and as B ran before D and in this case there were no C's, Marlene Benson's desk was in front of mine. Mrs. Fenske wrote her own name on the board and underlined it twice. Then she read "The Pit and the Pendulum" out loud. She stared at us when she finished and slammed the book down, got to her feet, walked down the aisles pinpointing her eyes.

"Mr. Edgar Allan Poe is a great writer," she intoned, as if she had forgotten he was long dead. "You kids can learn a great deal from Mr. Poe. Just as there is a pit and a pendulum in the story, there is a pit and pendulum in this classroom. The pit yawns dark and deep for those who think they can just sit back and believe their good looks will get them through or maybe the fact that their father is a big man in town, or those who foolishly think that nothing in books we will read bears any relationship to what you're going to do in your life. The pendulum will swing ever closer if you fail to study hard. In this class and the next, you will learn all you need to learn in order to get through high school, and if you try to stop it from happening, then you will see the pendulum shaving very close . . . and the deep pit yawns ever deeper on all sides of you!"

Mrs. Fenske showed us a stack of newspapers, and we took pages from the stack and made covers for all our textbooks and then sat silent in our seats until recess. Then Mrs. Fenske gave each of us a goiter pill and made us line up at the water fountain, and then she made us sit down again and learn all about polluted ground water. Marlene and I made sure we weren't anywhere near each other when it was recess. I played in a softball game while she sat on the merry-go-round with her friends, but inevitably we had to face each other at the end of the spelling bee after everyone else had spelled down. She stood on one side of the room, and I the other. She avoided looking directly at me, and I figured I would let her off the hook, so I misspelled 'cemetery,' one of my favorite words. She spelled it the right way, and I sat right down afterward.

After school, I decided to capitalize on it, and waited behind a tree at the edge of the schoolyard until she and Marion Hanson came down the sidewalk. When they reached the tree, I jumped out and said, "C – E – M – E – T – E - R – Y! I knew how to spell it all along but I wanted you to win!"

"Liar, liar, pants on fire!" she said, recovering. "Marion, don't let this pervert anywhere near me!"

Marion scrunched up her face and said, "What's this all about?"

"Look, what happened that day was not what you think."

"He's a sex pervert, that's what he is!"

What I said next bothered me for a long time, but I had to say it anyway: "That was my crazy aunt in the creek!"

She looked like she had something to say about that but changed her mind and walked off.

Marion said, "What are you two talking about?"

I knew then that Marlene was keeping it a secret. I ran and caught up with her. "Look, I made a big mistake."

"I don't care whether it was a big mistake or a little mistake!" she said, running off. "Stay away from me, you pervert!" Marion looked at me as if I might come after her, gave a little scream and ran off too.

That's where the saxophone came to the rescue.

Mr. Kaiser was the school band teacher, a tall man with broad shoulders and a beak of a nose, to which he clamped a pair of gold-rimmed glasses and tucked the wings away behind his long, slicked-back blonde hair. He looked a little like the pictures of Tommy Dorsey I saw in the newspaper. But Mr. Kaiser was more than a band teacher, he was a reformer, he thought the way to solve the Cold War was to have everyone up and marching around playing a musical instrument. His marching band and concert orchestra had already earned ten first-place silver cups at sectional and divisional band competitions, the copper drinking cups of which gleamed from behind the glass in the school trophy case. But he wasn't satisfied. He intended to take his next band to the state music tournament and get the gold cup, and to that end, had talked the school board into allowing him to invade the lower sanctity of the primary school in search of kids who wanted to start taking music lessons on tubas, French horns, clarinets, trumpets, trombones, saxophones, flutes, drums, triangles, sousaphones, even before they reached high school.

One day that fall he showed up at Mrs. Fenske's classroom and announced that at four o'clock Monday afternoon anyone interested in learning to play an instrument was to come to the band room and try out different kinds of horns. So, at four o'clock six of us appeared in the band room, Marion Hanson, Julie Strauch, Betty Halderman, Lily Kuckenbecker, Marlene Benson, and I. I was the only boy. We sat around in a circle in the band room, a large sunny room with lots of windows. The room doubled as the school cafeteria, and the cooks were cutting up carrots and chickens and looked as if they were coming for us next. They worked at one end of the room and the band played at the other as if food and music had nothing to do with each other. Marion announced she wanted to play the French horn, Julie the flute, Betty and Lily clarinets, and Mr. Kaiser went to the tall storage racks at one end of the room and fetched each of them a school horn. Marlene stared at me and said, "Saxophone." She had no idea the black box at my feet was an alto saxophone. The bandmaster fetched her an alto saxophone, and while the girls were adopting their horns, I took out my own alto saxophone and hung it around my neck, and I expected Marlene to change her mind right then and there, but she didn't.

The six of us played together as a little band for a week or so, and then one day Mr. Kaiser asked me to stay behind for a moment. "I'm a trombone player myself," he said, "but you know what, I love the saxophone. They call it 'the devil's horn', did you know that? It's only a hundred years old or so, and it had to horn in . . . if you'll pardon the pun, on the other symphonic instruments. It never made it of course, but that was long before jazz music. Do you know anything about jazz?"

"Maybe," I said, knowing nothing at all about it.

"I asked you to stay back because I can see you're way ahead of the others. I can teach you the usual things, like embouchure and sight-reading, but we need to get you going on theory and stuff like that. Do you want to do it? We'll have to set aside some afternoons after school."

I had forgotten about Gramma and Ned and . . . who were the others now?

"I have nothing to do anyways," I laughed. "I'll be there."

Then I learned how to read music, and in the spring Mr. Kaiser said, "I'm forming a German band next year, and since your name is Draeger, I'll let you in for free." He handed me a new saxophone book with major and minor scales and classical tunes to play and said if I took it home and practiced all summer, there was a good chance I could be in the band in the fall. My mother cleared a space in the cellar in among her sinks and washing machines, and then I began to practice in earnest. I went down into the damp dark underworld and practiced every day and all weekend, and whenever my old man wasn't around. My mother stood by me despite all the squeaks and blats and never said a word until she had to. "You better quit now," she'd yell down to me, "you played that song twenty times."

When I went back out to The Place the following summer, along with a bag of clothes and comic books, I took my saxophone and my saxophone book and spent an hour every day just after the noon dinner in the haymow, where I wouldn't bother anyone. They were all napping anyway. Vera said I could practice in the woodshed next to the house, but I liked the big sound of the saxophone echoing through the haymow rafters. Sometimes Nettie would come and sit in the hay and watch. Once I took the saxophone down the ladder into the cow barn and tried a tune out on the cows, but only that once. They took one look at me and the devil's horn hanging around my neck and began bellowing and strangling themselves trying to get out of their stanchions, and I beat a hasty retreat up the ladder and waited until things calmed down before going down and apologizing.

It looked as if it was going to be a case of cows *or* saxophones. The two of them weren't going to get along at all.

16

Uncle Ned lived most of his life in the company of animals.

He held long conversations with cows as he fetched them into the barn at milking time, and he gave long, detailed lectures to horses as they pulled him along behind a plow or one of the seeders or mowers or wagons. He seemed to think he was the one to start the conversation. "Ease up there," he'd say. "What are you doin'? I told you to ease up, now why are you headed that way?" Once I caught him talking to a heifer while he saw her off to the abattoir. I couldn't make out the words, but the little cow cried all the way out of the gate and over to Randall's truck, and then Ned went over to the driver and said, "Take it easy on this one, she's shy and she's scared, and remember she's only two months old." In the winter he left the barn and went into the woods, where he didn't so much talk as listen. He seemed to overhear what the wooly beasts were saying to one another because he could intercept their every move and finish them off even before they knew he was around.

But as for humans, Ned never had much to say.

When he *had* to talk, he surrendered up words one at a time. Or maybe two. A noun and verb. An adjective if he was called on to be eloquent. Most of his conversation with humans was about farm animals or wild animals or his crops. He never joined the Saturday night farm hegira into town after chores when everyone else went there to stand around lampposts making small talk in German. There were times during the week he had to go in to the grist mill or perhaps the blacksmith shop and stand around like a timid schoolboy listening to other men. If someone got him to talk, he would clear his throat first and then knot up his forehead and slowly lay out the words, like blocks of wood, and when it was over, he would pack them up and take them back to his truck.

But given the right circumstances – say, a confabulation of hunting cronies sitting around a fire or maybe a threshing crew at a cattle trough bearing a fleet of cold Leinenkugels or Pabst or Blatz floating about in it, or holidays with a bunch of kinfolk standing about on the tilting back porch off the kitchen – why then Ned could stand and deliver long-winded cantos of heroic verse without pausing to breathe. He would knock 'em dead with soaring iambic pentameter imagery. It was his custom to wait until someone else invoked the theme, and then he'd wait for his turn at the lyre. Like say old toothless Len Kregness, the little man who lost an eye on the job at the tire factory when a whitewall Goodyear blew up on him. Len might strum a chord like this: "I think I saw a huge stag up at Wilson Creek last week. Ned, wasn't you up in those limestone bluffs above the creek, you and Otto Krueger, that time you two had to square off against that big twelve-point buck with the arrow sticking out of its ass?"

That's all it took. Num num strum! Ned would start drumming his voice, waiting till the orchestra settled down. "I heard you two was just walking a regular trapping line," someone else would say, and another, " . . . and you'd left your shotguns back at the truck." A drum, a drum, Macbeth doth come! Ned would look up then, a little crazy in the eyes, and he'd launch forth into a story about buckled and bridled heroes and ancient grudges and burning cities, loosening his endless, trackless dreamlike mytho-sentences spinning a blood-curdling romance about hunters and hounds circling about in those mysterious fierce and final moments of man's unremitting combat against glorious and immortal behemoths.

"No, no, you heard wrong," he'd sing. "Me and Otto, we had just the one gun – it was a 30-30 – betwixt the two of us," Ned sang, "but I'd used up all the shot on those three beaver thrashin' about in the traps back at the creek, and so Otto, he wanted to go back and get his Overunder before we set out, but I says, No that won't be necessary, it's the wrong time of year, you ought to know that, and he looked kinda put out, and so we set out separate to look at those two traps up on the piney ridge, and when we come to the top of that bony knoll running behind Hermann Lander's place, down by his old planing mill? You know the one I'm talking about. Why this twelve-point buck, he come stumbling out of the jackpines, two arrows festering away in his hind quarters, bleeding and blind he was, but still somehow he must've picked up our scent 'cause he knew exactly where we stood and how many of us there were, and you know he never thought twice about it, he just dropped that cage of bones and pawed away at the snow to let us know he wasn't done by a long shot, snorting and gargling and carrying on real tough, and I see we didn't have any place to get to, so I says to Otto, I says, I'll dance a little off that way, and you back up real slow to the tree line over there, and when you get there, you make a commotion. That's the only chance we got, and then I see the old bull sorting out his chances and charging up a snowstorm with his hoofs, snorting away and ready to charge, but well, I stood still as a dead man already and Otto, he run straight back, and then he did some kind of Indian pow-wow and I took off, and at last here he comes, his head low like a sickle blade along the ground, his eyes all hot as a stove and white as the moon, and those horns flashing, blood spinning, snorting and growling, and I decide it ain't no use trying to hide behind a tree, so I turn around when he got to me, waited till I could get in a good whack, and then I let him have it right over the shoulders with the butt of my shotgun, just as hard as I could!"

I marveled at his mastery of words and song and his respect for and majesty of every animal he ever encountered in the woods – beaver, wolf, mink, bear and fox – and I was also amazed at his knowledge of every path and hill for a hundred miles around, and every creek and waterhole, hill, anthill, coven, every marsh, berry patch, beaver pond, and the location of every last whitetail deer salt lick in Bridge Creek County. Ned came down to us direct from the cave-dwellers, the Neanderthals, the Cro-Magnons, the Burgundians, the ones who lived the ways of the forest even after leaving it. My old man was a lot like him, except that he went into the woods to kill everything that moved because he wanted to prove something. Ned took his share out of the woods only because he was part of it, and it owed him something, and when he took it, he showed his appreciation, his reverence for it, because he knew he was part of the process, part of the renewal, vengeance, the climate.

Perhaps there was one thing that Ned loved more than wild animals, and that was the blueberry. In the late spring, when townspeople rushed madly out of their houses and drove deep into the woods in search of blueberries 'as thick as your thumb and ready to drum in the cavernous pail of the first one to come,' as Robert Frost used to say, they would meet Ned coming back out of the bush in his pickup and wave him down and ask him where the berries were, and he'd smile and look stupid and say, "Well, it looks like a lean year" or "It's way too early" or "Me I didn't find none," and then drive off and as usual, on his way back out to The Place, he'd stop off at our house in town and slip in through the back door and take off his cap and leave us two milk pails of the biggest, blackest blueberries you ever saw.

Ned was a professional bachelor. He avoided women whenever he could, slipping past them as if to avoid their needy eyes. On the other hand, I was divinely created, so far as he understood it. I was definitely not his brother's kid. We were summer's Real Father and Son, inseparable from the moment school let out to when it started up again in the fall. Just the two of us – you can't count Amos because he was just the "hired hand" who helped when we were haying or filling silo in September. Ned and I ruled over our little kingdom of forty acres of oats, thirty of hay, twenty of peas for the canning factory in town, and fifty of corn, thirty of pasture.

Though he never said a word to me about it, I knew he had one dream: that, if he could seduce me away from a fraudulent father and educate me into the ways of farming, I would graduate from high school and then take over the management of The Place, and that would thus leave him time to hunt and fish and trap and go blueberrying. Something deep in his genes directed him to make sure that the Draegers, who could trace their noble stewardship of the soil all the way back through the centuries to the Mennonite cadres of Catholic Holland and the regal peasants of Lutheran Prussia, would continue to steward the soil into the future through me.

Ned knew the soil and he knew the woods, but he didn't know a damn thing about saxophones.

It was early November, then. I had spent the morning in the cellar practicing minor scales, and my mother called down to me. "Would you please put that thing away? I don't think I can stand much more," she said. "I got a job for you anyways. I want you to take this blouse I fixed for Vera out to The Place. She needs it for church tomorrow." We had just had the first big snowstorm of the year, and the sun was high and blinding, and so I laid my horn aside, put on my winter gear and tied the paper bag to my Mars Rocket and towed it out to the farm. "Oh," said Vera, pulling the blouse out of the bag, "your mom did such a good job on this old blouse . . . my, my, she's so clever!" She made me some hot cocoa, and then I went out to slide down the hill to No Nothin' Creek. There were better hills nearer town, but I knew the menu for this particular hill featured something hot and sweet before I went home – maybe one or two of Gramma's hot buns with butter and maple syrup.

I slid down the hill a few times, and the sun went down, and it got cold. After a while I went inside and partook of another cup of cocoa and two hot buttery buns, and I played several hands of solitaire with Nettie. Uncle Ned finally came in from the barn around four and took off his boots and sat watching us play cards. He giggled with his eyes, and stretched his mouth a few times. I could see he was working up some words.

"Me and Uncle Otto, we went up and fixed the roof of the shanty," he said at last, as Nettie melded cards for another game. He was talking about the old hunting shanty up at Bear's Creek. It was where Ned and my father and all my uncles and all their cronies hibernated for two weeks during deer hunting season. "Squirrels or coons, somethin', they made an awful mess. We cleaned out the stovepipes and found a dead mink in one of them, and then we pointed up the two chimleys and split up two, three cords of wood and cut up the kindlin', and Uncle Otto, he set out the mousetraps and the Warfarin." He cleared his throat and looked away as if maybe he'd said too much. "Anyways, Uncle Otto says Kenny Strauch won't be coming out this year as cabin boy, and Arnie Zielsdorf, he was the second cabin boy last year, well, he can't make it this year, so I was wonderin' . . . maybe you'd be interested in being cabin boy this year."

For a few minutes I couldn't think of what to say. "Kenny and Arnie, they're seniors in high school," I said, grasping at straws. "Me, I'm only in grade seven."

"Grade seven's good."

"Well then, I don't have a gun. Just that old .22 for shooting sparrows with."

He leaned closer and fixed his eyes onto me. "I could teach you how to hunt. You're twelve now . . . that's when I started."

There was no avoiding saying it, so I looked straight back at him and said, "My old man didn't say anything to me about being cabin boy this season."

In a nasty voice, he said, "No, he wouldn't now, would he?"

"No, he wouldn't. And even if he did ask, I wouldn't go . . . *especially* if he asked me."

"You wouldn't go if he asked you?"

"No, I wouldn't."

"Would you go if I asked you?"

My old man drove my mother out to The Place later that day. He sat out there waiting in the car, and Mom came into the house. "We come to take Junior back," she said. "He's got a concert next week." Vera told her I was out in the barn helping Ned toss down hay for the cows.

"Ned wants to know if Junior can spend the night with us tonight," she said. She didn't mention his invitation to me to be a cabin boy this year. "Esther's going to take us to church in the morning, so we can bring him home on the way." My mother usually took me to the Methodist church every Sunday because my old man never went near churches, and sometimes she required me to sit through long sermons upstairs instead of sitting around downstairs drawing pictures of Christ on the Cross in Sunday School.

"Fine by me," my mother said, without the least suspicion it was all part of a huge plot of Ned's to steal me away. "I have to help out tonight at the Quality Store anyways. I can ask Mrs. Horton to look after Bits till I get back."

After chores we sat down to supper, and then I played double solitaire with Nettie while Ned rocked away nervously in his creaky chair below the clock, holding a newspaper up in front of his face, but I could tell he wasn't reading it. I knew he was still trying to figure out some way to talk me into becoming cabin boy. I left him to stew away and concentrated on outwitting Nettie at cards. Suddenly, Ned dropped the papers onto the floor and jumped to his feet as if he heard someone calling him from the barn. He hurried straight out of the room, and I heard him putting on his boots and going outside. Vera was watering her violets in the parlor, staring out the window at the road, and Gramma sat in a chair at the far end of the table pretending to read the Bible as she nodded off. I suddenly realized how comfortable it was in that room with these people. I said to myself, This is it, this is where I want to be on a cold and miserable winter night. No sign of the old man, sitting and staring, trying to find out what was wrong with me now. And Mom having to come to my defense and sending me over to Mrs. Horton's to play checkers.

Then I heard Ned coming back into the house and stomping the snow off his boots. He walked into the dining room carrying a long canvas bag, which he propped up against the table next to me. "Your Opa's deer rifle," he said, tossing me a small, intimate smile.

"Oh, Ned!" cried Vera, coming in with the watering can for her window flowers. "What's Junior want with that old thing? The least you could do is give him a proper gun."

"Pa wasn't no hunter," Ned said, ignoring her, "but he kept that gun oiled good, and clean too."

Nettie laughed and began a long story: "He used to take it out to the chicken coop when the trees was full of sparrows and he'd hide just inside the doorway, and then every time that gun went off, why those chickens, they'd go nuts and start squawkin' their fool heads off and fly out the doors and the dust would be just thick in there, you couldn't see a thing –"

"Well, Nettie!" snarled Vera. "Junior doesn't want to hear about Pa shooting sparrows!"

Gramma woke up and cackled away and said, "He shot more chickens than sparrows if you ast me."

"Nobody ast you," said Nettie.

I stared at the gun. I really didn't want to have anything to do with it.

"We'll go down to the creek in the morning after chores and shoot up some cannin' jars," said Ned, "and you can get used to the kick-back."

That night I went to bed and stared out the window at the moon and thought about my father. He hadn't asked me to go, not because he knew I'd refuse, but because he was afraid I might accept, and then shooting innocent and beautiful things wouldn't be any fun because he'd have to follow me around pointing out all my mistakes.

But wait! Maybe I *should* go if only to get his goat! And maybe I should bag me a deer using Grampa's old blunderbuss. What could he find wrong with that? He couldn't find anything wrong with that. Unless he could.

On Monday the following week Marlene stopped me after band

practice and said, "You think you're pretty good in there, don't you? You think you're better than me." We had been in a race since school started, but it was becoming clear I was going to beat her at playing saxophone. It had come easy to me, and also I had been working hard at it, but Marlene was having trouble. "You think maybe if you play better than me, I'll forget what happened last summer."

"What happened last summer? I forget now."

"Okay, okay." She looked at the floor and then at me. "Look, I've been meaning to say this for a long time." She tried on a sad smile. "Okay, I'm sorry about your Uncle Buck."

"You are?"

"Yes. Yes, I am."

I couldn't fight down a smile. "Me too."

"What I really want to do now is learn how to play the saxophone, and I was wondering if maybe . . . well, maybe you would stop off at my house on your way home and show me how to get better." She laughed nervously and got an angry look worked up. "I'm not taking any chances, you sex freak! My mother, she'll be in the kitchen keeping an eye on you . . ."

So stopping off on my way home from school became a routine that fall. We would sit in the swing on the porch, and I would show her how to tighten your lips around the mouthpiece, how to finger fast, support the airstream, that sort of thing. "Teach me swing music," she said, pushing us up into a long arc. "That's something," I said, "I can't teach you. You have to have it in your bones!" Whatever I did seemed to work, and in time we both made it into the high school band, taking over what was called 'third alto saxophone chair'. We tried to sound as if we were both making one note. But more often than not, there were two, and mine was more to the point, and so Mr. Kaiser moved me to second alto, and in time to first, and then I began playing solos at competitions and gradually making it to sectional and state competitions. Marlene seemed to think her failures were my fault. I was trying to prove I was better than she was. She tried getting angry, but she could tell it wasn't working. She started slipping me kisses and making strange sounds, but frankly, I was more in love with the saxophone than with her.

In time I began earning bronze and silver medals, and by my junior year I had started a dance band, a little trio we called 'Me and Annabelle' and went out and played at other schools, so that by the time I was graduated from high school, I was earning gold medals at the competitions which converted into a college music scholarship which took me out into the world in a way that Marlene would never come to.

17

My mother got my black wool coat out of the attic and sewed four flags of red flannel across it. "I won't need this," I complained. "I'm just peeling spuds and cutting up carrots, I plan to catch up on my comic books!" She said Ned had left specific instructions for her to sew red patches on my coat, and that was what she was doing. I knew I couldn't back out now. I kept on bitching, saying, "Well, he's crazy if he thinks I'm going out into the woods carrying a gun."

On the day we were to leave for the hunting shack, my old man drove out to The Place without me, and I had to walk clear across town wearing the scarecrow black winter coat with all the red patches on it. Old Man Senske was shoveling his driveway and giggled when he saw me, said, "You look like a target." Sandy Roberts and her sister were building a snowman. "You look like a pirate flag!" they laughed, and further out Main Street Mrs. Roberts stood on her porch and stared at me as if she didn't even know me. "You look like a visitor from another world," she said. Mrs. Taggert said, "Where you from anyways?" At the cemetery, staring at the graves of my ancestors, I waited for them to pop up out of the ground laughing at me.

The hunters were already gathered around a line of five muddy black ModelA's and Ned's red Chevy truck, looking like dog sleds packed up for a trek across the tundra. There was Ned, and there was my old man, and there was Len Kregness, and also Uncle Harry, whose left heel was shot off in the Ardennes and wore an oak one instead, and Frank Lipke, beard bristling with frost and flashing his three gold teeth, and Leonard Lone, whose wife died when thrown from a plow, and Henry Futz, who owned a great big hardware store in Bayport, Minnesota, but came back home every deer season to join in the bloodbath. Hanging around looking as if he didn't belong was Kenny Schwock, homely, tall and skinny, red with pimples, a senior in high school known for warming the bench at basketball games till it was a sure thing Herring High had lost the game. He was going to be head cook this time out, and his only chore was to make sure I knew he ran the kitchen. The men drifted over to Ned's truck when Esther came out and told them she wanted to take a picture of them with her new Brownie, and I made sure where my old man was standing before I went and stood beside Ned.

Nettie, Gramma, Vera, Esther, Aunt Ollie and Aunt Doris, the ladies all came out and stood around the pump on the porch. They had that worried look of women who figured they might not ever see their loved ones again. Uncle Harry finally said it was getting late, and so we climbed into our caravan without saying goodbye and circled out into the road, cars rocking back and forth as if they might just tip over given half a chance. Abandoned now, the women walked out to the front yard and waved, and I was the only one who rolled down a window and waved back.

I thought somebody should go tell the Japanese they should go ahead and invade the country because only the women and children and the old folks were left holding the fort.

I watched the farm getting smaller and smaller until it vanished, and then I leaned over against the window in Ned's truck and tried to go to sleep to prevent what was happening. I remembered last winter after deer season walking up to the knoll facing the road, where the carcasses of all the murdered deer hung like trophies, and the cruel eye of the moon came out to illuminate the ruffled grey fur of the dead beasts. Such beautiful animals, I observed, such sleek, regal heads, crowned with arched horns, snouts emblazoned with black flaring nostrils, heroic black eyes, glassey and hard, such delicate, long bodies sparkling in the night.

Last summer I had seen the movie *Bambi.* I didn't really care that it was a manufactured myth coming out of Beverly Hills, California, where snow and roaming herds of wild deer were but distant memories of Minnesota cartoonists sitting around air-conditioned rooms and making sketches drawn from their own boyhood memories, men who caused owls to sing and fawns to be born, who created Thumper and all the other pretty little choir of animals and birds to gather in a circle to watch the fawn climb for its first time onto its long wobbly legs. Disney had matched the world of children perfectly. I remember sitting in the dark theatre watching with only my eyes working. Bambi was more than real. More real, say, than the mother holding my hand and the sister who leaned into her and giggled but finally wept. And I was horrified to encounter all those horrible brutes called 'human beings' who came and caused a forest fire that killed the king of the deer. I prospered in the Technicolor forest until the final golden flicker and all the lights came up, and then I had trouble finding my way out the door and into the black and white world of Herring.

I said, "Mommy, you should take Dad to see this movie."

"You know he doesn't go to movies."

"Make him go!"

"Why? He loves deer just as much as Walt Disney does. Why do you think he spends all his winters with them?"

"To shoot them."

"Some of them maybe!"

"I'm never going deer hunting."

"Never say never."

"Never," I said. "Never, never!"

My sister bawled out, "Me neither!"

I had to remind her of my pledge when she wrote a note to Mr. MacLaughlin asking him to excuse me for a week because it was hunting season, and I had been selected to help out up at the cabin in Coon Gut. He wrote back saying it was not his custom to excuse students who want to go deer hunting, but since I had a decent scholastic record and was a rising saxophone star, he would make an exception.

When Mother showed my old man the principal's letter, he said, "Whose idea was this?"

"Ned's," said my mother, in a smarty-pants voice. "He asked Junior to help out in the kitchen this year."

My old man looked across the table at me and said, "Think you're old enough to wash the dishes?"

She knew Ned had bought me a deer license behind my old man's back and had said nothing about giving me the family heirloom gun.

It snowed hard the first two days we got to the cabin in Coon Gut, and so we stayed inside, the passionate hunters indulging in pinochle and blackjack, drinking scotch whiskey and beer, smoking wildly, laughing at each other's jokes, Ned telling more of his hunting stories. I helped Kenny Schwock in the kitchen and washed dishes and set table. We got to know one another, and I discovered he wasn't such a bad guy after all. My old man made it a point to ignore me altogether. He treated me as if I wasn't there. But this time I was there. I was *there* there.

Early the third morning Uncle Harry looked out the window and announced that the snow had stopped, and Kenny woke me and I helped him fry up the pancakes and bacon, and that was when Ned made the big announcement: "I'm going to take Junior out to the blind to keep me company. Anyway, there's already the six of you driving, that's enough."

"You sure about that, Ned?" said Len Kregness. He fixed me with his glass eye, no matter what the other eye was up to. I think maybe it was watching my old man to see how he was going to react. "It don't look to me like Junior there knows which end of the gun is which."

"Well, that's why I figured to take him along with me. I can straighten him out on that."

"Has he even got a gun?"

"Well sure," laughed Ned. "It belonged to his grandpa." Then, to my astonishment he let loose an absolute lie. I don't remember him ever lying before, but he lied this time, even if it was to protect me from the likes of my old man. "I don't even know if it works," he said. "This'll give us a chance to look it over. They used to use these Remingtons in the old days, and they was pretty accurate back then."

"Watch your backside, Ned," said my old man, looking at me for the first time. "You don't want to be anywheres near that boy if it goes off!" He laughed, but lacked company, and so he shifted gears. "I remember that old blunderbuss was real slow and off to the right." The others said nothing. They knew something hard was going on between the two brothers, and they figured they ought to stay out of it. "All right, all right," said my father, making wild concessions, "we'll take Kenny along with us then to even it out. At least he's not dangerous."

"I ain't got a coat," said Kenny.

"We'll have to take Junior then," said Uncle Harry.

"No, I'm going with Uncle Ned," I said.

Kenny and I went over and washed up the dishes. I looked over at Kenny, and he tried to smile to distance himself from me.

I hung back with Ned while the crew crept away through the trees to the crossing lanes to surprise and then drive the deer down toward Ned's blind. They carried small flashlights pointed at their heels as they found their way through the woods to their position, where they would hunker down until first light when the deer would stroll forth from their secret caves to dig in the cornfield or stroll down to the creek to look for running water. The men would wait until the herd got between them and Ned and then jump out and drive them down toward the blind.

"Your dad sure needs some cheering up," said Ned.

"That's about as happy as he gets."

Along the path Ned held his flashlight low behind his legs to show me through the white blackness. He stopped after a while and turned around. "Now you watch me close," he whispered. "If I drop, you drop. And don't make no noise. If you have to sneeze or something, cuff it. When we get to the blind, you have to make yourself small and don't move about even if you hear something. Stay low till you see the herd come."

I whispered, "I can do that."

"Of course you can."

At last we reached a thicket of pine branches cleverly woven through a beech tree on the top of which perched a snowy moon. You could see a little room made in the heart of the darkness. We crept up inside, and Ned said, "When I tell you, slip your gun through those branches but don't fire till I tell you to. Aim at the king, the big one out front, the one leading the charge. Aim for the front shoulders. You try and hit him in the hind-quarters, it'll only slow him down and make him mad as hell and then he'll hightail it into the trees and we'll have to go look for him. And if you miss him, try for the rest of the herd. You might get lucky but probably not." He loaded both guns and handed Opa's to me.

I took it and wondered what I would do with it. I thought about the movie. How had I got to this point? The gun was heavy. The bullets must weigh a ton. I looked at my uncle. What I could see of him was all nose, ears, eyes. Looked like an animal. He wasn't even breathing. Maybe he was trying to find his animalness. I tried the same thing, but all I heard was my own small human heart murmuring, "You got yourself into this bind, didn't you? You said you wouldn't, but you did it anyways."

Gradually, imperceptibly, the darkness lifted into a foggy definition of trees and long white meadows. I looked at Ned and tried to remember I wanted to be just like him. I didn't want to be like my old man. I wanted to be like Ned. Against my better judgment I was trying to fit into his definition of the trees and the moon and the mauve sky.

Then I heard what sounded like the wind suddenly springing up.

I looked at the darkness that was Ned. “Shhh!” he whispered as if he had smelled my fear, and then, “You’ll hear them before you see them.” Then it was as if the wind had gathered itself at the far upper end of the clearing. I turned and looked away up the long meadow, but there was nothing to look at.

Then suddenly there was nothing but whirling snow, and then . . . I thought I saw something like huge flying arrows . . . a blur of snow and something maybe brown behind it.

“Just breathe slack and slow!”

I said, “What about you? Aren’t you shooting?”

“Just get ready and remember you got only the one shot!”

I pressed my gun through the pine branches and watched them come. I tried the trigger. It wouldn’t move. It would take two fingers to move it. Then they were there. A flock of Whitetail flying through the deep snow as if it wasn’t even there . . . long, graceful leaping arches, their great heads held high, long legs spindling, white throats flashing. When I saw the great king out in front, a great prancing beast, I froze.

“Lead him now!” said Ned. “Lead him, lead him!”

I knew I had no choice, I had to do it. I would do it. I would do it now. I would do it because I had to do it because Ned expected me to do it because there was no way not to do it.

I aimed at the nose.

The trigger was hard to pull and the gun slammed me back into the brambles and flew up and away from me. I was sure my shoulder was shattered. My hearing was gone. I got up slowly and looked for Ned, and he was saying something I couldn’t hear. Then I looked out. I could see something down and trying to get up. The rest were all gone. It was the big buck. He whirled about and fell and began thrashing about, the blood spattering the snow.

I could hear a little now. “You missed the shoulders!” said Ned, thrusting aside the green covers and pushing his way out of the blind and into the heavy snow. “Bring your gun, Junior, we got to get out there fast!”

I followed Ned out through the hip-deep snow to where the great king thrashed about in red snow trammeled down by the enraged dying animal. We stopped and watched him whirling about looking for some way to join the rest of his family. I could see he wanted to live, he wanted to run, he wanted to rule, to dance, to have more children and live a long happy life, but he had to sing a dying song now, it was caught in his throat, his gorgeous head lolling about, the large warm black eyes fixed on us, his long legs dancing.

Ned cocked his rifle and handed it to me.

"Shoot him in the chest, Junior!"

"Me?" I cried, in deep pain myself. "No way! Not me, no way!"

"You've hurt him, he's in a lot of pain."

"I . . . I just . . . I just can't do it, Ned!"

Ned turned and looked at me and said, "What? You're going to let him drown in his own blood and die a long and painful death?" That much was true. Terrified, I looked at the king and burst into tears. "You have to do it!" said Ned. "Do it, do it!"

"You betrayed me!" I sneered. But I lifted the rifle and pointed it at him. The eyes of the great buck were on me. They said, Listen to your uncle. Pull the goddamn trigger. You started all this, now finish it. There's no way out of this, just finish what you started.

I closed my eyes and pulled the trigger. The gun threw me back into the snow, the already-injured shoulder stinging again with pain, and the explosion rolled around the woods and down across the meadow and out into the whole world, where it published my murder to everyone. I lay in the snow stunned, and Ned picked up the gun and came and took my hand and pulled me to my feet. I looked at the dead animal. I had killed him. I had killed one much more noble than I was, much more gracious, more beautiful, one that had more to live for.

Behind me I heard the others yelling as they ran toward us. I took one look at Ned and charged off through the blood-drenched snow toward the woods, leaving everything and everyone behind forever.

* * *

My old man didn't know what to make of it that night when I was invited to sit with the men at the dinner table, and afterward, when Len made me inhale his cigar and everyone laughed, a shadow of regret and fear hung over the old man's features. Kenny stood at the stove regarding me now as an enemy. I was asked to take a hand at the whist table. The next morning Frank Lipke got out his Brownie and took a picture of me and my gun. He wanted to take another one with me and my old man, but I spared my father the pain by walking back into the cabin.

The days of the week went by in single file, and I tried to stay out of the woods and close to the woodstove. "You go with Ned this time, Kenny," I said. "I've had enough." I considered walking out to the road and heading home on my own. But Ned made me go with him the following morning to the stand. "You don't back out of these things once you're in them," he said. "Go talk to your dead buck if you have to and have it out with him." Which I did, but the conversation was all one-way.

One day I went out with the drivers, and once more with Ned to the blind, but I left Ned to do the shooting. Before we packed it in, he killed three more bucks, which he distributed among the others. And when the crew had its limit – on the seventh day of deer season – we packed up and headed back to the world of women and children.

Uncle Ned ordered me into his truck for the long journey home, and when Kenny asked if he couldn't come along, Ned said, "You ride with the others. Me and Junior, we got something to sort out between the two of us."

18

It was snowing so hard you could barely make out the road, but I thought Ned gave up too easily when he pulled into a tavern hidden in snowbanks. The Leinenkugel beer logo barked out a code of loneliness, and somewhere under the snow were the words 'Ratty's Lagoon'. The parking lot was empty, but that didn't stop Ned from turning off the engine and saying, "Let's go have a little drink to celebrate your first buck, what do you say?"

"If we don't show up back at The Place, won't the others think we got lost in the snowstorm?" I asked, ever the worrywart. "They'll be stringing up the deer and telling stories, and my old man will claim *he* bagged my buck."

"Give your Pa some room." He waited to see if I knew what he was talking about. "He's learned something he still don't know he's learned." He didn't wait for me to agree, he climbed out of the truck and headed for the bar. Kids weren't allowed in taverns, but I had no choice. If I sat in the truck, I'd freeze to death. I got out then and examined the two stiff carcasses roped across the front fenders, their racks of horns draped over the headlights, furry trunks lashed along the sides of the truck, legs arranged so they looked as if still in flight. I ran my fingers through their thick hair and then followed Ned and knocked the snow from my boots just as he had done. The door squawked open as if to announce that here was another boy taking his first step toward becoming an alcoholic. The tavern itself was as empty as the parking lot, but there was a roaring fire that made the place look real homey. And of course the delicious fumes of dead cigarettes and spilled beer and mustard on frankfurters. The barkeep, a man I had heard about but never seen, Ratty Zielsdorf, stood enshrined below a yellow lamp behind a long polished bar and smiled at us as he whirled a beer glass through a long white towel.

"Gentlemen," he said, nodding. "You must be on your way home from Coon Gut."

"That's right, Ratty," said Ned as he climbed onto a stool and patted the one beside him, said, "A couple Leinies if you got 'em."

The man stared at Ned and then at me, and I climbed up and leaned forward on my elbows just the way I saw Ned do it. The bartender gave me a hard look. Then he turned around and with a flourish, balanced a clean beer glass on top of a pyramid of glasses and tossed away the towel and plucked a cigarette from an ashtray, propped it in the corner of his mouth, inhaled and blew the smoke menacingly through his nostrils, and then he looked at me again and said, "You and Junior here."

"Junior just bagged his first buck."

"Well now!" said Mr. Zielsdorf, conceding a small grin. "That calls for a celebration." He glanced out through the icebound windows at the empty parking lot and then stepped to a cooler and fished out three bottles. "How big?" he asked, toweling the bottles dry while listening to Ned's statistics, prying off the caps, and setting two bottles before us, lifting the third into the air. "Twelve points, hunh! Well then . . . *Weisman's Heil!* to you, young man."

"*Weisman's Heil!*" echoed Ned.

I lifted the bottle to them but had no idea what they were talking about. Ratty looked at me and said, "Don't suppose you'd like to tell me how it happened?"

"I'll let Uncle Ned tell the story, he's good at it."

I tipped the bottle back. The beer was cold and sour and burned my throat. I gagged on it, set the bottle down and tried wiping away the tears as the two of them began laughing until they cried.

"Well, here's what really happened, Ratty," said Ned. "I give him Pa's old 410. Junior, he couldn't hardly lift it, but we did a little target shooting with it before we went up to Coon Gut, and then I took him out to the blind with me that first day, wicked cold it was, too, and soon's it got light and the boys found the herd heading out of the creek bottom, they drove it down toward us, and Junior, he picked up the gun and fired . . . of course, the old buck, he was flyin', you know, but Junior, he hit him in the haunches, knocked him down, spun him about, that twelve point rack sharp as jack-knives . . . why the snowbank was red like you'd thrown a bucket of barn paint around, and oh sure! he was ready to cut you to ribbons if you come anywhere near him, but Junior, he went right at him with that gun and polished him off . . ."

I listened as Ned stretched the story further than it would go. He couldn't let what actually happened hamper the spell of his epic narrative, and I wondered how many other tales had been stretched out like this one. The two of them then moved onto other topics, like trapping and fishing, and so I pushed my misty bottle of beer away and drifted across the room to the Mighty Wurlitzer, softly glowing like a hot marble chocolate fountain, wheezing away, the vapours moving out in spheres. The menu on the front of it was mostly Six Fat Dutchmen, Whoopee John, Blue Barron. Polkas, schottishes, waltzes. But at the bottom of the menu, I saw that Glenn Miller song I had heard on the train that day, the one called "In the Mood". I went and asked Ned for a nickel, and he dug out three of them, and I went back to the machine and dropped one into it. Saxophones, lots of saxophones. So, I thought, that's how saxophones are supposed to sound. Mr. Kaiser hadn't said anything about this. Maybe it was a secret. Maybe I wasn't supposed to know about them till later. I got two more nickels out and listened to the record again, remembering the people on the train and how that delicious sound had danced across the fields, and now, closer and more distinct, I thought it even more fascinating. The colours, shifting rhythms, the groove, the ideas, the flourish of trombones and trumpets and especially saxophones . . . I could scarcely breathe.

* * *

"You going to wear that record out, boy," said Ratty Zielsdorf, when I went back to the bar and climbed onto a stool. "That's coon music, you know. You're too young to listen to coon music."

"Whatever it is, I like it," I said, and Ned sat looking at his hands and wearing a goofy smile. I figured they figured I was getting drunk. I had seen Ned drunk only that once. The time he missed evening chores, and Gramma, Vera and I did all the milking. When he drove up to the milkhouse just as we were going to the house, he climbed out of the truck and stumbled and sat on the ground. Vera laid into him, and Gramma just cried. Nettie started laughing and telling the long story about the bum who spent the night in the haymow and got good and spiked.

"You know, Junior, your dad . . ." He stopped then as if that was all he was going to say and looked over at Ratty Zielsdorf. Then he looked at me again. "Your dad, he was seven years old when . . ." He stopped again and took a swig of beer and then wiped his lips on the back of his hand. "I wonder if I could have a private word with Junior here," he said to Ratty, and the bartender looked at the two of us as if he figured we were up to something and wandered down to the far end of the bar. Ned studied himself in the mirror for a while and tried to steady himself. "Well, you see, your grandfather give your Pa a Guernsey calf when he was seven years old, and your Pa called her 'Princess'. Opa was sick all that winter, so I was doin' most of the chores on account of that. I noticed your pa wasn't feedin' Princess right, and so I fed him, and then your pa, he comes over to me and says, 'Ned, you don't know nothin' about feeding Guernsey calves, so just stay away from my Princess.'

"I says to him, I says, 'All I know is you feed them when they get hungry.' Why, I never saw nothing like it! Your pa treated that calf like it was Mary Christ." Ned paused and signaled to Ratty Zielsdorf for another beer and waited until he brought it, and then Ned stared at him till he went back to the end of the bar. "Then one day your dad said he was goin' to enter the calf in a 4-H show at the county fair. Our Dad, he just laughs, he says, 'It's only a cow, Colvin, for Chris'sakes! This is a farm, we milk cows here, we eat cows here, but we don't fancy up to them ever!' But your Pa . . . well, I don't have to tell you how stubborn he is, do I? After that little talk all they did is quarrel. I found out your Pa kept a book on that calf. It was buried under some old harnesses in the barn. I looked at it, and I see how he wrote down what that calf et, when she et it, what she weighed after she et it!

"Then towards spring that year we got a telegram from Aunt Lena, out in Montana. She said Uncle Henry had fallen off a binder and broke his hip and got pneumonia and up and died, and the funeral was coming up. My mother says well then we have to go, but Opa, he says someone has to stay and do the milkin' and the chores, and he can't do them all by hisself, and my cousin Doris says, okay, she'll stay and cook his meals and run the house. The rest of us, we get packed and head on downtown and get onto a train and take it all the way out to Aunt Lena's, and we stay maybe a week and then head for home, and when we get home, Opa meets us at the station with a rig and drives us all out to home, and Doris, she's got supper on the table. Hot beefsteak, mash potatoes, gravy, cream peas, sauerkraut, apple pie, you name it. Your Pa, he hasn't eaten all day, says he's got a stomach ache . . . didn't like the food on the train. And so there he sits, stuffin' his mouth with all that hot beefsteak and sayin' how good it was to be home and then he says, 'My goodness, this is awful good beef, Doris!' And she gets this funny look on her face and stares at Opa. It gets real quiet then, and everybody stops and looks around the table. "Where'd that beef come from?" your Pa asks, and Doris is still looking over at Opa, and finally Opa says, 'Doris, tell him where that beef come from,' and she tells him, she says, 'I'm glad you like it, it's your 4-H calf.' And they all sit around the table waitin' for him to laugh.

"But he just sits there starin' down at his plate, his face gettin' all red, and then he starts to gag and gets up real slow to his feet and pukes all over the table. Then he bolts out the door, and of course we all sat there hearing him still pukin' away in the yard, and Opa, he says, 'Rosella, that boy has to be taught a lesson, and you know it! Around here a cow is for milking and eating. It ain't for paradin' up and down before a lot of school teachers and dry goods merchants.' Then your Gramma, she gets up and runs outside, and we get up too and run after her. We can see your Pa now, he's headin' for the barn, and so we light out after him, none of us knowin' what to do, just run after him, I guess, but when we get to the barn, we can't find your Pa nowheres. We look in the haymow and climb up the silos and look into the calf pens . . . but he ain't nowheres. We figure he's run out the horsebarn door and out into the woods and probably won't be back before it's dark. But you know what? He didn't come home that night at all, nor even the next one. Why, he stayed out there in the woods for three whole days before he come home. You see now why he's the way he is."

Don't say that, I'm thinking, don't say that! I'm not used to thinking of my old man as someone who needed any figuring out. He was just as plain to me as were Hitler and Tojo. There was nothing to figure out. Ned pushed my beer bottle closer to me. I thought it was a disgusting story. I was mad as hell. "I don't want to start feeling sorry for my old man," I said. We had worked so hard building up the wall between the two of us. What is the point in trying to tear it down? What good would it do? Why tell me the story? I'd have to make sure the story worked to my advantage. I'd have to think about it for a while before I could act on it.

"After that," said Ned, "your Pa wouldn't eat no beef. Only chicken and nothin' but. He never lifted a finger around the farm, never helped out with chores, nothin'. When he was growing up, he'd get up in the morning and take an old shotgun out to the woods and come home around suppertime with a squirrel or two but he wouldn't eat them neither. Nothing but chicken. He become a real sourpuss, too. He used to throw kittens up against the silo or go around kicking pigs. Why, soon as he got out of country school, he went to stay with Uncle Melvin in town till he got out of high school, and then he found a job in town."

When I figured he was done, I said, "Do you have any more nickels?"

It was the middle of the afternoon by now and almost dark. We'd been in the tavern for over two hours. Ned grinned at me as we walked back to the truck, and then he dredged the truck key out of his pocket, handed it to me, and said, "You better stick with 'G', it's a little longer maybe but that way you stay off the highway." I was twelve and had only a wartime farmboy driver's license. It was good for driving pickups and tractors over country roads around the farm, but I had to stay off the highways.

We got in the truck, and Ned went right off to sleep. I had the wipers going, and the headlamps were busy trying to pick out the road. We left the woods and came to the open fields of Thompson Valley. It began to snow harder when we reached the Steinmetz Place, where I turned off 'G' north onto County Trunk 'F', which would take me right to The Place. I could see maybe twenty feet ahead of me and kept my eyes on the ditches on both sides of the road. I was doing maybe fifteen miles an hour. Fortunately, there were no cars or trucks out that afternoon. The snow let up a little at Harmon's Mill School. Ned was snoring away now, slumped over against the window. That, I thought, that was real trust. I never got that from my old man. My old man . . . what was I going to do about him now? Well, he had problems with his old man. As I said, all in the family. But I wasn't going to change things. Next time he turned on me, I'd let him know I'd heard all that about his 4-H heifer.

That would fix him. I had to let him know it was my turn to know things about him.

By the time I reached Diamond Valley and came down along the creek and across the tracks, I was rehearsing my lines. Turning at last into the driveway at The Place, I saw five deer dangling from a long two-by-six nailed into the yoke of the two elm trees on the knoll below the windmill. They were visible from the road. That's where they wanted them. We wanted everybody to see we bagged our limit. I parked beside the milk house and nudged Ned. "We're home, Ned," I said. "Are you okay? Can you walk?" He looked over at me as if he had forgot who I was. "Sure," he mumbled. "Sure, I can walk, why can't I walk?" The yard light came on, and as we climbed out of the truck and into the cold night, we heard them talking in the house. Then the door opened, and out flew my mother, her coat drawn about her shoulders, and then Vera and Nettie, pulling on coats, and the three of them came and stood and watched the two of us unlashing the bucks from the fenders. Vera could see Ned was tight. Of course, that didn't stop him from doing what he had to do. We followed him up the knoll as he dragged one of our trophies and laid it on the ground at the foot of the other five dangling there.

"You been drinking, Ned!" growled Vera. "And you took Junior to a tavern!"

Nettie, her fingers doing a war dance, said, "Your Pa told everybody you killed your first deer, he said you only wounded him the first time around and then you ran out and shot him dead, and then he said it was just laying there and thrashing around and there was blood all over, and he said you done real good –"

"Oh stop it, Nettie!" Vera growled. "You don't have to stand there and tell Junior everything his Pa said, maybe he wants to tell it himself. Anyways, it's too cold to stand around out here listening to you gobble away like that."

"Nettie's right," my mother said, looking at Ned. "We're real proud of Junior. Maybe we shouldn't even call him 'Junior' anymore." Vera reached out for Ned, but he pushed her off and started for the house. My mother threaded an arm through mine and after giving me an exultant smile, steered me down the knoll and over toward the glowing farmhouse that held all the complications that stood between me and my old man, and after him, all the meaning of everything else that happened to me the rest of my life.

PART THREE

The Amish

19

The screen door on the back porch yarrs and snaps, and my mother steps out into moonlight that augments her sad depletion. "You just got up and walked out on me," she says, "and I wondered if maybe it was something I said." I smile up at her and shake my head. The television drones on behind her in the living room as she slips into a chair beside me. "What are you looking at out there, there's nothing to look at."

How would she know, I think. She's lived here for forty, fifty years now and has lost her bearing, and I had sailed the seven seas. "I was just sitting here thinking about Ned," I said, "and remembering that winter I shot my first buck." We sit awhile contemplating the half moon, and then, as if even mentioning Ned actually conjured up the actual past, there is a faint but swelling rustle of a train, and we turn to look across the valley toward the railroad tracks. "Well, well," I laugh, "right on time . . . coming down The Cut."

"The nine-thirty."

"We could set our clocks by it."

"No, it's not that one. That one's gone, Junior." She pauses and clears her throat. "I'm sorry, I'm just used to calling you that. I mean 'David.'"

"Let's just go with 'Junior.'"

"All right, Junior. That train's long gone."

"Gone? How could it be gone?" I look over at her, and her wrinkles tell me how long I've been gone too. "They're all gone, then? The passenger trains, they're all gone now?"

She coughs, and I listen to more than I want to hear. "It's just freights now," she says, and I watch her stretch out an arm and roll her shoulder back and forth as if she's had to carry something heavy around for a long time. "I remember your dad sitting out here on a night like this, waiting for the passenger trains to come back. He said it wouldn't be long before they took the freights off, too. She laughs and says, "He was wrong about that."

"He was wrong about a lot of things," I laugh.

She waits for me to say something nice about him. She'd tried twice at supper, an angler with a clever fly, and I had to remind her she was the one who told me not to bother coming home when he came out of the hospital because she said he wouldn't have known who I was. For nearly a week he didn't know who *she* was. And then he died, and she called and said there was no point in coming home for the funeral either, since it was going to be a simple affair at the 'funeral home', and only Ned, Vera, and Nettie were coming and nobody else. I caught the first plane out, of course, and it was a good thing too because I had a chance to stand beside her at the coffin and make my peace once more with the old man.

"He was right about a lot of things too," she urges.

"He never once got onto a train," I say, as the freight rolls like a fat slug through town, iron wheels grinding away over worn rails. "Never went anywhere."

"I don't think he *could* go anywhere," she says after deciding I hadn't disfigured his effigy. "He didn't like change." We sat for a while thinking about him. "Everything's changed anyway." She studies me. "You've changed too. I don't see a thing in you that reminds me of that little boy who used to carry his suitcase clear across town and out to The Place." That hurts a little, and I look away. "It was such a different way of life in those days, wasn't it? We all got along even though we were way different. And everybody knew everybody. They knew who your mother was and your father and your grandfather, and they knew where they came from too and what kind of work they did and whether they were good or bad, and everybody stayed at home all year and worked the year around, no one ever took a holiday. It was our own little world right here in Herring, and you could go to the edge of it and gaze out into space. It was all out there somewhere. You were here, and they were there, and that is how it was going to always be." She pauses and listens to the caboose whisking up the dust as it clears the canning factory and out to the farms on the edge of town. "These days everyone's busy driving all the way to Clearwater to work and shop, and around six they all come back to eat and watch television till they go to bed. You meet people on the street you never saw before and probably won't ever see again, and it doesn't seem to bother anyone one way or another."

"Bother?"

She yawns and collects herself. "That's enough philosophy for tonight," she says. "I'm tired, I'm off to bed. It's been a long day. I'm not used to driving. Your father did all the driving."

"He didn't like other people driving *his* car. I learned that lesson early on."

She smiles like a pussycat and refuses to be drawn into an argument. "I cleaned out the cellar last fall . . . and the garage, of course, and Jack Helmer came over and helped me with the yard sale. Quite a few people stopped by, and a couple buggies of Amish ladies. They took all my old green canning jars and the pots and pans and all the old kitchen things. One young man with a beard saw your father's carpenter tools and wanted to buy them. The hammers and saws, the leather aprons, all that sort of thing. But I said no. I told him my husband wanted his own son to have them."

"What? Me? If he ever caught me using one of his hammers or saws, he'd have to climb out of the grave and come after me."

"You know he wasn't like that at the end," she cries, narrowing her eyes. "You two got on very well last time you were to home. Remember that? It was just before you left for China. I remember the two of you standing at the front door and hugging each other and saying the nicest things." She fights away sudden tears, and we listen to the loud silence freight trains always leave behind. "Anyways, let's not talk about that now." She turns away. "Do you want me to leave the television on for you?"

I am overwhelmed by the memory of that day when my old man and I hugged each other in the front doorway. I had just told my mother I had hired a neighbor to drive me up to the bus. "No," he grumbled, "he's not goin' to catch no bus to Clearwater. No son of mine is goin' to have to catch no bus to Clearwater."

It was the first time in his life I had ever heard him claim me as his son. And as it turned out the last time.

"You can turn the TV off," I said. "I think I'll just take a little walk around town."

"This time of night? Where do you want to go? There's nothing to see here." She laughs and tilts her head to appeal to me. "It isn't Vancouver, you know."

"I need to stretch my legs. Been sitting on airplanes all day."

"All right, but please don't forget to lock the door when you come back."

"You lock the door now?"

"You just don't know, do you?" She opens the screen door and steps back into the house and stands for a moment looking out at me. "Anyway, it's sure nice to have you home again, even if I had to get good and sick to do it. It's been a long time."

"Thirty years."

"Where did they all go, Junior . . . I mean, David?"

"Junior," I said.

I walk past a row of tall white clapboard houses nailed to a stiff Lutheran imagination, high pious windows, sharp angular roofs, brick chimneys like fingers pointing up to Heaven, long lazy lawns and backyard vegetable patches, small tilting garages with the backside of fat Fords and Chevrolets, yellow dogs leashed to clotheslines and yaowling at nothing. Down along Main Street, the solid but now weathering wall of redbrick stores: the bank, the lawyer's office, the post office, the hardware store, the meat market, and then way up there, astride the village like a visitor from outer space, the silver water tower with bold letters HERRING on it, its lightning rod stabbing the sky. And somewhere alongside the silver belly, resting on one of its steel ribs, the siren that still warns children it's ten o'clock and home to bed. The taverns are still open. A jukebox swells from within the Sportsmen's Grill, a cowboy tune from the Urban Jungle. Within, there's talk and laughter, words lost in the thuck of billiard balls. Cigar smoke sifts through the open door, the snap of cards at a pinochle table. Someone steps out into the cool night and, without a lick of curiosity, watches me walk past him and down toward the corner, where I turn the corner and encounter the Grace Methodist Church and the old railway inn, and then I head back home along a street I used to take everyday to and from school.

I know all these houses. They are as familiar to me as my own features in the bathroom mirror. The Schoendiensts, the Erdmans, the Kreutzers. The Bensons. I remember the Benson house only too well. Tall and narrow. Gothic without the fussiness. Turn of the century but maybe a bad turn. I remember these skinny windows, this high-swept roof, such tightly held confidences. Sitting back amongst the elm trees way off the street, as if embarrassed. The sidewalk is narrow and winding. Pitted with rain and snow, wind and hail, and I remember how often I stumbled over its broken, buckling plates running into this house and running back out.

Back in the darkness is the screened porch . . . and in it too the porch swing where Marlene Benson and I used to come sit after school and play saxophones together, or maybe deep in the night, after movies, just the two of us. We'd sit together in the dark. She didn't want to talk about saxophones that time of night. She wanted to touch and be touched even if she was worried about her mother, whose bedroom was back there on the ground floor. She'd make sure all the doors were closed, and we'd sit there debriefing the movie and whispering all the love songs we'd heard that week. Over the Rainbow, I'm Beginning to See the Light, Long Ago and Far Away, Kiss Me Once and Kiss Me Twice. We'd caress all the soft places where we thought the most beautiful things in the world lay waiting, coiled to spring once we were married, beyond the royal city, beyond the Munchkins, waiting for us beyond the Yellow Brick Road.

The light from the street doesn't reach the porch and I can't see the swing. I wonder if it's there. No, things change.*Tempus edax rerum.* Well, I don't need to see it. Or maybe I do. I take a few steps up the sidewalk. I still can't see inside the porch. Suddenly, I want to see that swing. I need to see if it's still there, maybe even sit in it once again.

"Hey, who's that out there?" A voice knifes through the dark. I step back. "Who's out there, goddamn it!"

I'm trapped. What can I say? I have to say something.

"I'm . . . sorry," I manage at last. "I didn't know anyone was home."

"What the hell!" she screams. "Is that you, Junior?" It's Marlene's voice! Ravaged by time, but a voice I knew as well as my own. "Jenny Meister told me you were coming home, and I said, 'Well, I'm sure he'll look me up.'" I'm unable to fork my tongue or even to breathe. "It's you all right, Junior, or I'll eat my goddamn panties! "

"Marlene?"

"Jeezus Keerist, who else would it be!"

"What are you doing here?"

"Well, for one thing I live here."

"Your mother . . . I thought only your mother lived here."

"My mother? She's gone, didn't you know? Your mother didn't write you about that?" Boards weep, the screen door swings open, the spring yammers just the way it used to unless you were careful. I can't help it, fifty years along and still I worry about that damn porch spring! A stout white arm appears out of nowhere, a palm collects the moonlight. "Oh, come on in here, you asshole! Come on in and set down for a minute, I won't eat you!"

I smell dentures, I smell alcohol, misery, and defeat. I can't see much of her, but she doesn't look at all like the Marlene I remember. I take a few steps toward her. She's in the shadows. Long ghostly hair settles like snakes about her shoulders, eyes sunken, she flutters about the porch doorway like a big white moth.

"You're supposed to be up in Canada somewheres. What in hell are you doing back here in this dump?"

"My mother's going into hospital."

"I heard that." She was quiet for some time. "So, dear fellow . . . whatever happened to you? You were gone a long time. I hope you got a good excuse."

"It's a good excuse."

"I got time. It's about all I have left." She turns around and deposits herself on the swing. "Now, damn it, come on in here and sit down and tell me the whole goddam story. You owe it to me."

20

When I think about it, I realize it's a story I'd rather not tell. Maybe I'll just make something up.

"Where do I start?"

"Start anywhere."

"Fine, let's start with the war then."

"Which one?"

"The Vietnam one."

"I have a hard time keeping them all straight." Marlene lifts a long arm into a shaft of moonbeams and cups her hand around it. "Wasn't that the one where we dropped napalm on straw houses that just happened to have babies in them?" I'm a little surprised at the hard edge of her voice. It is definitely not the voice I remember. The Marlene Benson I knew had a voice that always made you want to listen to it because it had such promises in it, a confident innocence, a flower planted in every word. In the spelldowns we had in the classroom, when she went down, she went down with a voice that made you prefer the way she spelled the word and hate the way others spelled it.

I want to talk about that one to see if I could learn anything by listening to my own telling of it. But I take one step forward and say, "I certainly haven't forgotten this porch, that's for sure." Then I open the screen door and step inside. "Or this swing. I taught you how to play the saxophone on this swing."

Marlene ignores me, grumbling, "Forget about the goddam swing. What about that fucking war in Vietnam? Were you in that one? Were you busy dropping napalm on straw houses with babies in them?"

"No, no! I was too old by then, and anyway I was a post-graduate at a university at the time, and, oh I don't know . . . kind of ambitious about getting somewhere in life. I had gotten off on the wrong foot teaching at rich boys' schools back East and wanted to teach at university, so I came out to Berkeley. At first I tried sticking to the books, but something more interesting was going on outside on the sidewalks. Protests. Megaphones. Crowds. Sit-ins. I found myself listening to students now, not their professors. And it was hard not to hear what they were talking about. They were talking about dropping napalm on straw houses with babies in them, and the government was denying doing that. It was a showdown with the Communists." She went suddenly very quiet, and I walked over to the swing and looked down at her. She had leaned back against a pillow, and her eyes were closed. "Hey, you asleep or something?"

"No, I'm busy listening to you. I could be putting those words into your mouth, I know them so well. I knew what we were doing over there and I didn't need a bunch of snotty-nosed kids holding posters with bad spelling parading around and telling me what was going on over there."

"Me too. But you know, there didn't seem to be anything you could do about it. I finished writing my dissertation and . . . well, it seemed at the time all my friends were going up to Canada. Lots of my classmates had already gone up there, and many others were planning to do it when they got out, and so I went on up there looking for a teaching job at a university, figuring to sit the war out. I thought I'd just hang out up there for a while and then come back. One thing and another . . . It seemed to me that Canada was a kinder, more gentle, more humane place, and then, well, things got a little complicated. Jobs, opportunities, relationships, and of course I got married and had kids –"

"Traitor!" she barks. "Walking out on your own country just when it needed you most. How could you do that?" I let myself down beside her on the porch swing, and she pushes us off into space, swinging back and forth, and then she takes one of my hands into hers. It's a warm hand, soft and inviting.

"It still makes that squeaky sound," I say.

"You loved it, didn't you?" She breaks out in a horsy laugh. "God, you were all hands in those days!"

"Look who's talking!"

"Remember that time I caught you and your auntie skinnydipping in the creek out at your Gramma's farm!"

"I'd hoped you had forgotten all about that. Anyway, I thought I explained all that to you."

"First thing I made Derrick do when mother died was to put this swing back up," she said, ignoring me, "but I didn't tell him why." She smiled at me. "But I think you know why."

I try to avoid her pinning me down: "You remember the night the damn thing come right off its hooks and fell crashing to the floor?"

"How could I forget, Jeezus Keerist! My mom come running across the kitchen, but you were halfway home before she got to the door!" She laughs and slaps her thigh, a heavy, dead sound. "I had a hell of a time trying to explain how the swing came off the hooks, just me all by own self out here!" She pauses and snickers to herself. "Well, you *do* remember that, don't you?"

"That's about all I remember. I've forgot just about everything else."

"Not me. I never forget a damn thing."

"Best to forget."

"Oh, but you *have* to remember! If you don't remember things, they might as well never have happened in the first place."

We swing and sway together without talking for a while, and I feel I have to get the conversation going again, so I say, "You married some guy who wasn't around when I was."

"Derrick? He came to town after *you* deserted us. All he wanted to do at first was screw. Not like you, always playing hard to get. Always worrying whether your folks caught us at it. But anyways, you knew me when screwing seemed such a big thing, but when you get a few miles on you, you know screwing's not so bad. So I decided to play along with him with the idea of civilizing him." She roars with fake laughter. "Make a man out of him, which is more than I could do with you!" She places a hand on my knee and squeezes it playfully. "You were always such an amateur, you know that? If only you could've played me like you played the saxophone . . . of course, that's the way you played the whole world, so far as I can see."

Two can play the game of ignoring the other one. "Where is Derrick now?"

"He's down at the Buckhorn playing pinochle with Bernie Schafft. Derrick and Bernie go down there and play pinochle two, three times a week. Derrick's home by eleven just in time for the news on channel thirteen. He's usually half sloshed when he gets home. He says he has to drink to make it through the eleven o'clock news. Me, I never listen to the news on TV."

"No?"

She clears her sinuses. "Say, can I get you something to drink?"

"No thanks."

"Okay, fine. I'll drink for the both of us." She leans over and lifts a tumbler of ice-cubes off the floor. "Look, Marlene, it's late," I say, climbing to my feet, teetering there, telling fibs. "I should be home when my mother goes to bed."

"No way!" she screams, winching me back down onto the swing. I'm surprised at her strength. "Not this time, boy! We let you get away with it once! It ain't going to be so fucking easy this time."

"What do you mean?"

"We sat around in this stinking town for years waiting for a sign from you," she says, her voice souring. "You promised you'd send us a sign, but you never did. You probably forgot all about us."

I should have left when I had the chance. I try to get the proper kind of reproach into my voice: "You're being silly now, Marlene, just like you used to be."

She empties the glass and munches on an ice cube. “When you come home from college that time . . . you got your draft notice? Surely you remember that! Anyway, you decided to escape the army by joining the navy when they told you you could play your saxophone for four years instead of going over to Korea and shooting at all those gooks. Don’t you remember saying that? I remember you saying that.”

“I don’t remember saying that.”

“I remember you saying that. And I remember you made a whole lot of promises to a whole lot of people in this town . . . especially me!”

“God, that’s fifty years ago, Marlene! We were just kids, we made a lot of silly promises –”

“*You* made a lot of silly promises!”

I don’t have to sit here and listen to a madwoman. “Well, maybe you shouldn’t have listened!” Oh, that is too loud, too nasty. I settle back in the swing and try to sound offended. “Anyway, look . . . I didn’t stop off to rake over the rubble.”

“Rubble? What rubble?”

“Old times, you know.”

We wheel away for a time in silence. I imagine she’s raking through the rubble of childhood infatuations and schoolyard games.

“So you went up to Canada,” she says, proving me wrong again. “Are you famous in Canada?”

“Famous?”

“We always said you’d be famous. We took refuge in that. One of us was going to make it. We all figured it was you. What was it they wrote in the school yearbook? Said you’d be a famous saxophone player and then a big band bandleader. I’ll bet you’re a famous bandleader up there in Canada and you’re not telling anybody.” She laughs in an ugly way. “You remember what you wrote in my yearbook? Probably not. I’ll go get it if you want.” I put my hand out to stay her. “You wrote one day you’d get your own dance band and come back here and put this stinking town on the map." A wild cry comes from way down in her throat. "Damn it! If you *are* famous up there in Canada and you never told anybody, I'm going to kill you!"

"Look, I'm not famous up there, okay? You can relax."

She sits back, and I can feel the heat of her disappointment. "Oh no, don't tell me then you're a failure!"

"I wouldn't say I was a failure, no."

"Well then," she shouts so loud they can hear her up and down the street, "where's that goddamn dance band you promised us!"

I collect myself, and then I say, "It didn't take me long to find out there were lots of good saxophone players and not enough dance bands to go round." I try not to sound too disappointed, but the disappointment is there anyway, and so I try playing some major chords in words. "Anyway, I gave up on the saxophone a long time ago. I don't even own one anymore. I gave up a lot of things I never figured I would give up." I laugh, falsely I think. "But I took up other things, too. I taught for a while at university. I got married and of course divorced. I started writing. People have said nice things about what I've written, but . . . that hasn't really worked out for me either."

But my tragedy apparently doesn't interest her.

"You know we sat here in this goddam burg year in year out thinking, hoping, trusting, believing . . ." she exhales loudly, as if maybe she hasn't been listening to my story at all. "We sat here and told each other, we said, any day now he'll come back with that dance band and rescue us!"

"Rescue you from what?"

"So you never got up a band or nothing?" She says, ignoring my question. I shake my head hoping she will change the subject now, and she does. "Well, maybe it doesn't matter, you took up other things."

It is time to go. I step toward the door.

"Marlene, it's late, I have to go."

"Yes," and there's a new misery in her voice, "I think you should. You really should. I think I've heard enough. You should."

"Maybe I'll stop by again –"

"You do that. You stop by again. But I want to know just this one thing before you go. How come you never come home again and told us about all this?"

"Told you about all of what?"

"You owed us a goddamn explanation!"

In the half-light of anger I can see Marlene worming her way off the swing. She lumbers toward me, but I'm half out the door before she can grab hold of me and pull me back onto the porch. It's not a violent action, it's something more like a hard caress. I twist about and try to see what she's up to. I still can't see her face. I know she's older and fatter and still got gutsy strength. But now I see a white cane in her hand. She swings it at me, but I'm able to grab hold of it. She's strong but I'm able to twist it out of her hand. I toss it to the floor and at the same time smell the sweat and the whisky and feel her hot tears splashing my face, and I'm embarrassed and shriveled and lost, and I can only push her back from me. Too hard. She reels back, tries to get her footing, and then collapses onto the swing, which groans and wobbles beneath her weight and wheels about screeching. She mutters something and then shouts at me as I cross the lawn, but I'm too far away now, I can't make out the words, or maybe it's only that I don't want to make them out.

21

I'm reading yesterday's *Clearwater Times-Leader* at the breakfast table, and I see where a man walked into an office and shot three women dead, one of them pregnant, and in yet another story two children were abducted from a campground in Yosemite Park and found later raped and hastily buried in shallow graves alongside a logging road, and then there were the awful earthquakes in Bhutan burying thousands.

"Good morning," my mother says sweetly, walking into her sunny kitchen. She is holding her side as if it might slide away from her. I watch as she limps past me to fill the kettle and set it on the stove. "Have a good walk last night?"

"Went downtown, looked around and then walked down to the tracks. I see the train station's gone."

"Been gone for twenty years."

"Nobody miss it?"

"Don't need it anymore, nothing stops here." She looks out the window to see if her neighbors are still there. "Meet anyone you know last night?"

"No." I want to keep it simple, but there's something still bothering me about my encounter with my old girlfriend. "Come to think of it I *did* meet someone . . . Marlene Benson. I was walking past her house on my way home and she was sitting out on the porch swing and called me over . . ."

"She sits out there a lot. Some people say she's out there drinking, and her hubby is in the house watching TV."

"She was drinking last night, that's for sure."

"You have to call her Marlene *Schroeder*, that's her name now. Did you even recognize her? She doesn't look good, does she? Put on a lot of weight. Some say she's an alcoholic. It's too bad. I don't think she ever got over the accident."

"Accident?"

"Didn't I write and tell you about the accident? Wait. I'm sure I sent you a clipping from the newspaper."

"You sent me a lot of clippings. But I don't remember anything about Marlene." Chances are I saw it and just let it go, like so many other things. "When did it happen?"

"Oh, well!" She gets milk from the refrigerator. "When?" I remember now the strange thing my mother does with her lips when trying to remember something. "Let me see. Must've been the late Seventies."

Bad years, the late Seventies. Nothing my mother sent me in the mail would have touched me in the late Seventies. Floods, famine, earthquakes, or more likely in this part of the world, tornadoes. I wouldn't have been surprised if she had written to say a funnel had fallen out of the clouds and flattened the whole town. And I remember 1978 was an especially bad year. My own house had been flattened by a tornado of my own making. I remember quite clearly walking dazed about the wreckage while the divorce lawyers circled like vultures picking up the pieces.

I say, "So what happened?"

"Why the poor woman . . . what? I think she put the wrong drops into her eyes." The water begins to boil. "Yes, that's right." She gets out the tea bags. "She'd been having eye troubles and had some eyedrops sitting on the kitchen counter, and somehow she picked up the wrong bottle . . . I forget what was in it now. Bluing? Plant food? Something. She was probably drunk at the time. Anyhow, one eye went and then the other. She's as good as blind now."

"Blind!"

"I sometimes see her walking downtown wearing dark glasses and pecking away at the sidewalk with a white cane."

The white cane, of course! She had come at me with a white cane, and I had taken it away from her. "Funny she didn't mention it to me." I find it hard to breathe and I'm about to faint, but I can't let on. "No, really, Mother, I didn't notice anything out of the ordinary."

But then I remember something she said . . . what was it? Something about *listening* to television. People don't listen to television, do they?

"Oh, you can tell by looking at her if she hasn't got her sunglasses on. Didn't you look at her?"

"Mother, you forget I told you it was dark!" Too strong, I think, pulling back. "Anyway, I didn't look too closely. She was . . . well, as you said, she was drinking. In fact, she was quite drunk and she was saying things."

"What kind of things?"

"Oh, lots of silly things."

"Can I make you breakfast?" My mother brings the two cups, sits at the table and sips her tea. "I don't really eat breakfast if I don't have to, but what about you, you need a good breakfast? Why don't I make you breakfast? Eggs, bacon?"

"No, I had a bowl of Wheaties already and a glass of orange juice before you got up."

"I'll make a nice lunch then." She looks out the window and inhales as if in deep pain and takes her cup to the sink and pours it out. "My doctor tells me I should go for a short walk every morning. So I usually walk down to the post office to get the mail. Maybe I'll do that. Want to come along?"

"Tomorrow . . . I'll go with you tomorrow," I smile in a silly way. I really want to go somewhere and hide till I can catch my breath. *Blind!* Why hadn't I seen it?

At that point I get up and walk to the back door and look out at the back porch. "I thought I'd take a hike out to the cemetery and then to The Place this morning. It's been twenty years or more since Ned died and they sold the farm. I'd like to go see what it looks like after all these years."

"There's nothing left to look at. All the sheds are gone, and last month, well, I meant to tell you when you called. I should have. The barn burned last month. Ralph Thornquist says it was something electrical. Old man Hoehn, he wasn't interested in farming The Place, and that barn sat empty for years."

"Which Hoehn?"

"Tom Hoehn, he's the one who owns The Place now."

"So tell me about the barn."

"He didn't want to pay the insurance on it, they say. The Amish already rent out the fields . . . and the city rents the house. That's all that's left, the house. They keep welfare families in it. Bunch of single mothers and kids and dogs. The police are always running out there for one reason or another."

Huge cumulus clouds and a few close-clipped blue lawns, a Beethoven sky, and then the scruffy, dry grass of the East Lawn Cemetery, and at the far end, a cluster of mossy, gray granite Draeger headstones. But you can see, just beyond the rusty, silver-painted wire fence of the cemetery, how the land dips down toward a bridge and then rises to a knoll. There's a solitary house sitting amidst the big old oak trees now, and nothing else.

The graves at the south end of the cemetery are as close as you can get to The Place without actually being there. Opa Draeger, Gramma Draeger, Vera, Esther, Ned, Buck, Nettie. Nettie's grave is of course a little way from the others. People I have loved are just flat stones now. A small flag snaps proudly in its holder beside Buck's headstone. I dig out the moss with my fingers and brush the grass clippings from the graven letters on Nettie's hard pillow. My father's gravestone is in the second row, my mother's next to his. Her birth date is inscribed but followed by a long dash to remind anyone who wishes to know that she's still among us, but for how long?

There's an open area beside Mother's place, probably left for me and my sister Bits, but Bits now lives in Illinois, and is not interested in making a return appearance. I look at the open places and imagine myself laid out there for all eternity. I remember as a kid being struck dumb by thinking of myself lying down there in the dark wormy mud. Eventually, I got over it. It seemed like just a bad dream at the time, but now it doesn't appear to be so distant and horrible.

I think about it. I don't want to be buried in the back row alongside my folks. I want to be buried in front between Buck and Ned. My hero and my pure father. But that isn't going to be possible. I'll probably go with cremation. I'll be in a drawer somewhere in Vancouver.

I sit and face Nettie's tombstone. My eternal sweetheart. I miss her terribly. It would be poetic justice if I were but a sift of ashes beside her? Maybe I will do that.

The sun suddenly bursts forth and embraces me like a major chord, and I use the light to break away from the flat stones of my ancestors, and I hurry out through the cemetery gate and into the road and down across the old iron bridge above No Nothin' Creek, still trickling along golden over white sandbars, and somewhere up the creek I see the fat naked Nettie ankle-deep in the crystal water and the shocked Marlene clutching her handbag and watching us. And then I hear a P-38 somewhere up there, just beyond Beyond.

A huge rusty truck is sitting in the road. A yellow caterpillar tractor has been launched and is busy pushing wood and stones into a crater. It's what's left of Ned's great gothic cathedral. The man in the caterpillar has a look of grim determination about him as he solemnly goes about his business. All the old timbers and the yellow fieldstone foundation stones, the whole barn is being buried in that hole.

"They'll have to bury The Place," Vera had said ever so many years ago, "after they bury the rest of us."

I stand in the road and wait for Nettie to come around the corner of the house, fussing away, gobbling the words – 'Oh, don't you worry about all this, it ain't really happening, none of it's happening, don't believe none of it!' She's gathering me up now in her arms and urging me across the lawn and into the house, where Gramma and Vera are busy baking food fit for the gods, and the kitchen brimming with heavenly breads and cakes. And there goes Ned. Walking from the horse barn. He won't say a word, will he? I run to him. We walk together over to the machine shed and the Junior-sized tractor and it's time to get out to cultivate the corn patch . . .

But instead, what licketysplits out from behind the house is a scrubby brown dog with great red eyes, snarling in yellow saliva at me. It ambles across the lawn yaowling and stops at the ditch and issues a guttural growl.

I'm an intruder now.

The house looks much smaller. Shriven, defrocked, subdued, sheathed in some kind of sanitary white vinyl siding already dented from hail and violent summer storms. And where once Vera stood watching the road and waiting for something which will never happen nor does she wish it would happen, or maybe she wants it to happen . . . The windows are gone now and in place of them, one big picture window in which you can see nothing. The sloping porches are gone, the screen doors, the summer kitchen. Just a bare-bone house. Standing all alone, treeless, alien, skeletal. The out-buildings – the woodshed, pigpens, chicken coop, granary, machine shed – all gone, as if a tornado had come and swept the place clean. Only the small milkhouse remains. It's a garage now. One fieldstone wall has been demolished and a blue canvas cover flaps in the wind, the rusty buttocks of an abandoned car protrudes through it.

I walk around the caterpillar's jaws and out to the road that leads to the back acres. Out there the sky is blue, the clouds are swept away, the sun is high, the air is fresh and sweet with promises of hay and corn. I take to the road and search for the brilliant green crops and for signs of a small naked boy riding a Ford tractor with Ferguson tools. But I know he is long gone too and Ned is gone and Vera and Nettie, all gone, and now the barn.

And yet the land is still there, still rich and green, promising as always yet another splendid and fruitful harvest.

Then, seeing No Nothin' meandering through the pasture, I remember Marlene Benson too and wonder why I hadn't been able to answer her questions last night. They were good questions. Of course, I owe her nothing. I never promised her a dance band. Never promised anyone anything. And yet her questions sound through the quiet air of the creek. Still, what do I owe her? And, more, why had I forgotten her? Say for the moment she is right, why had I run off on her and never returned with a dance band . . . or for that matter without a dance band?

How had I so easily turned my back on all this? What had compelled me to seek another world?

I leave the asphalt road and climb the barbed wire fence and stroll across the cornfield. The corn stalks are six, seven feet high. Green, oh so very dark green! And the cobs are already full out, the tassels yellow and silky. I stroll down between the rows, disappearing from sight, and walk deep into the cornfield. The rich smell of the purple earth. I stand in one place. Then I feel it. It is the earth pushing its way up through the soles of my feet and then all the way through my knees and into my thighs.

It says Welcome Home, and it cries out, This is your soil, which has been broken and given unto you, take it and . . . I am whirled about by some mystic wind and I'm down on my knees. I hear the high whine of a tractor. I smell the sweet wine of the fruit. The ground is warm. I climb slowly to my feet, watching, waiting. I turn and rush across the rows of corn, sharp blades of the leaves slashing at me, stalks pummeling, the tassels powdering my face, I'm being pushed out toward the barbed wire fence along the road. What is it? I remember how to climb the fence, holding to the post, climbing strand by strand, watching the '400', then hopping down, running down through the ditch and up onto the hot road. A light warm breeze is in my face, the corn patch rustles farewell behind me. Where did it come from? Where did it go? I turn and head for the train tracks, trying to slow my breathing. The sun is in my eyes. Down the road, glazed by a mirage lake as the sun moves slowly, I see the white diagonal crosses, the red lights now dark, the steel wands. And there it is, California! Just the other side of the tracks!

I look south by southeast, north by northwest. Nothing coming. No. No yellow cars bearing the mystical phantoms from distant cities. Never again will I look at them and hope for a magical existence. I turn back toward town. I'm sweating profusely. I've got a headache. I shouldn't have come out here. I'm going to have to pay for this.

I'm walking away from it all when I hear a clip-clop clip-clop coming up behind me. I spin about and see a horse drawing a black buggy. The gelding canters along playfully, all decked out in simple leather harnesses. Has to be Amish. All their horses are retired racehorses, so I heard. The tack and traces are jingling as the buggy slows when it reaches me. Out of the dark interior, a pair of hands holding the reins, and then a face.

It is Ned. Ned as a young man, long before cars and tractors. Ned at twenty, handsome, a dignified black vest, a straw hat. The same Ned as the Ned in the old yellow pictures hidden now in family albums.

The boy lifts his hat and reins in his horse. *"Morgen!"* he says, frames a bright farmer's smile, simple, honest, neighbourly. *"Schöne Tag!"*

"Yes, good morning to you."

He doffs his hat and wipes his forehead and smiles. "It's hot, isn't it?" and I nod, but I can't think of anything to say. He smiles and puts his hat on again. "May I give you a lift to town?"

I stumble into the conversation. "No . . . I mean, well, yes, why not?"

"Do you need a hand up?"

"No, no I'm fine." I climb up and sit beside him on a simple plank seat. "Thank you so much," I say, and we ride for a few moments looking for words that might get us all the way to town. "I was just out for a walk," I decide to start the conversation. "It's been a long time . . . forty years or more since I walked down this road." His brow is creased. I'm making no sense. "This farm, all of this," my hand sweeping the landscape, "it used to belong to me, well, not me personally of course but my family. . . well, what I mean is it used to belong to my uncle Ned."

A smile creeps into his sleeping features, he says, "You mean Mr. Draeger?"

"You know my uncle?" I laugh perhaps harder than I should. I don't know whether I should say it or not, but I have nothing to lose. "You know, for just a moment when you pulled up, I thought *you* were him. You look . . . well, you look a lot like him. I mean of course in his younger years."

"Pardon?"

I'm just being silly. "Nothing, sorry."

"My father, he knew Mr. Draeger. Mr. Draeger used to come out and help us during harvest. He was not afraid of us. He could speak good *deutsch*. We all knew him. He was a plain man, a good neighbour, a good farmer." He thought about it before he said it. "But I think he has passed some time ago now."

"Yes."

"I'm sorry."

"I left this farm a long time ago," I said, "when I was about your age. As a boy, though, I worked all these fields . . ." And once again, I waved my hands about my head in a holy circle. "I spent all my summers out cultivating in these cornfields . . ."

"Now you are here to visit?"

"My mother is not well. I have come home to take care of her."

"I have heard too of Mrs. Draeger. My aunt bought all of her canning pots and her jars when she auctioned them off."

"May I ask, what is your name?"

"Fisher . . . Karl Fisher. Our farm is back not too far the other side of the tracks."

I laughed. "California."

"Pardon?"

"A family joke."

"You must come sometime and visit us."

"Thank you, I will."

He drives me to my mother's house in town, pulls up at the small path to the house and stops. I climb out. "Well, thank you, Karl. Perhaps I will take you up on your invitation. Do I need an appointment?"

"An appointment, what is that?"

"Nevermind. *Auf Wiedersehen* then."

"Auf Wiedersehen, Mr. Draeger," He tips his hat like they used to do. I stand until the black buggy turns the corner and heads into town. I will make it a point to visit the Fishers before leaving town. Tomorrow I have to take my mother to the hospital in Clearwater. She will be there a few days. Maybe when she comes home again, when things settle down, then I will visit the Amish and take her along. She needs to make sure they are using her pots and pans right. And another thing, while she's in hospital, I will try clearing up matters with Marlene Benson. Maybe together on the porch swing late some night while her husband is out we will discover the very point at which the past ended and the future should have begun.